Praise for
HOMETOWN VENDETTA

"*Hometown Vendetta* is Traci Hunter Abramson at her best!
I fell in love with Luke and Amberlyn and am counting the days
until the next Luke Steele adventure."

—DANI PETTREY, BEST-SELLING AUTHOR

"Fast-paced and fun, characters to root for (and a few to dread)—
Abramson brings her A-game with *Hometown Vendetta*!"

—MICHAELBRENT COLLINGS, BEST-SELLING AND AWARD-WINNING AUTHOR

"*Hometown Vendetta* is the latest example of Abramson's mastery
of this genre; intriguing political thriller woven through with a
satisfying romance sure to exceed readers' expectations."

—JOSI S. KILPACK, BEST-SELLING AUTHOR OF THE SADIE HOFFMILLER MYSTERIES

Praise for
TRACI HUNTER ABRAMSON

"The nonstop action keeps the pages turning. . . .
Readers looking for excitement will find plenty to hold their attention."

—PUBLISHERS WEEKLY, FOR ON THE RUN

"A heart-pounding suspenseful adventure
that you won't want to put down!"

—IND'TALE MAGAZINE, FOR NOT DEAD YET

"An edge-of-your-seat hostage rescue thriller."

—PUBLISHERS WEEKLY, FOR UNSEEN

A LUKE STEELE NOVEL

HOMETOWN VENDETTA

also by
TRACI HUNTER ABRAMSON

For Apostle Frank R. Lacey
Your dedication to service and unity is truly an inspiration.

CHAPTER 1

AMBERLYN REINER DROVE across Memorial Bridge and approached the Lincoln Memorial. The early morning sunlight illuminated the white granite-and-marble structure that always reminded her how lucky she was to work in Washington, DC, even if the Monday morning traffic had once again slowed to a crawl. While she certainly wouldn't have minded an easier commute, part of her appreciated the ritual and the time alone with her thoughts each weekday.

Within the hour, she would tap into her knowledge of human behavior to search for terrorists, murderers, and other criminals who, if not identified and stopped, would likely strike again. But for now, she focused on the Washington Monument in the distance.

Her phone rang, her car's audio announcing the incoming call was from her best friend and former coworker. The mere sound of Chanelle's name brightened her mood.

"Hey, Chanelle. How's everything going?" Amberlyn said after she answered the call.

"I have to admit, after spending ten years working in the counseling office, it's still weird to drive by the high school and not turn into the parking lot."

"I'm sure it is, but you were ready for a change. Burnout is real."

Amberlyn had never experienced that particular sensation. She had taught for a year at the high school where Chanelle had worked as a counselor and then had joined the FBI and left Missouri behind. When she had started her master's degree in psychology, she'd never thought

1

she would use it to help profile criminals, but her progression from student to teacher to special agent had occurred as though she had been destined to work in one of the FBI's behavioral analysis units.

"I have some news," Chanelle said, changing the subject. "Are you going to be around next week?"

Amberlyn inched up another few car lengths, drawing closer to the Lincoln. "Yeah, why?"

"FEMA is sending me to DC for training. I'm flying in on Monday, but I thought maybe I could stay through the weekend."

Amberlyn's smile was instant. "That would be great." Her coworkers at the bureau were amiable, but spending time with someone from her old life would give her a taste of home without leaving her adopted city. "I can show you around."

"I was hoping you'd say that." Chanelle's enthusiasm carried over the line. "I can't wait to see you."

"Me too." The road in front of her opened up, and Amberlyn finally made it off the bridge. "Call me when you know your schedule."

"Will do."

"Stay out of trouble."

"Who, me?" Chanelle asked. "I always stay out of trouble."

Amberlyn laughed. "I know better." They said their goodbyes, and Amberlyn continued to FBI headquarters.

She parked in employee parking and made her way to her office. Kiera, one of Amberlyn's team members, stood by the secretary's desk, two boxes of Krispy Kreme donuts open beside her on the counter.

"I thought you were giving up eating sugar." Amberlyn peeked inside the box closest to her. Traditional glazed. Her favorite.

"She was," Robin, the unit's secretary, said.

Kiera shrugged. "The Hot Doughnut sign was on."

Amberlyn laughed. "That's what happened the last time you decided to eat healthier."

"I know. It's like Krispy Kreme senses when I'm about to go on a diet and has to tempt me." Kiera put a donut on a napkin.

Robin stood and peered into the second box of donuts, selecting a cream-filled one for herself. "Maybe you should give up and just balance your morning sugar fix with a salad at lunchtime."

"That's too logical." Kiera headed toward her desk. "You both need to have some so I don't eat them all."

"Ian and Jeff will take care of that problem for you," Robin said, referring to their boss and one of the other special agents in their unit.

Both men held degrees in psychology, and neither had an ounce of willpower.

Robin turned her attention to Amberlyn. "Those new reports came in on that bombing in Nebraska. Ian wanted me to let you know they had some updates."

"Great. Thank you. I'll look through them now." Amberlyn had spent the past five months trying to get a handle on the suspected anti-government extremist group. Forever Freedom had claimed responsibility for a bombing at a library on primary election day, but despite Amberlyn's many conversations with the other members of her team, so far, no one had been able to determine what was motivating the group or who was leading it. Maybe the updates would include a lead that could finally break this case open.

She grabbed a donut and continued to her cubicle. She reviewed the latest reports and updated her notes, but the only new information was the copy of the ballot for the local voting districts. Somehow, she doubted Forever Freedom had bombed a library and killed six people because of a bond referendum for road improvements. The election for the local sheriff didn't seem like a high probability for a target either.

Setting that case aside for the moment, she pulled up her file on a suspected serial killer in Atlanta. The local authorities had worked the case for nearly two months before reaching out to the FBI's behavioral analysis unit. The range of differences in the victims—a twenty-eight-year-old white male, a thirty-four-year-old Hispanic female, and a fifty-seven-year-old Black male—suggested race and gender prejudices weren't a significant factor.

Amberlyn tried to look at the statistics without thinking about the victims' families and friends. She tried and failed. Lives had been cut short because the victims had been in the wrong place at the wrong time or because someone had specifically targeted them. Amberlyn's job was to find out why and to figure it out before another family lost a loved one.

When she had started with the FBI, she had assumed it would get easier to face all the evil in the world. She'd been wrong. In truth, if she hadn't experienced firsthand the aftermath of a violent crime, she doubted she ever would have taken this job. Thank goodness her boss and coworkers were always willing to talk things out when work became too intense or overwhelming for any of them.

She was an hour into her workday when Jeff approached her cubicle, a file in his hand. "Hey, I thought you'd want to see these."

Amberlyn opened it to reveal the back of a man sitting in a restaurant booth, a ball cap on his head, what appeared to be part of a tattoo on his wrist, and some sort of class ring on his finger. The man across from him also wore a ball cap, a wolf tattoo visible on his forearm. "What am I looking at?"

"A patron in a restaurant in St. Louis said she overheard a couple guys talking about getting into a building without being noticed."

"Sounds like a report that should be filed with the local police."

"It was, but when they pulled the surveillance video, they saw this." Jeff leaned over and slid the top photo aside to reveal another photo of the two men leaving, their heads lowered, both of their faces hidden by their ball caps, which were embroidered with the logo FF.

The symbol for Forever Freedom, the same symbol that had been left behind at the library bombing.

Amberlyn straightened. This was the first real development they'd had in months.

Jeff gripped the top of her cubicle wall. "The woman said she didn't hear the word *bomb*, but she was afraid they might be trying to plant one."

"What made her think that?"

"One of them said something about the blast radius. They also said this would take them to the next level," Jeff said. "They never said what *this* was, but the mention of a blast radius sure makes it sound like they're planning another strike. The complete copy of her statement is in the file."

A sense of urgency rushed through Amberlyn. "When was this taken?"

"Three days ago."

She looked through the images again. "Any idea about the target?"

"Nothing. All the witness said was that it sounded like an office building."

Which left them far too many possibilities.

"Has an alert already gone out to the St. Louis field office?"

"Ian is on the phone with them now, but he wants us to look for likely targets." He motioned to the file. "You take everything within the city limits. I'll work on the suburbs."

Jeff headed back to his desk three cubicles down. Amberlyn pulled up a map of St. Louis and tried to think like a terrorist. If she wanted to make a point about not wanting federal oversight or to make a case for less governmental interference, where would she target?

For the next two hours, Amberlyn made her list, including everything from local polling spots to the various federal buildings. After she emailed her list to her boss and cc'd Jeff and the special agent in charge in St. Louis, she turned her attention back to the details of the shooting in Nebraska. Surely there had to be some clue as to why they had chosen that target.

Amberlyn's phone rang, and she picked it up from where she'd left it charging on her desk. When the caller ID didn't reveal anything beyond a number, she answered, "Special Agent Reiner."

Chanelle's voice carried over the line. "Ooh. Special agent. Look at you being all fancy."

"Hi, Chanelle." Amberlyn fought to switch from investigative mode to normal-person mode. "I didn't recognize this number. What's up? You still coming Monday?"

"Guess where I'm calling you from right now."

"The FEMA office building in Kansas City?"

"Well, yes, but I'm calling from *my* office in the FEMA office building in Kansas City," Chanelle said excitedly. "My very own office, with my very own phone."

Amberlyn smiled. "You're moving up in the world."

"Yeah. It only took six weeks for me to finally get assigned to my own space. I even have a view of—" The line went dead.

"Chanelle? Are you there?" Amberlyn held out her phone. The call had dropped. She pulled up her recent contacts and dialed Chanelle's work number. It rang once before an annoying chime came over the phone along with an automated voice stating that the person she had dialed was not currently available and that she could leave a message after the beep.

Amberlyn pulled up her favorites and hit Chanelle's name to call her cell. This time, the phone rang twice and went to voice mail. Strange.

———

Luke Steele sat beside the grandfather clock in the Oval Office as the secretary of commerce and two of her aides discussed the trend reports for consumer financing. The topic might be of interest to many in the country, especially if someone who didn't speak in monotone delivered the information, but Luke personally preferred to be on duty when significant events in history were unfolding.

He still wasn't sure why he'd been selected to serve as the Marine Corps' military aide to the president, but he was quite certain no one from his childhood ever expected he would graduate from college, much less work every day with the president of the United States. He supposed the distinguished service medal he'd been awarded after orchestrating a rapid evacuation of a hostile area had helped his chances to receive this assignment.

"As you can see, Mr. President," Secretary Gutierrez continued, her voice low and smooth, "if the Fed raises interest rates again, it will have a significant impact on consumer spending." She was interrupted when a quick knock sounded on the door.

Dale Ellis, the chief of staff, rushed in, his distress obvious. "Mr. President, there's been an incident in Kansas City. The FEMA building was just bombed."

"What?" President Frazier closed the report he'd been reviewing and stood. "Give me details."

Luke stood as well, his body tense.

"The initial reports are just coming in," Dale said. "We don't even have a casualty count yet, but it doesn't look good."

"How bad are we talking?"

"It's not on the scale of 9/11, but it could rival the bombing in Oklahoma City."

Luke had studied the Oklahoma City bombing during college. Hundreds injured, over a hundred fifty killed, more than a dozen of whom had been children. Just the thought of the tragedy made his heart ache.

Dale passed the president his phone, likely showing him whatever data was already available.

The president set the report on his desk and directed his next comment to the secretary of commerce. "I'm sorry, Emily. We'll need to table this discussion."

"Of course, Mr. President." She nodded and excused herself from the room.

As soon as the secretary of commerce and her aides left, Dale closed the door.

"Any indications yet of who we're dealing with?" the president asked.

"The FBI is working on it now."

"I want someone in here to brief me. ASAP." The president handed the cell back to Dale.

"I'll put in the call." Dale tapped on his phone screen. "In the meantime, I suggest we put all our federal buildings on high alert and have Yvonne cancel the rest of your meetings for today."

"Make it happen." The president headed toward the door, and Luke followed. "I'll be in the Sit Room."

A sickness settled deep in Luke's gut.

President Frazier continued forward slowly and mumbled to himself, "Why would someone do something like this?"

Luke knew the president wasn't waiting for an answer. Anyone with any sense of right and wrong would never deliberately seek to destroy lives the way the bomber had. No, this someone was without a moral compass or any knowledge of good and evil. Understanding such a person was beyond comprehension and not something Luke would ever have to worry about in his profession. Luke had only one objective, one mandate—to stand at the president's side no matter what.

CHAPTER 2

SMOKE AND FLAMES rose from the windows of the FEMA building, a huge part of the structure no longer intact. Amberlyn stared at the television screen in the corner of the conference room as hope and fear tangled inside her. Her entire team, analysts and support staff alike, had crowded into the room, everyone glued to the live news broadcast.

Firefighters were already on scene, and the evacuation of the survivors continued as one person after another stumbled out of the building, many aided by rescue personnel.

Amberlyn scanned for any sight of Chanelle, but the distance between the camera and the emergency exits was too great to distinguish one dark-haired woman from another.

From the information they'd already gathered, the timing of the explosion coincided with Amberlyn's call with Chanelle ending so abruptly. But even though the timing was suspicious and Chanelle's phones were down, that didn't mean Chanelle hadn't survived. Amberlyn had assured herself of that fact repeatedly over the past thirty minutes and every time she'd dialed Chanelle's cell phone again. The blast could have simply downed the building's phone system and interrupted the cell signal in the area. She prayed that was the case.

Amberlyn also wouldn't put it past Chanelle to stay in the building and help others evacuate. Nearly every time Chanelle got herself into trouble, it was in her efforts to help someone else.

A man exited the building, his arm around a woman as they stumbled out together. Any minute, Chanelle would appear looking just like that, her arm supporting someone who needed help.

Ian picked up the remote from the conference room table and muted the TV. He motioned to the man to his left. "Zane, keep watching for any clues on the news, and coordinate with the Kansas City office. Someone needs to contact the various stations to get copies of their video stream. If the agent in charge wants your help, give it to him."

Ian handed over the remote. "Kiera, get in touch with your contacts at the CIA. Work together to identify possible foreign threats."

"Got it." Kiera left the room.

Turning his attention to Amberlyn, Ian asked, "Are you okay to keep working today? I know Chanelle meant a lot to you. We'll all understand if you need to take some time off."

Though tempted to go home, where she could stare at the TV, she knew that would only make her anxiety worse. She shook her head. "I'll stay. I can use the distraction."

"Then, go ahead and get started on the assumption that this could be Forever Freedom's work."

That wasn't the assignment she'd been hoping for. Rather, she preferred to be among the first to find out about Chanelle's fate. "Maybe I should work the phones for the information line. I have experience with this sort of thing." Not that she had ever wanted to gain firsthand experience with grief counseling.

"I know you're worried about your friend, but you have more insight into Forever Freedom than anyone else. You dig into that angle. Jeff can help you."

With Amberlyn's thoughts so wholly focused on news about Chanelle, Jeff would likely need to do the heavy lifting on this. She couldn't think. She just needed to know her friend was all right.

Amberlyn focused on the TV, not quite able to get her feet to move.

"Come on." Jeff put his hand on her shoulder. "We can work in your office."

The brotherly nudge worked as intended. Amberlyn tore her gaze from the fire and smoke and left the conference room.

Jeff grabbed his chair as he passed his cubicle and rolled it behind him until he reached her workspace.

Using every ounce of energy she had, she typed in her password to access her computer. "Where do we start?"

"You need to talk first." Jeff sat and swiveled his chair to face her. "Tell me about your friend. What makes her so special to you?"

"Ian said—"

Jeff waved a hand toward the conference room. "The damage is already done. And you aren't going to be able to concentrate until you talk out your fears."

And she couldn't deny that with each passing second that she didn't hear Chanelle's voice, her fears were magnifying. "I was on the phone with her when the bomb went off."

"I know."

Tears welled up, and Amberlyn blinked them back. "She was a counselor at the high school where I taught. She's the one who convinced me to get involved with helping the kids after one of the students was murdered. If it weren't for her, we probably never would have found out who was behind it."

"How did she end up at FEMA?"

"She got burned out working in the school system and wanted a change." A tear spilled over. "She's only been there six weeks."

The realization that she should let the school know Chanelle was at the FEMA building rushed into her head. "Those poor kids. If something happens to her—"

"For now, let's worry about you." Jeff pulled his cell phone from his pocket. "I'll call the victim hotline and make sure that when your friend's status is identified, you get a call."

She should have thought of that. "Thanks."

"No problem." He dialed the number. "In the meantime, let's take another look at those photos from St. Louis. That's only about a four-hour drive from Kansas City."

Amberlyn nodded. She opened the file and spread the photos out on the open space of her desk between her computer and her inbox.

Not a single image revealed any part of the two men's faces. As soon as Jeff put in the request with the hotline and passed along her phone number, Amberlyn held up one of the photos. "Look at how both men look down as soon as they head toward the security camera."

"They knew where it was."

"Any chance there might have been a camera outside or a traffic camera or an ATM nearby that we could pull feed from?"

"I'm afraid not. The diner is across from a golf course on an open stretch of road." He furrowed his brow. "We might be able to access the traffic cameras in the intersections on either side of it though. It could help us narrow down what vehicle they were driving."

"As long as it isn't a heavily traveled road."

Footsteps pounded toward them, and Zane stopped beside her cubicle. "The news just broke."

Ian rushed out of his office and joined them, as did Kiera. "What is it?"

"I don't know where they got the information," Zane said, "but according to CNN, the organization claiming responsibility for the bombing is Forever Freedom."

Amberlyn's already fragile emotions shattered, and an indescribable pain shot through her. If they could have identified the people behind that organization, they might have been able to stop this bombing before it ever happened.

Forever Freedom. Luke didn't know where they'd come up with their name, but as far as he was concerned, whoever would cause such destruction of innocent civilians didn't understand the definition of either of the two words.

The reports had been coming in steadily. Twenty-two confirmed dead, dozens more missing.

Luke couldn't begin to imagine what the families and friends of the FEMA employees must be going through right now. He had taken a twenty-minute break to eat a quick lunch, but even though Parker, the air force military aide, had offered to take over for him for longer, Luke had wanted to be where the news was most likely to be accurate, and that was here in the Situation Room.

"How long until Simon gets here?" the president asked, referring to the FBI director.

Dale looked down at his phone. "He already passed through security."

The phone in the corner rang, and the communication officer answered. After a brief moment of silence, she nodded. "I'll pass that information along."

The moment she hung up, she said, "They have updated casualty numbers. We're up to thirty-eight confirmed dead. A shelter has been set up at a nearby elementary school to allow victims' families to gather while they wait for news."

"Does anyone know what this Forever Freedom group wants?" President Frazier lifted a hand in frustration. "What was the point of all this?"

"I don't know," Dale said, "but if anyone does, it's the FBI's behavioral analysis unit."

Which meant that until the FBI analysts showed up, all they could do was wait.

———

Still no news. Amberlyn had been handpicked to accompany the FBI director to the White House—she was going to meet the president of the United States—and all she could think about was whether her friend had survived the day.

Her throat tightened as she and Director Thompson followed their escort down the stairs to the Situation Room, and Amberlyn struggled to focus on the briefing she would soon give. They each placed their cell phones in one of the small lockers by the entrance and collected the miniature keys used to secure them. Their escort opened the door and waited for them to pass through.

When Amberlyn entered the conference room, she expected to see it filled with admirals and generals. Maybe even the director of the CIA and a few cabinet members. Instead, only five people sat inside: the president, the chief of staff, the national security adviser, a communications officer at the desk in the far corner of the room, and a man in uniform sitting beside the back wall.

Amberlyn did a double take at the man in uniform. Luke Steele?

She had met him briefly when she'd gone through the FBI Academy and he'd been stationed at Quantico, but he'd made quite the impression. During a shared meal with mutual friends, she had considered herself lucky to end up seated beside Luke. He was good-looking and had seemed friendly enough when he'd been talking to their friend Kevin. But when she had asked Luke about his work, all he'd said was, "I'm a Marine." Like she hadn't already figured that out from his haircut and posture.

Every attempt at conversation after that had been met with an "I don't know," an "I guess," or a shrug. Yet when Kevin or his wife had said anything to him, Luke had chatted with ease, offering interesting answers and insightful comments. By the end of the dinner, Amberlyn had come to the sad conclusion that Luke hadn't wanted anything to do with her. Every interaction between them had solidified the fact that her mere presence had been an annoyance he'd been forced to endure. Then when dessert had been served, he'd managed to drop her piece of cheesecake, complete with strawberries and whipped cream, into her lap.

He had apologized and offered to pay for her dry cleaning, but despite her personally typing her number into his phone, he'd never called.

Amberlyn came back to the present as the people in the room stood.

Director Thompson shook the president's hand. "Mr. President, this is Amberlyn Reiner. She's the analyst who's been profiling Forever Freedom."

The president shook her hand before motioning toward the empty seats in the middle section of the long conference table. "Please sit."

As soon as they complied, the president asked, "What do we know about this group? What are they after?"

"We're still trying to piece that together, but so far, their actions are consistent with a group who believes their voices aren't being heard, and they're convinced they won't achieve the changes they want without taking radical actions." Amberlyn shared the rehearsed narrative she and Jeff had worked on. "Their targets have little in common other than being aimed toward the government. We believe they have a grudge against government agencies, but we haven't identified why."

"How big of a group are we talking about here?" President Frazier asked.

"We aren't able to determine that at this time," Director Thompson said.

"Can you give us a ballpark?" President Frazier held up both hands. "Are we dealing with a few radicals or a group in the hundreds?"

Director Thompson gestured to Amberlyn, his silent command for her to answer.

A brief spurt of panic momentarily paralyzed her. This wasn't part of the practiced speech she had rehearsed, but the information the president asked for had been the subject of much of her research over the past few months. "Our initial analysis suggests the group is small." Amberlyn clasped her hands together. "Thus far, Forever Freedom appears to operate very much like a religious cult, with a single unifying leader and the members sharing the same vision. Unfortunately, we haven't been able to determine who the leader is or what he or she hopes to achieve."

"We believe two of the men involved in the bombing were spotted in a restaurant outside St. Louis three days ago." Director Thompson passed a paper to the communications officer. "Can you bring those up for me?"

"Yes, sir." She accessed the secure drive and brought the photos up on the large screen opposite where the president sat.

"The men kept their faces hidden," Director Thompson continued. "But we did find several identifying markers." He nodded for Amberlyn to take over before telling the communications officer to advance to the next photo.

The image of the hat with the Forever Freedom logo came first.

"We believe these letters on the baseball cap is Forever Freedom's logo," Amberlyn said. "It's small enough to go unnoticed by most people, but it's possible it's being used for the various members to identify one another."

"Any chance someone could track down whoever did the embroidery on those caps?" the national security adviser asked.

She and Jeff had shared the same thought. "One of my associates is working on that, but it's a long shot." Amberlyn nodded to the comm officer for her to click to the next image, this one of the wolf tattoo on the forearm of one of the men. "We also have analysts working on identifying the tattoo artist."

"That's another long shot," the chief of staff said.

"Yes, but if we can narrow down the range of where these men are from, it could help identify them." She glanced at the comm officer. "Next slide, please."

The close-up of the other man's hand came next.

In her peripheral vision, she caught the way Luke straightened suddenly. Ignoring him, she focused on the television screen. "We're also trying to identify this championship ring. We can see the initials PHS and the year."

"There are hundreds, if not thousands, of high schools that start with the letter *P.*"

"We're contacting the jewelers that cater to the high schools to determine which schools ordered the rings."

Behind her, Luke stood. "Can you zoom in on the center of the ring? The part between the PHS and the year?"

The officer at the communication desk glanced at the president as though asking permission. When the president nodded, she complied.

"What's that symbol in the middle?" the national security adviser asked.

"It looks like a one with something over it."

"It's supposed to be the state of Virginia," Luke said. "The ring is from Pineview High School in Pine Falls, Virginia."

Director Thompson swiveled in his chair to face Luke more fully. "Are you sure?"

"Yes, sir. The football team won state that year."

"Captain Steele, is this ring from your high school?"

Luke visibly swallowed and nodded. "Yes, sir."

CHAPTER 3

LUKE DIDN'T THINK today could get any more surreal. A terrorist attack, a possible connection to his hometown, and Amberlyn Reiner staring at him with her gorgeous brown eyes. Not that Luke should be thinking about her appearance right now or the fact that his revelation had everyone's focus on him, a sensation he didn't like any more now than he had when he'd been a kid. He fought the urge to squirm.

"Nina, get a replacement down here for Captain Steele," President Frazier said. "Captain, I want you to work with Special Agent Reiner to identify the man in that photo."

"Sir?" A storm of nerves jumbled in Luke's stomach. Surely the president wouldn't want him to step away from his duties to work with the FBI.

"I know this isn't orthodox, but this situation is bigger than you and me," President Frazier said. "If me working short-staffed means we can find the person behind this bombing sooner, so be it."

Despite his reservations, Luke answered automatically. "Yes, sir."

Over the next few minutes, Amberlyn, Director Thompson, and the president discussed possible psychological profiles of the bomber. All the while, the ramifications of what Luke had been asked to do pushed to the forefront of his mind.

He'd never told any of his coworkers about the incident with Amberlyn in the restaurant when he'd tried to pass her dessert to her but had instead managed to drop it in her lap. Never had he been more mortified. He had wanted to impress her so badly that he'd been tongue-tied every time she'd spoken to him. Then he'd had to settle for getting her attention by enraging her and embarrassing himself to the point that he'd wished he could disappear and hide under a rock.

But he'd swallowed his pride and offered to clean her dress. She'd resisted at first, but when she'd finally consented, he'd experienced a brief glimmer of hope that he could apologize again and maybe even take her out. That plan had died a quick death when he'd tried texting and calling her only to learn the number she'd typed into his phone belonged to some guy named Todd Hart.

And while working with Amberlyn would be beyond awkward, facing the memories of his hometown would be much worse.

Just the thought of the way Russ Gibson used to bully him relentlessly brought back those awkward years of trying to stay invisible and steer clear of the popular crowd. Or more specifically, the bullies in the popular crowd, most of whom had been on the football team. Being forced to push pennies with his nose across the bathroom floor, the wedgies that had followed when he'd lost the races every time against the football team's other victims. Then there were the invitations to parties that didn't exist, getting blamed for things he didn't do, having his locker broken into and cleaned out the day before he'd needed to turn in his three-week research project. And the list went on.

Tom, the army military aide, entered the room and relieved Luke of his current duty.

"Captain, accompany Special Agent Reiner and work in the watch room." President Frazier stood. "I want an update by the end of the day."

"Yes, sir." Luke turned to Amberlyn and moved to the door in the corner of the room. "This way."

They walked out of the large conference area of the Situation Room and entered the watch room, with its two curved rows of workstations. Three watch-team members already occupied the spots on the upper row, and one more sat at the end of the lower section. Urgency simmered in the air as Luke led the way to two vacant spots and pulled out both chairs. "We can use these computers."

"This would be easier if I had access to my files," Amberlyn said.

"You can log into your server from here and pull up anything you need." Luke waited for Amberlyn to sit before he lowered into his chair. He logged her into the secure system and instructed her on how to access her own files. He didn't mention that he'd only been trained on this particular system three months ago.

"What exactly do you do here at the White House?" Amberlyn asked.

"I'm a military aide to the president."

"Which means what?"

"Among other things, I'm basically the guy who carries around the nuclear football." At her blank stare, he added, "The nuclear codes. They always have to be in close proximity to the president."

"Oh." Amberlyn motioned to the phone situated beside her computer. "Can I use that to get my team working on this with me?"

"Go ahead." Luke logged in and looked up the phone number for the only jeweler in his hometown, the one that had likely coordinated the order for the championship rings for his high school's football team. At least, it had been the only jeweler in town when he'd moved away fifteen years ago.

Amberlyn spoke into the phone. "I need a favor. We may have identified that championship ring. We think it was from a high school in Virginia, the Pineview state champion football team." She paused, clearly listening to the person on the other end of the line. "I want everything. Social media, yearbooks, newspaper articles, death records." Another pause. "I don't think I'll be back in the office today, so just email it to me. I'll work on tracking down the jeweler and see if they have a list of everyone who received a ring." She hung up the phone.

Luke handed her the note with the jeweler's name and phone number. "This is probably who handled the orders for the rings."

Surprise flickered over her face. "Thanks." She picked up the phone again and put in her request. As soon as she hung up, she asked, "Any idea which of your old teammates might have leaned toward violence?"

"My old classmates," Luke corrected. "I was never on the football team." His scrawny high school self would have been broken in half had he even dared try out for the team. Plus, he wouldn't have wanted to spend more time than he had to with the people on the team who were determined to make his life miserable.

"If you weren't on the team, how can you be so sure that ring is from your school?" she asked.

Because Owen Lester had flaunted it in front of him every day in their learning strategies class. Luke censored his answer. "A few guys on the team were very proud of their rings. Trust me. That's the ring from my school."

"I don't suppose there was anything familiar about the guy in the photo."

Luke shook his head. "I'm sure everyone has changed a lot since I graduated." He certainly had.

"When was the last time you saw any of them?" she asked. Her eyes brightened. "Do you have any photos from your ten-year reunion? If we can identify who was still wearing their championship ring then, it could help us narrow down our suspect pool."

"Sorry, I didn't go." He hadn't had any reason to. High school was his past, a past he preferred to leave firmly behind him. He could happily live the rest of his life without ever seeing *those* people again.

"There have to be photos online." Amberlyn tapped her finger on her desk.

"Can you show me the images from the diner again?"

Amberlyn retrieved the images.

Luke pointed at the one with the championship ring. "Can you zoom out on that one?"

She did, part of a tattoo barely visible at the edge of the man's sleeve.

"That tattoo will help us narrow down the field a bit."

"You can't see what it's of."

"It's two curved lines that look like the outside of a football." Anticipating her next question, he added, "A bunch of the championship team got the tattoos after they won. The center part is different, usually the player's number, but the outside looks the same."

Amberlyn's expression brightened. "You're sure about this?"

"Positive. I can't tell you who got a tattoo besides one of the guys who sat next to me in class, but I think several of them got one."

"Any chance you know where they had them done?"

"Pine Falls only had one tattoo parlor, but I don't remember the name of it."

"I'll ask one of my colleagues to look it up," Amberlyn said. "For now, let's start with a list of people you remember from the football team. That will give us a head start while we wait for my office to get us the complete roster."

"I don't remember the names of that many, but I'll give you what I can."

She opened a blank document on the computer. "I'm ready. Who's the first one?"

"Owen Lester."

For a guy who'd said he didn't remember many people, Luke had been far more helpful than Amberlyn had expected. He'd given her nine members of the football team; those names expanded to twenty-three, thanks to the people those initial few had tagged on their social media accounts. Luke was now helping her scroll through Facebook and Instagram for photos that might reveal who was still wearing a ring and eliminate anyone who didn't have the tattoo.

She glanced at the phone on her desk. Someone had to know whether Chanelle had made it out of the FEMA building alive, but if anyone had tried calling Amberlyn, the call would have gone to her cell phone, which was still locked outside the Situation Room.

A sense of dread spread through her, her heart literally aching in her chest, and she glanced at the phone in front of her. She might be able to make a quick call and have Jeff check on Chanelle for her. But what if she received bad news while here at the White House?

"Owen Lester and Jackson Scott both have their rings on in this photo, and you can see Jackson's tattoo," Luke said, bringing her back to the task at hand.

Amberlyn leaned closer. "When was that taken?"

"Four years ago."

Still struggling to keep her mind on her work, Amberlyn made a note in her spreadsheet. "Try Zachary Upton and Timothy Vincent next. I'll take the next two."

She looked up the first one, the last posts on his feed containing comments about friends missing him as well as a funeral announcement. A quick check confirmed what social media indicated. "We can take Kyle Moran off the list. He died three years ago."

"I hadn't heard." Luke motioned to her screen as though the news of his classmate's death were no big deal. "The pictures Zach is tagged in are of him skiing and hunting, but there aren't any photos that show his wrists. And the only ones that show his hands are ones where he has gloves on."

"Maybe we'll be able to find him in someone else's reunion pictures." She glanced at the phone again. Her anxiety hiked up another notch.

Oblivious to her churning emotions, Luke tapped on his keyboard. "Timothy Vincent doesn't have any kind of social media presence. You might want to check death records for him too."

Amberlyn did a search with Timothy's name and an estimated birth year. A hit popped up on her first try. "Good call. Timothy was killed in a motorcycle accident when he was nineteen."

"Who do you want me to look up next?" Luke asked.

"That's it for the list of people you gave me." Amberlyn opened her email to check for a message from Jeff. Sure enough, one topped her inbox. She prayed it would contain news about Chanelle, but that prayer went unanswered. "Looks like we have the full roster." She opened the attachment. Sixty-two names.

"Forward your list to me." He pulled a business card from his pocket and handed it to her. "My email is on there."

Amberlyn glanced at the rest of the contents of the email from Jeff to make sure there wasn't anything she would be uncomfortable forwarding on. Of course, the man had open access to the Situation Room in the White House. His security clearance was most certainly higher than hers.

She hit the forward button and clicked Send.

"Want me to start from the bottom of the list, and you can start from the top?" Luke asked.

"Sounds good."

With the watch team buzzing about surveillance feed in Kansas City and some unrelated incident in north Africa, Amberlyn and Luke worked for the next hour in silence, except for when Luke gave her information to add to the notes on her spreadsheet.

Amberlyn typed in her comments on the last suspect for her half of the list and noted the time on the computer screen. Four thirty-two. She glanced at the phone again. Maybe she could take a quick break to leave the Situation Room and check her cell phone for messages.

"It looks like Lance Herrick didn't get a tattoo," Luke said. "I found photos going back ten years, and he didn't have the tattoo in any of them."

Amberlyn added the final details to her spreadsheet. "That gives us four who fit the general description of the man in St. Louis, who we're sure got a championship tattoo and have also been photographed wearing their ring within the past five years. We still have twenty-three we aren't sure about."

"That knocks the list down by more than half."

"I'll forward this to my office and the Kansas City field office. I'm sure we'll have people working around the clock tonight."

Concern filled his eyes. "Including you?"

"Probably." She wouldn't be able to sleep until she knew Chanelle was safe. She glanced at the phone again.

"If you need to call someone, you can use one of the privacy booths."

"Actually, I did want to take a quick break and check my cell phone."

"Send your email. After you do, I can either escort you out to get your phone, or I can show you where you can make your call."

Amberlyn typed up a quick note to Jeff and shared her spreadsheet. Luke stood. "This way."

He led her to what looked like a phone booth of sorts, the rounded glass door allowing the occupant privacy while still being able to see his or her surroundings. "Will this do, or would you rather go out and get your phone?"

Amberlyn debated briefly before accepting the offer of privacy. "This will work great. Thanks." She stepped into the phone pod, picked up the receiver for the unsecure line, and dialed Jeff's cell number.

"This is Jeff."

"Hey, it's me. Any chance you can get me an update on the survivor and casualty list?" Amberlyn asked. "I had to turn over my cell phone when I came into the briefing."

"I've been staying up on that," Jeff said, his voice grave. "I'm so sorry, Amberlyn. The news just came in a few minutes ago."

Amberlyn braced against the words she didn't want to hear. Her throat tightened. Her breath backed up in her lungs.

"Chanelle Mays was identified as one of the casualties."

"No." The single word came out in a whisper, and immediately, Amberlyn's eyes flooded. For the past six years, Chanelle had been the sister Amberlyn had never had. They'd spent Christmas together when Amberlyn's parents had abandoned her to go on a holiday cruise. They'd binged on ice cream and chick flicks after Chanelle's last break up. And the list went on and on. They'd done everything together. Chanelle had even helped Amberlyn pick out a new suit for her interview with the FBI.

"I am so sorry," Jeff repeated.

Amberlyn lifted her chin and sucked in an unsteady breath, fighting to keep the tears from falling. Several spilled over despite her efforts.

"I can talk to Ian about trading places with you," Jeff went on. "I was already planning to work late tonight anyway."

She swallowed the lump in her throat. "No."

"Amberlyn, you need time to process this. Working isn't going to do you any good."

Sniffling her tears back, she shook her head, even though he couldn't see her. "I've already been cleared to work in the Situation Room. You haven't."

"And you know we have dozens of agents working on this case right along with you."

"I know, but I need to keep working on this. I'm not ready to think about—" She broke off. "A distraction will be good for me."

"You have my number. Use it anytime."

"Thanks." Amberlyn hung up and leaned against the wall of the tiny space. Using both hands, she wiped away the tears that had spilled over, then opened the glass door.

Luke turned at the sound, a look on his face that held far too much understanding.

CHAPTER 4

AMBERLYN KNEW ONE of the bombing victims. Luke couldn't say how he had come to that conclusion after reading the expression on her face, but with the way she'd kept looking at the phone and checking the time and her email, he suspected she'd been hoping for much better news than what she'd received from her phone call.

She swiped at her eyes and stepped out of the privacy booth. Blinking rapidly, she opened her mouth as though to say something, only to close it again.

At a loss of what to say, Luke went with the standard, "Do you want to talk about it?"

She shook her head and shrugged at the same time. The contradiction suggested she didn't know what she wanted any more than he did.

"Who was it?" he asked sincerely.

She drew a deep breath and let it out slowly, blinking against the tears shimmering in her eyes. "Chanelle Mays. We used to work together."

"I'm sorry." Luke gestured toward the exit. "I can escort you out if you need to leave."

Before Amberlyn could answer, a member of the watch team approached. "We're getting ready to finalize our evening report. Can you give me whatever details you have so far on the investigation?"

Luke nodded. "I'll get that for you right now." He turned to Amberlyn. "I can find someone to escort you out."

She shook her head. "I'll help you put the report together."

Even though Luke suspected Amberlyn was desperate for time to herself, he didn't argue. He headed back to their workstations and waited for her to sit before he reclaimed his seat. Hoping to simplify their task, he said, "We should start with the email you sent to your office. It'll have the same information the president will want."

She nodded, still looking like she was buried in the sand after being slammed by an emotional tidal wave.

"Forward it to me. I can add the summary and share it with the watch team."

She tapped on her keyboard and forwarded the email.

Luke skimmed her analysis, impressed by the depth of information she had provided. Beyond the list of potential suspects, she had detailed the reasons the others on the list had been eliminated, ranging from the two who had passed away to those whose race didn't match their suspect to the ones who matched the general description but didn't have the tattoo that had been partially visible on their suspect's wrist.

She had also added a section of a witness statement that highlighted the conversation the woman had overheard. Most of the conversation had been summarized, the two men talking about the blast radius when parked beside a building, but the witness had quoted one line, and it jumped out at him: *This is our turn to show we're serious about making a difference.*

Luke couldn't fathom how killing innocent people could ever bring about someone's end goal to make a difference.

He skimmed over the report a second time. Satisfied that everything the president could possibly need was in there, Luke copied the core email and pasted it into a new one. After adding a summary of the data, which was most likely what would be included in the evening report, he added Amberlyn to the cc line, included his own contact information, and sent the email.

"It's sent," he called to the watch-team member.

"Got it."

Luke turned his attention back to Amberlyn. "Did you drive here?"

"No. I drove in with the director, but I planned to walk back to headquarters. It's not far."

Not sure how she was managing to keep her emotions under control, he said, "Maybe you should consider going home."

"I'd rather work."

Luke glanced at the time. Technically, he'd gone off duty an hour ago. He stood and motioned toward the exit. "This way."

They both retrieved their cell phones from the lockboxes in the hall outside the Situation Room, and Luke dialed Tom. As soon as he answered, Luke asked, "Are you still on duty?"

"Yeah," Tom said. "I'm staying overnight."

"I'm taking off. I need to go over to FBI headquarters."

"Is the rumor true that you went to high school with one of the terrorists?" Tom asked.

"It looks that way."

"That's crazy."

Not wanting to dwell on his high school years any more than necessary, Luke changed the subject. "I'll see you tomorrow."

"Yeah. See you then," Tom said. "And let us know if you find anything."

"I will," Luke agreed, though he suspected the FBI would control that information, and he might be limited in what he could say to whom. He ended the call.

Amberlyn stared at him. "You don't have to come with me."

"I know more about your suspects than anyone at the bureau." Luke guided her toward the exit. "If you can get me a visitor's parking pass, I can drive you over. That way, we don't have to walk. And if you want, we can grab something to eat on the way."

"I'll worry about eating later. I just want to get to my office."

"We need to swing by my office so I can grab my things," he said. When she didn't respond, he started walking toward the east wing. Thankfully, she fell into step with him without needing any additional prodding.

They were halfway to his office before he realized what he had done. He'd offered Amberlyn Reiner a ride . . . in his twenty-year-old Honda.

After the fiasco of their dinner together years ago, it was already too late to make a good first impression. He suspected once she saw his car, her second impression of him wasn't going to be much better.

Amberlyn wasn't going to cry in front of Luke. She wasn't. That thought repeated in her mind even as tears threatened and the heartbreaking reality of a future without Chanelle formed in her mind.

She walked with Luke along the Ellipse, the trees shading the parking area, the leaves just beginning to turn color despite the overly warm October day. Though it was nearly five, only a handful of parking spots were open.

Luke stopped beside a Honda Civic that looked like it had seen better days. He unlocked it and opened the passenger side door before circling to the other side.

As soon as he climbed in and started the car, Amberlyn ran her fingers beneath both eyes, wiping away the moisture lingering there. She took a deep breath and slid into her seat, warm air blasting from the air conditioning vents.

Despite the worn appearance on the outside, the interior was surprisingly clean. No empty cups or soda cans on the floor, no old fast-food containers. Not even a trash bag in sight.

Only the hat to his uniform, or cover, as she now knew the military called it, lay neatly on the back seat, his bag stored on the floor behind him.

The warm air turned cold, providing relief from the heat that had been trapped inside the car, and she closed her door.

Amberlyn's gaze was immediately drawn to the White House, dozens of tourists crowded at the fence to take photos. Always before, she had considered the iconic home to be a symbol of freedom. After today, it would be a reminder of the worst day of her life.

New tears threatened. She glanced out the window to hide them.

Luke drove in silence as he navigated the few blocks between the Ellipse and FBI headquarters. When he got closer, he asked, "Where's the entrance to the parking lot?"

She drew a deep breath in an effort to settle her emotions and directed Luke to visitor parking. After they had the appropriate credentials for Luke to accompany her, they made their way to her office.

As soon as they entered, Kiera spotted her. Immediately, she crossed to Amberlyn and enveloped her in a hug. "I'm so sorry."

The offer of condolences broke Amberlyn, and instantly, she was fighting back tears again.

Kiera released her. "Is there anything I can do?"

Amberlyn's throat closed up.

Thankfully, Luke spoke before she had to make an attempt to speak. "I'm Captain Steele. I'm here to help Special Agent Reiner with the investigation," he told Kiera. "Is there a workspace I can use?"

"We're set up in the conference room." Kiera motioned to her left.

"Would you mind showing me?" Luke asked. "I'm sure Amberlyn needs to get her files."

"This way." Kiera gave Amberlyn's arm a squeeze. "We're here for you."

Amberlyn blinked against the newest wave of tears threatening, stopping when she reached her cubicle. She dropped into her chair and snatched several tissues from the box on the corner of her desk. She blew her nose, wiped her eyes, and silently thanked Luke for giving her this moment alone.

She let her head fall back on her chair, her face toward the ceiling, her eyes closed as she gathered her strength. Then she pulled herself up, grabbed her laptop, and carried it to the conference room.

As soon as she entered, Jeff shot her a sympathetic look, but he didn't say anything. He most certainly didn't want to see her tears any more than she wanted to shed them.

The large evidence board on the far side of the room already held photos from the diner, a photo of the Pine Falls championship football team, and individual photos of the members who were currently listed as their top suspects.

Amberlyn set her laptop on the empty spot beside Luke and sat down. As her coworkers brought her up to speed on the latest developments, she prayed she would be able to separate her personal life from the task at hand. She added an extra silent prayer that Luke's memories of his high school years would provide insight into the adults his former classmates had become.

When Luke had offered to help, he'd done so because he hadn't wanted Amberlyn to be alone after receiving such devastating news. Now that he was staring at photos of his high school past, he was rethinking the wisdom of that decision.

Kiera had introduced him to Jeff Iverson when they'd arrived in the conference room. From what Luke gathered, the rest of their staff had been sent home so they could work the investigation in shifts.

"Captain, how many of these guys are you still in contact with?" Jeff asked.

"None of them."

"Have you seen any of them since graduation?" Kiera asked.

"Only Gavin Pennington, but that must have been five years ago."

Beside him, Amberlyn spoke for the first time since walking into the room. "Where was that?"

"National airport."

"Any idea what he's doing now? Where he works, that sort of thing?"

"I didn't talk to him." Luke had been both surprised and relieved that one of his former high school tormentors hadn't noticed him at the time.

"But you saw him," Amberlyn said.

"Yes." Digging the memory out, Luke tried to let the details form. "He was with a woman, but I don't remember seeing a wedding ring on either of their fingers."

"What was he wearing?"

"The usual, I guess. Probably jeans and a T-shirt."

Amberlyn tapped on her mouse pad. "According to his social media, he went to Old Dominion University for college and is currently living in Pine Falls."

Yet another reason not to go back to his home town.

"Captain, tell us what Owen Lester was like during high school. Was he a good student? A nice guy? A bully? Was he into drugs?"

"He was on the fringes of the popular crowd." Luke couldn't count how many times he'd wanted Owen to shut up when relating every single moment one of the popular kids had let the guy join them at lunch or at a party.

"Drinking? Drugs?"

"He drank, but I don't know that he ever did drugs. At least, he never said anything around me about it."

Kiera looked up from her laptop. "I just got the high school transcripts. Looks like Owen Lester wasn't the best student, but he wasn't failing classes either. Mostly C's."

With the way Mrs. Bailey had ridden the guy in their learning strategies class, Luke was surprised Owen had managed to do that well.

"Let's go through the other three who have been seen wearing their rings who also have tattoos," Jeff suggested.

"Any chance you've been able to contact the tattoo parlor in Pine Falls?" Amberlyn asked.

"I'm afraid that was a dead end. It went out of business eleven years ago," Jeff said.

Amberlyn sighed. "Looks like we're back to searching online for anything that will help us narrow our suspect field."

Together, the four of them pulled up notes, transcripts, and news articles to build a profile for the other three teammates.

Hayden Barry had attended one year of community college before he'd enlisted in the army. Within months of joining, he had married his high school girlfriend and had had the first of two kids less than a year later. After eight years working as a mechanic, he'd left the service and now worked in a garage in Chesterfield, Virginia.

Jackson Scott was also married, with two daughters and one son. He had attended trade school after high school and was now an electrician.

Less was known about Randy Cole. His social media hadn't been terribly active over the past ten years, but all indications were that he was single and had graduated from Mary Washington University with a degree in political science.

"I'd put Jackson Scott at the top of the list." Jeff settled his elbow on the table. "With his knowledge of electricity, building a bomb would be child's play."

"I don't love that we have so little on Randy Cole," Kiera added.

"Can you make sure he's not working for the government?" Amberlyn asked. "The timing would be consistent with someone who had gone to college and then been recruited into an intelligence role."

Kiera nodded. "I'll reach out to the CIA to see what they can give me."

"While you do that, we can start on the rest of the list," Jeff said. "Captain, since you and Amberlyn have already looked through their social media, why don't you keep going with that and search through their friends' pages? Maybe we'll get lucky and find photos that will tell us if these guys have wrist tattoos and if they're still wearing their championship rings or not."

"Whether they're wearing their ring is less important than the tattoos," Amberlyn said. "Jewelry is something they can put on and take off."

"That's true," Jeff said, "but if we find evidence of them wearing their rings, it shows us that their ring still fits and that they do wear it sometimes."

"True." Kiera picked up her cell phone but didn't dial. "For social media, I think their girlfriends and wives would be the best place to start."

Luke glanced at his watch. "What time is the next shift supposed to take over?"

"Ten o'clock," Jeff said. "In the meantime, I say we order some dinner."

"Agreed." Kiera nodded toward Amberlyn. "That's the only way we can be sure Amberlyn eats."

Luke had entertained a similar thought. He might not look forward to reviewing the social media posts of the people who had tormented him during high school, but when he went home tonight, he would do so knowing his few close friends were still breathing.

CHAPTER 5

FROM THE MOMENT Amberlyn had entered her home, she'd cried until she was certain she had no more tears left. Throughout the night, she'd tried to quiet her mind, to let herself pretend today had never happened. She'd even called Chanelle's phone again just to hear her voice on her voice mail, but the cheerful greeting telling her to leave a message only reinforced the truth: Amberlyn would never hear Chanelle's voice in real life again.

Amberlyn had finally fallen asleep a bit before one. At one thirty, her phone rang, the call coming from Chanelle's mother to make sure Amberlyn had heard the news. How the woman could even speak on the phone was beyond Amberlyn's comprehension, but she had to admit, speaking with someone else who knew and loved Chanelle had given Amberlyn an outlet she'd very much needed.

After the twenty-minute conversation, Amberlyn had only managed to sleep in short stretches, more tears coming every time she awoke to remember the events that had cost so many lives.

She still couldn't believe she had cried in front of Luke Steele, of all people. Yet she couldn't deny that he'd been far more sensitive than she'd expected. He hadn't acted at all like a guy who would insist on paying for her dry cleaning and then never call.

Her alarm went off, serving as a reminder that today was a work-day. She headed for the shower, hoping the water would wash away the evidence of her repeated crying jags throughout the night. When she looked in the mirror fifteen minutes later, her puffy eyes proved her hope hadn't been realized.

Though she dreaded facing her coworkers looking like this, she dressed for the day.

She was debating whether to eat breakfast when her phone rang. Ian.

"Hey, anything new?" she asked.

"No, but I spoke with Jeff already this morning. I understand you came in and worked a shift last night."

"The early one."

"Then you've put in enough hours on this for the time being. I want you to take today off."

"What?" She couldn't have heard him correctly. "I've been running lead on Forever Freedom since we first heard of them."

"Yes, but you also need time away from the office," Ian said. "And I need the rest of the team to stay focused on the case, not on whether they need to pass you another box of Kleenex."

Amberlyn glanced at the empty box of tissues at her bedside. "That's not fair."

"I'm thinking of your mental well-being."

"And I'm thinking of the victims and their families and friends who deserve answers."

"Including you."

"Yes." Her grip tightened on the phone. "Including me."

Ian sighed. "If you really want to stay on this, you can work from home today, but I don't want to see you in the office until tomorrow morning, at the earliest."

It wasn't the ideal situation, but it was better than nothing. "Fine."

"And, Amberlyn?"

"Yes?"

His voice gentled. "I'm truly sorry for your loss."

"Thank you." She hung up and reached for a new box of tissues.

With the directive to work from home, she changed out of her business attire and into a pair of yoga pants and a neon-pink T-shirt. She needed something to brighten her day, even if it were only the cheerful color of her shirt.

Amberlyn retrieved her laptop from her bag and set it on the desk in her guest bedroom that doubled as an office. This was the room Chanelle would have stayed in had she made the trip to DC that she'd told Amberlyn about.

After Amberlyn turned on her laptop, she pulled up the live news feed on her iPad and set it beside her. Not surprisingly, the current segment was on yesterday's bombing and the broadcaster's speculation that Forever Freedom had chosen the FEMA building as a target because of a bungled response to a hurricane that had hit Texas last month. Amberlyn didn't know how the newscasters had come up with that theory, but she wasn't buying it. Texas wasn't even in the same region as Kansas City.

If those photos from the diner outside St. Louis had come to light earlier, maybe they would have been able to stop this attack. Maybe they would have thought to expand their warnings as far as Kansas City. Maybe Chanelle would still be alive.

Amberlyn sniffled and crossed into the living room, where she'd left the tissues. She carried it back into her office and set it on her desk. Time to get to work.

Luke stifled a yawn as he walked down the hall in the White House Tuesday morning. Working until ten last night and then getting up at five this morning hadn't given him much time to recharge, but he and Amberlyn's team had eliminated five more people from their likely suspect list.

He still couldn't believe Amberlyn had managed to work for so many hours after finding out about her friend. Her sense of determination would have been inspiring if Luke weren't so worried about the way she was ignoring her grief.

When Luke walked into his office, Parker, his air force counterpart, stood by his desk, his go bag in hand. "Grab your bag. We fly out in fifteen minutes. Ankara."

A trip that wasn't supposed to happen for two more weeks—first to France and then to Turkey. "Why didn't someone tell me?"

"I tried calling twenty minutes ago, but you didn't answer."

"Sorry. I was on 395, and I couldn't reach my phone."

"You know, if you had a new car, you would have the hands-free option."

"So I've been told." Luke grabbed his emergency pack he kept stored under his desk. "Any idea why the trip got moved up?"

"No. The president announced in his address to the nation last night that he was postponing his visit to Paris," Parker said. "I'm not sure why he moved this part of his trip up."

"There must be something important in Turkey for him to leave the country before we have answers on who set that bomb."

"My thoughts exactly." Parker headed for the door.

"Who all is coming?"

"Just the two of us," Parker said. "Wyatt is on duty right now, but he'll hand off the football when we board Marine One."

"Any idea how long we'll be gone?"

"Word is it'll be a quick trip. Two days. Three tops."

Two days of freedom from the questions about his high school and the football team. That thought should have brought him relief, but instead, an uneasiness snaked through him. What if his knowledge would help stop the person behind this and potentially prevent another attack?

He shook that thought away. Any number of the people he'd graduated with would be more useful in providing information than him.

"So what happened to you yesterday anyway?" Parker asked.

"What did Tom tell you?"

"Just that you had to help the FBI with something to do with the bombing."

Though his instinct was to protect information, Parker's clearances were as high as his own. Luke had to remind himself that Parker was a friend, one he trusted. "They think one of my old high school classmates may have been involved."

"Involved, as in planted the bomb?"

"That's their working theory." They passed through the east wing diplomatic reception room. "I was at FBI headquarters until after ten last night, trying to help them narrow down their suspect list."

"Sounds like you need to take a nap as soon as we get on board Air Force One."

"I wouldn't say no to another hour or two of sleep."

"I hope you can sleep on planes."

They reached the West Colonnade as the Marine One helicopter lowered onto the South Lawn. Luke and Parker waited beside the rose garden until the president and his security detail passed by.

Wyatt handed the case holding the nuclear codes to Luke. "Have a good trip."

"Thanks." Luke fell in line behind the president and boarded the helicopter.

Less than an hour later, they were aboard Air Force One with more questions than answers.

Amberlyn was done crying, and she was ready to do whatever was necessary to identify the men responsible for Chanelle's death. She'd already received word from Chanelle's parents that the funeral would be on Saturday, four days from now. Amberlyn would need to be there, but it would be far easier to attend if her friend's killers were already identified and in custody.

Still with more questions than answers, she went back to the beginning. The beginning of this attack anyway.

She settled onto her couch and retrieved the original diner footage that had produced the image of the championship ring and the partial tattoo. Setting her laptop on the coffee table in front of her, she played the surveillance feed in slow motion, projecting it onto the flat-screen television hanging on the wall opposite her couch. The clip started with the two men sitting at their table, both of them far enough into the booth to make it impossible to see anything beyond their arms and shoulders.

A waitress stopped by their table, carrying a coffeepot. She refilled both men's cups, her focus on the man with the wolf tattoo. A short chat ensued before she turned toward the camera, a little smile on her face.

Amberlyn froze the image. That smile indicated one of two things: the waitress was hoping to get to know the man with the wolf tattoo better, or she already had a relationship with him.

Amberlyn stood and moved closer to the TV, studying the pretty brunette's face. Attraction, expectation. Both of those were clear, but was there a hint of familiarity as well? She couldn't tell.

Amberlyn sat back on the couch and hit the button on her laptop to save the screenshot.

Then she hit the Play button and continued.

A long stretch of time passed before the waitress reappeared, her lips twitching into a half smile as she approached the two men. This exchange was much shorter. She stacked two plates on one arm and headed toward the kitchen. Moments later, the two men slid out of the booth. The one with the wolf tattoo dropped a few bills on the table before heading for the door, his ball cap obscuring his face from the camera.

She rewound the feed until the waitress appeared the second time, and then she played the segment again. Something was off during the exchange, but she couldn't quite put her finger on what it was. She played it a third time.

When the waitress turned toward the camera with the dishes in hand, it dawned on Amberlyn. "She never gave them their check."

Amberlyn watched the rest of the surveillance feed, all the way through the men leaving. The man with the ring nodded slightly, likely in response to something his friend said. A moment after they left, the waitress returned and cleared the coffee mugs left behind. She then returned a second time and wiped the booth down thoroughly—table, bench seats, even the napkin holder and salt and pepper shakers.

Amberlyn looked up the name of the special agent who had forwarded the surveillance video to her office, and she snatched up her phone.

"This is Ray," a man answered after Amberlyn had dialed.

"Special Agent Franco?" Amberlyn asked, making sure she had dialed the right number.

"That's right," he said.

"This is Amberlyn Reiner with the behavioral analysis unit. My records show you were the one who identified the two men in the restaurant outside of St. Louis as belonging to Forever Freedom."

"Yeah." The word came out on a sigh and carried with it a healthy dose of regret.

"By any chance, did you question the waitress who served them?"

"Yes. I talked to her yesterday morning, about a half hour before the bomb went off."

"What did she say?"

"She didn't remember anything about the guys," Ray said. "I can send you the interview transcripts if you want, but there wasn't much to them."

"I'd appreciate it." Amberlyn looked down at the screenshot on her laptop. "What about the surveillance feed of the two men entering the restaurant?"

"The owner sent me as far back as he had. They said they clear the surveillance feed every forty-eight hours unless there's a problem. We got lucky that we were able to get to them before all of it was deleted."

"Or someone there erased it before you arrived."

"You think someone was protecting these guys?"

"It's possible." Amberlyn set her laptop aside and grabbed a notepad and pen. "What else can you tell me about the waitress who served our suspects?"

"Let me pull up my notes." He went silent for a moment, save for the clicking of a keyboard sounding over the line. "Jenny Armstrong, twenty-one. She's been working at the diner since high school."

About ten years younger than the man who'd likely gone to high school with Luke.

"I'm helping out in the Kansas City office right now," Ray continued, "but I can drive back to St. Louis and conduct another interview tonight."

Amberlyn zeroed in on the coffeepot. "I have a feeling the person we need to talk to won't be at the diner tonight." She pushed to a stand and paced to where a cluster of photos hung on the wall, one of her with Chanelle at the center of them. "Stay where you are for now. We may get more information if we send someone in there she hasn't seen before."

"Let me know what you find out."

"I will." Amberlyn hung up and dialed a different number, this time her boss.

Ian's voice came on after the second ring. "I'd ask how you're doing, but I can't imagine you want to answer that question right now."

He had that right. "I think I found something. How would you feel about letting me fly out to St. Louis?"

"Why?"

Amberlyn told him about her suspicions that the waitress was familiar with at least one of the men spotted at the diner. "The agent investigating left the diner before the bomb went off. Now that it's clear what those men were up to, it's possible I can tap into some new emotions."

"Hoping the waitress feels guilty?"

"Guilty, smug. I don't care which, but the emotions are likely fresh enough to help me trip her up."

"I can send Jeff or Kiera."

"I need to do this," Amberlyn said. "Besides, I want to go out to Kansas City to visit Chanelle's parents."

Silence stretched over the line for several seconds. Finally, Ian said, "I'll put in for your travel order. You book your flight."

"Thanks, Ian. I appreciate it."

"Just take care of yourself."

"I will."

CHAPTER 6

"THAT'S THE PRESIDENT of Georgia," Parker whispered. "What's he doing here?"

Luke had the same question. More importantly, why had President Frazier made a secret trip to Ankara for a meeting with him and the prime minister of Turkey?

Luke was currently on duty, but whatever was happening in that conference room was confidential enough that he hadn't been invited inside. Since they had already checked out of their hotel, Parker had taken position with him outside the embassy conference room, both of them in their dress uniforms.

A group of four arrived a moment later, including the president of Armenia. Luke's curiosity heightened.

Parker waited until the Armenian president and one of the men with him entered the conference room, the two members of the security detail taking position beside the door.

"What do you think?" Parker whispered. "Problems with Russia or Azerbaijan?"

"Could be both." Or increased tensions with Iran. An aggression by any of those nations could quickly evolve into a full-fledged military conflict, particularly with the rumors of Azerbaijan having hidden nuclear capabilities. The number of Russian scientists who had moved to that country over the years was alarming in itself.

Luke's phone vibrated with an incoming message. He pulled it from his pocket and read the text. *It's Jeff Iverson. Any chance you can come in again today and help us dive into our suspect list?*

"Who's texting you?"

"One of the FBI agents I met yesterday."

"The girl I saw you with?"

"No. One of the guys in her office. He wants to know if I can come in and help them out today." Luke held up his phone.

"Just say you're on duty." Parker looked at his watch. "We should be back in DC around eight or nine tonight, so it's a fair bet to say you won't get off duty until midnight."

Luke nodded and typed in a response. An instant later, Jeff texted back.

How about tomorrow? We could really use your insight.

"Now he's asking about tomorrow."

"That's up to you. We'll both be off tomorrow," Parker said. "Do they have a suspect yet?"

"No. That's what they're hoping I can help them figure out."

"Then you need to say yes."

Parker's words mirrored what Luke's conscience was already telling him. But that didn't mean he wanted to do it. It didn't even mean he had to say yes.

When he didn't immediately text back, Parker asked, "What's the problem?"

"High school wasn't a good time for me," Luke said, trying to put the past into perspective. "It's hard looking through photos of people who made my life a living nightmare every day."

"They obviously had no clue who you really were." Parker motioned to Luke's phone. "And you aren't going to rest easy knowing you could have done something to catch these guys, especially if they plan to strike again."

"I know." Gathering his courage, Luke sent a text. *I can do tomorrow. What time?*

Seven. I'll leave your name with the guard at visitor parking.

Luke hit the Like button on the last message. "Looks like I'll be spending my day off at FBI headquarters."

"If you need some extra time off, the rest of us can help cover you."

"I may take you up on that."

The conference room door opened, and Luke and Parker both rose to their feet.

The occupants filtered out, starting with President Frazier and the rest of the American contingent.

Luke took only one look at the president's face to decide that whatever had gone on in the meeting was enough to worry him.

Parker leaned close and whispered, "It doesn't look like that went well."

Luke shook his head. "No. It doesn't."

The aroma of bacon and waffles hung in the air when Amberlyn entered the diner in St. Louis Wednesday morning. Her stomach grumbled, a reminder that she hadn't eaten before leaving for the airport. She'd slept through the beverage service of her 6:00 a.m. flight, though she doubted the little snack bag would have satisfied her hunger, especially after she'd eaten so little over the past two days. Maybe she was finally getting her appetite back.

After making her travel plans, she had checked in with Ray again. He'd opted to return with her and now stood watch by the back door in case she needed backup.

Amberlyn looked around the cozy diner, with its red upholstery and chrome accents. She spotted the surveillance camera mounted to the ceiling in her first sweep. A dozen patrons were seated around the room, three at the serving counter lined with stools. The rest were seated in booths that lined the wall with windows. The first booth was far enough forward that it didn't have a window, the perfect spot to dine if one didn't want to be seen by anyone outside. Based on the surveillance feed, that was where the suspects would have been seated, away from possible witnesses.

The hostess, a blonde woman, approached holding a menu. "Just one?"

"Maybe. I'm hoping a friend will be able to meet me." She waved toward the front two booths, which were currently empty. "Could I sit over there so I can watch the door?"

"No problem." She walked to the second table from the front, likely the table where their witness had sat. "Is this okay?"

"This is perfect." Amberlyn slid into the booth and accepted the menu the waitress handed her.

"Your server will be right with you."

"Thanks." She opened the menu and skimmed through the options. Comfort food. She needed comfort food. She made her selection quickly, but she left her menu open as though still trying to decide.

Amberlyn spotted the waitress from the surveillance feed across the room. When the woman approached with a glass of water and set it in front of her, Amberlyn's heartbeat quickened in anticipation.

"I'm Jenny. I'll be your server today. Can I get you anything else to drink?"

Amberlyn took in the woman's appearance. Despite her age, little worry lines marred her otherwise smooth brow. "Some orange juice would be great."

"I'll get that right out to you." Jenny headed to the counter and poured her juice.

Amberlyn glanced down at her menu as she approached.

"Here you go." Jenny set down the juice. "Have you decided?"

"I think I need another minute."

"No problem." Jenny crossed to the serving counter and then disappeared through the door leading to the kitchen.

An older man sitting at the counter paid his check and headed for the door. The waitress behind the counter cleared his dish and used a rag to wipe the counter.

Jenny returned a few minutes later, and Amberlyn asked for french toast and a side of bacon. Again, when the woman left Amberlyn's table, she retreated to the kitchen.

The next time she came into the main part of the diner, she brought with her Amberlyn's order and a tearful expression.

Amberlyn keyed in on the woman's obvious distress. "Hey, are you okay? You look upset." She had to swallow before she added, "You didn't know someone who died in that bombing yesterday, did you?"

"No." She gave a quick shake of her head, but she blinked rapidly, as though fighting back rising emotions.

"I did." Amberlyn forced herself to keep her gaze on the young woman's even as she fought against her own rising emotions. Though the words caught in her throat, she forced them out. "My best friend died in the bombing. It was her first day in her new office at FEMA."

Jenny's eyes widened, a look of complete agony on her face. She took a step back and then another. With a jerky movement, she gestured toward Amberlyn's plate. "Let me know if you need anything else."

What Amberlyn really wanted was answers. For now, she'd settle for some syrup. "Oh, wait," she called after Jenny. "Can I get some syrup, please?"

Jenny nodded without turning around. She stopped beside the hostess, whispered something in her ear, and continued into the kitchen.

The blonde brought Amberlyn a little cup of syrup a moment later.

"What happened to Jenny?" Amberlyn asked.

"She's had a rough couple days."

"Any idea why?"

The blonde looked over her shoulder as though to make sure no one was listening.

The woman knew something, and she wanted to talk. Despite the flood of adrenaline that pumped through Amberlyn, she kept her voice calm. "I know you don't know me, but I only want to help. Really."

After another quick glance over her shoulder, she leaned closer. "I'm not sure, but I think she's afraid her boyfriend was mixed up in that bombing in Kansas City."

"I remember hearing the name of a suspect on the news. I think it was Bill Thomas. Is that her boyfriend?"

"No, his name is Eli Duffy. But she hasn't heard from him since last Friday."

"I hope she gets some answers soon."

"Me too." She stepped back. "Enjoy your breakfast."

"Thanks."

Amberlyn spread the ball of butter out onto the triangular-shaped pieces of french toast and poured on more syrup than she should. She took her first bite and tasted home.

She ate half her breakfast before Jenny reappeared, but instead of entering from the kitchen, she walked through the front door, Ray at her side.

With his hand gripping Jenny's arm, he escorted her to Amberlyn's booth. "Have a seat." Ray gestured for Jenny to slide into the booth across from Amberlyn. "I caught her trying to leave through the back door."

"I was going home. Is there anything wrong with that?" Jenny asked.

"You don't get off until two." Ray had clearly checked.

"I was taking a lunch break."

Determined to give Ray an upper hand, Amberlyn said, "I gather you haven't arrested her yet."

"Arrested me?" Jenny's words came out with a squeak.

Ray shook his head. "I thought you'd want to talk to her first."

Jenny immediately shook her head and focused on Amberlyn. "Who are you?"

"Amberlyn Reiner. FBI."

"I didn't do anything wrong."

Amberlyn took another bite of her french toast, chewing slowly. As though oblivious to the young waitress's rising anxiety, Amberlyn slid her plate of bacon closer to Ray. "Did you want some?"

He plucked a piece off her plate. "Thanks."

"I want to leave." Jenny motioned toward the door. "You can't keep me here."

"Oh, yes we can," Ray said evenly.

Amberlyn slid her plate aside and leaned forward. "Withholding evidence is a crime." She waited for Jenny's gaze to meet her own. "It's called 'obstructing justice.'"

"And don't forget the tampering with evidence." Ray held up one finger, as though making a point. "She must have been the one to erase the surveillance feed that showed her boyfriend walking in last Friday."

"That's right." Amberlyn nodded thoughtfully. "And we're both trying to give her the benefit of the doubt that she didn't help Eli plant that bomb."

"I didn't." Jenny shook her head, her panic now full-blown. "I swear I didn't know that's what he was going to do."

"But you know more than what you told Special Agent Franco," Amberlyn said.

"Yes."

"Great. Let's start at the beginning."

Jenny shook her head. "Not until you promise I won't be arrested." She paused as though searching for the right words. "I want immunity."

"Tell us what you know, and we'll see what we can do."

"No." She shook her head again. "The promise comes first." She held up her trembling hand and pointed at the table. "In writing."

So much for the information coming easily.

CHAPTER 7

LUKE SIGNED IN at the reception desk at FBI headquarters and slipped the lanyard holding his visitor's badge around his neck.

"Do you know where you're going?" the woman behind the desk asked.

"Yes, ma'am. Thank you." Luke made his way to Amberlyn's office. The outer door was locked, but as soon as he knocked, Jeff opened it.

"Right on time." Jeff waved him inside. "We're just getting ready for a briefing from the St. Louis office."

"Why St. Louis?" Luke asked.

"We have a lead on a suspect there." Jeff led him past Amberlyn's empty cubicle. "That's where the photos were taken of the man wearing that championship ring."

They reached the conference room, where Kiera waited, her laptop open on the table and the flat screen on the wall already turned on.

The question of why Amberlyn wasn't present burned on Luke's tongue, but he swallowed it.

A man in his early forties walked in behind them. "You must be Captain Steele."

"Yes, sir."

"I'm Ian Yardley." Ian offered his hand. "Thanks for coming."

Luke nodded. They all sat around the table, and Luke set his briefcase on the floor beside him.

"Kiera, let Amberlyn know we're ready," Ian said. "Jeff, go ahead and log us in."

Kiera sent a text. Jeff opened a secure video-conference channel. Within moments, Amberlyn's image came on the screen. At first glance, she looked like a professional with nothing on her mind but the case at hand. On closer inspection, the sadness in her eyes was hard to miss.

"Sorry to make everyone come in so early," Amberlyn said, "but we have an update on the waitress."

Luke had no idea what waitress they were talking about, so he remained silent and hoped someone would eventually think to clue him in.

Ian tapped his pen against the file in front of him. "Did you finally get her to talk?"

"Yes. The DA granted her immunity late last night."

"And?" Ian prompted.

"She was dating one of the men in the diner, the one with the wolf tattoo," Amberlyn said. "His name is Eli Duffy, and his last known address is here in the St. Louis area."

Where the photo was taken. Luke leaned forward. "I don't recognize that name."

"Our initial background on him indicates he grew up here in Missouri. We have a surveillance team at his house now. No sign of him so far." Amberlyn seemed to focus on Luke before shifting her attention to Ian. "We're waiting on the search warrant before we go in."

"What about the other guy?" Jeff asked. "Did she give you a name?"

"No. She said she hadn't seen him before the day he was at the diner," Amberlyn said. "According to her, she even introduced herself, and he didn't give her his name."

"Any chance she was able to identify any of our suspects?" Ian asked.

"No. I don't know if she never got a good look at him or if she didn't recognize him, but she wasn't able to give us much," Amberlyn said. "The sketch artist tried to work with her, too, but he said her memory wasn't enough for him to create anything usable."

"What else did she say about her boyfriend?" Kiera asked. "Did she know he was building a bomb?"

"No, but she did say she thought it was odd that he just bought two used cars when he bought a new truck last year."

Ian lifted both hands, the movement a combination of surrender and frustration. "You think one of them was where the bomb was hidden?"

"Yes. We believe the Nissan Altima was the one that housed the bomb at the FEMA building. The second vehicle is a Toyota Camry."

"Any idea where the second car is?" Luke asked.

"We won't know if it's accounted for until the search warrant comes in." Amberlyn focused on Luke. "But if you're concerned that he bought the second car to create a second car bomb, you aren't the only one. I had the same thought."

"Keep us up-to-date on your progress," Ian said. "And be careful."

"I will." She picked up her phone and looked at the screen. "The search warrant just came in. I'll call as soon as I have an update."

The video chat ended.

Ian stood. "I have some calls to make. Jeff, you see what you and Luke can come up with on our suspect list."

As soon as Ian left the room, Jeff opened a file folder and spread out nineteen photos. Based on what they'd accomplished last night, six of those photos represented people who fit the suspected bomber's description and also had a football wrist tattoo. The rest, they weren't sure about.

"Did your team make any progress after I left?" Luke asked.

"They eliminated one from the suspect list. They also tracked down the owner of the old tattoo parlor in Pine Falls. I'll follow up on that in a couple hours." Jeff tapped a finger on the file folder. "For now, I'd like your help with the backgrounds on your former classmates, particularly those who might still be close to the members of the old football team."

"I already told you, I hardly spoke to any of them in high school. I don't have anything to tell you."

"We understand that, but we have another way of gaining information."

"How?"

Jeff reached for a printout and passed it to Luke. "Your high school reunion."

"What?" Luke couldn't have heard him right.

"Your fifteen-year reunion is in less than two weeks. We want you to attend to see what you can learn about our suspects."

Go back to the high school? The mere thought of walking those halls, of seeing the people who had either ignored him or bullied him through the four years he'd spent there made him sick to his stomach.

He shook his head. "Look, I'm fine with telling you what I know, but going to the reunion wouldn't do any good. Those guys didn't talk to me then. They aren't going to talk to me now. Neither will their friends."

"We'll send you with a date, then, someone who can help you mingle and who can chat with any of the suspects who attend," Jeff said.

"I don't know . . ."

"We need this." Jeff waved his hand to encompass the photos before them. "We have to narrow this down if we're going to find out who's behind this. And if your concern about a second bomb is realized, we don't have time to do the legwork by setting up surveillance on this many people one at a time."

Luke focused on the various photos on the table. Despite the queasiness in his stomach, he nodded. "If I can get my leave approved, I'll do what I can."

"Good. In the meantime, we have a lot of work to do."

Amberlyn shouldn't be here. She knew it. Ray knew it. But with Eli Duffy's house in front of them and half the St. Louis office currently helping track down leads in Kansas City, Ray and his team were willing to take whatever help anyone offered—even if it was in the form of a woman who was too emotionally involved in this case, someone who hadn't been a field agent for nearly two years.

Trying to keep her emotions in check, Amberlyn sized up the single-level house on the quiet street. The yard needed to be mowed, the grass ankle high, and a large maple tree partially obscured her view of the large living room window.

"Reiner, cover the front." Ray tightened the strap of his body armor that had FBI emblazoned across it in bright yellow.

His voice came through her earpiece, but he was also still close enough to hear without equipment.

"Be careful," she said.

Ray gave a curt nod, then moved into position by the front door, opposite one of the other special agents, where he was protected in the event of instant gunfire.

Amberlyn stepped behind the hood of the SUV they'd arrived in, drew her Glock 19, and took aim at the front door.

Ray rang the bell.

No answer.

Ray knocked.

Still no answer.

The curtains in the big picture window twitched.

Amberlyn spoke in a low voice, trusting her communication earpiece to pick up her words. "I've got movement at the window."

Ray pounded on the door three times and this time called out, "FBI. We have a warrant. Open up!"

The curtains twitched again, but the door didn't open.

Ray's voice came through her earpiece. "Tucker, you ready?"

"Ready."

"On three." Ray counted them down. Then moving with precision, Ray and the other agents, one with Ray in the front and two at the back door, all rushed inside.

Almost instantly, gunfire erupted.

Within seconds, Ray's voice carried to her. "Agent down!"

Amberlyn's heart seized before the adrenaline kicked in. She took aim at the door in case their suspect made it past Ray and his partner.

Then gunfire sparked toward her, and the front passenger window shattered.

Amberlyn ducked, shifting behind the main part of the SUV.

Another shot fired, but this time, it wasn't aimed at her. She moved back into position as a man jumped out of what had been the front window. Eli Duffy!

"Freeze!" Amberlyn shouted.

Duffy lifted his gun, and Amberlyn squeezed off two shots. The first one went wide, but the other clipped him in the arm.

The gunman stumbled behind the tree and lifted his gun again.

Amberlyn ducked. A bullet struck the SUV's windshield only inches from where she had been a moment ago. Her heart raced. That was close. Too close.

Keeping her head low and her weapon aimed at the ground, she rushed to the back of the vehicle to give herself a better angle.

She peeked around the back bumper at the same time she spotted Ray in the now-broken window.

Hoping to keep Duffy's attention on her, she fired at the tree. Bark flew into the air.

Ray aimed at Duffy and shouted, "Drop it!"

Amberlyn could see only the suspect's shoulder and back as he whirled to face Ray. Two shots from Ray's weapon pierced the air, and Eli Duffy fell to the ground.

Amberlyn rushed forward and stepped on the man's wrist before relieving him of his weapon. She then put in a call for an ambulance.

Tucker rushed outside. "I'll take him. You two search the garage."

"How's Ben?"

"He took one in the vest, but he'll be okay," Tucker said.

Relieved, Amberlyn started toward the garage door. It opened a moment later. A newer-model pickup was parked in the middle of the two-car garage.

Ray cleared the back end of the garage while Amberlyn ensured no one was hiding in the front corners or inside the vehicle.

"Check out the truck. I'll search the rest of the grounds."

Amberlyn donned a pair of gloves before opening the door. She searched the glove compartment first. Napkins from a fast-food restaurant, registration and insurance, a pair of needle-nose pliers, and some copper wiring. She looked under the seats. A semiautomatic Smith and Wesson 9mm under the driver's side. Three half-empty water bottles on the passenger's side. The back seat contained only a St. Louis Cardinals sweatshirt and an empty Coke can.

Ray walked into the garage. "Anything?"

"No. There's a pistol he had hidden along with a few water bottles and a Coke can. Hopefully, the forensics team can pull some DNA off them. Maybe one of them belonged to our second suspect." Amberlyn closed the door. "What about you? Is the white Camry here?"

"No." Ray jerked his head toward the front of the house. "Let's see if our suspect is in any shape to tell us where it is."

They returned to where Tucker stood beside the ambulance attendants. Only instead of treating their suspect, the paramedics were standing by while Tucker documented the scene.

Amberlyn's heart sank. Their suspect had died, and all of his knowledge of Forever Freedom had died with him.

Tucker finished taking photos of the victim before moving aside for the paramedics.

"So much for getting intel from him." Ray shook his head.

"You didn't have a choice," Amberlyn assured him.

"Let's hope you're right about the DNA on those drink containers," Ray said. "If that other vehicle is intended to house a second bomb, we need answers fast."

"Yeah, I know."

Agent down. After hearing those words come over the live feed during the raid in St. Louis, Luke had refused to leave FBI headquarters until he'd received an update.

The suspect had died on the scene. The wounded officer had been transported to the local hospital and was expected to make a full recovery. And Amberlyn had walked away uninjured.

Though Luke had hoped to see evidence of that for himself in the form of another video conference, the latest reports had come via email.

Now, with a copy of the top suspects' bios and current photos in his inbox and a temporary transfer request from the FBI, Luke walked into his boss's office. Never before had he considered that he would be loaned out while working as a military aide, but the president was right. This situation was bigger than any one person, and whoever had killed those people at the FEMA building had to be stopped before they could strike again.

The deputy director of the White House Military Office looked up from his desk. "What are you doing here?" Deputy Director Hobbs asked. "I thought you were off today."

"I was. Sort of."

The deputy director motioned for Luke to sit in one of the chairs opposite his desk.

Luke complied and set his cover on the empty seat beside him. "I've been at FBI headquarters, helping look through potential bombing suspects."

"Parker mentioned you worked with them on Monday. Are you all done with that?"

"I believe that's up to you." Though the mere thought of going back to his hometown brought with it every insecurity of his youth, Luke forced the words out. "The FBI is proposing that I go to my high school reunion a week from Saturday so they can insert one of their agents as my date."

"I see." Deputy Director Hobbs leaned back in his chair. "How many people are left on their suspect list?"

"We've narrowed the likely possibilities down to nineteen."

"That's still a lot."

"Yes, sir. One of the suspects was killed in St. Louis about an hour ago, but he wasn't the one who went to school with me." Luke shared what little he knew about the case.

"I guess I'd better redo the schedule for the next couple weeks," he said. "How soon do they need you to leave?"

"They didn't say," Luke said. "When I left headquarters, they were focused on finding the second bomb."

The deputy director instantly straightened, his chair jerking forward as he did so. "A second bomb?"

"The FBI believes that possibility exists."

The deputy director tapped on his computer keyboard. "The president is holding a nationwide memorial tomorrow morning at ten. If we have you work through Saturday night, I can rearrange everyone else's schedule to cover for you until you get back from your reunion."

A stone of dread sank in the pit of Luke's stomach, but he kept his chin up. "Thank you, sir."

Deputy Director Hobbs nodded. "Get some rest tonight. I'll contact the FBI and let them know you're all theirs after Saturday at twenty-two hundred."

Luke pulled out the business card Ian had given him, took a quick photo with his phone, and handed the business card to his boss. "This is the man who requested I help them."

"I'll give him a call." He picked up his desk phone. "And, Captain?"

"Yes?"

"Good luck."

"Thanks." But luck wasn't going to help him. What he needed right now was a healthy dose of courage. Without it, he didn't know how he would face the high school demons he had escaped fifteen years ago.

CHAPTER 8

AMBERLYN RAN FULL speed on the hotel treadmill, her heart racing and her breathing heavy. She hit the button to increase her speed by another tenth of a mile per hour. Maybe if she reached the point of complete physical exhaustion, her body would finally stop shaking.

It had been nearly twenty hours since the shootout yesterday, since bullets had struck the car only inches from her. That reality paled to the four days she had survived since Chanelle had died.

Ian had insisted she take the morning off so she could watch the president's memorial address. After meeting with the man in person, she didn't see the need to listen to some eloquent speech someone else had written. She'd already seen the devastation on the president's face and believed he would do whatever was necessary to stop Forever Freedom from harming Americans again.

Amberlyn finished her five miles and hit the button to start her cooldown.

Her breathing was nearly back to normal when her cell phone rang. She squeezed the tip of her AirPod to answer. "This is Amberlyn."

"It's Ian." He paused. "Are you on a treadmill?"

"I'm just finishing up." She hit the button to stop her workout with a minute left on her cooldown. She crossed the empty workout room and grabbed a towel. "What's the latest?"

"I have an assignment I need to run past you."

She dabbed at the sweat on her forehead. "If you're asking if I want to stay out here and help with the investigation, the answer is yes."

"I want you to continue with the investigation, but I have a different assignment in mind."

"What?" She tossed the sweat towel into the hamper.

"Jeff found out the fifteen-year reunion for Pine Falls High School is a week from tomorrow. We want you to attend to try to identify our second bomber."

"Pine Falls is a small community. I can't just walk in there and pretend to have graduated from there." She had barely said the words before she guessed at the rest of the assignment. "You want me to go as Luke's plus one."

"His leave was approved to help us," Ian said. "He helped you identify the men on our suspect list. You do what you can to find our guy."

"If there is a second bomb in play, it's unlikely this guy will even be at the reunion. Fifteen years isn't the reunion most people get all excited about." At least, she doubted she would rearrange her schedule to go to her fifteen-year reunion, unlike her ten-year, which most of her friends had attended.

"It turns out that because the high school football coach is retiring this year, there will be a special program at the homecoming game on Friday night to honor him and the former championship team. That will be the kickoff event for the reunion."

Amberlyn crossed to the glass door leading from the gym into the hotel hallway to make sure no one was nearby. Then she closed the door, remaining in the empty workout room. "Maybe that will bring our suspect out."

"Even if you can help us narrow down the field, it will make our investigation a lot more manageable."

Pretend to be Luke Steele's girlfriend. The guy who had barely spoken to her the first time they'd met, the guy who had handed her tissues while she'd cried after receiving the news about Chanelle. Her cheeks colored at that thought.

"I can send Kiera in, but Jeff thought you and Captain Steele would make a more convincing couple."

Even though she wasn't sure why Jeff would make that assumption, the ruse would only be for a weekend. Surely she could handle that. "I can do it."

"What time is the funeral tomorrow?"

"Eleven." She crossed to the water cooler and filled a paper cup.

"I'll have travel book you a flight for tomorrow afternoon. I want you and Luke down in Pine Falls in time for church on Sunday morning."

"Sunday?" She lowered her cup without drinking any water. "As in two days from now?"

"Yes. The sooner the two of you start mingling with the townsfolk down there, the better. And from what we've dug up on the captain, his best source of information will come from attending Sunday services."

"Okay." She took a gulp of water. "I'll touch base with Luke tomorrow after the service."

"I'll text you his number."

"Thanks," Amberlyn said. "Where do we stand on the rest of the investigation?"

"No luck yet on who embroidered the hats. The tattoo parlor in Pine Falls was a bust. The owner didn't keep records when he closed the business, and we gave up on finding the other one since we identified Eli Duffy."

"And our suspect list?" Amberlyn drank the rest of her water.

"We cleared two of the men who had tattoos," Ian said. "Randy Cole works for the NSA."

She tossed the empty cup into the trash can. "That explains why he didn't have a social media presence. Any chance he could still be our guy?"

"No. He was out of the country, attending a seminar when the photo was taken."

"Who was the other person you cleared?"

"Jackson Scott. We confirmed he was in Phoenix on both of the days in question. There was one other we found with a tattoo, but he had an alibi too," Ian said. "As of now, we're back to a total of nineteen suspects, three with evidence that they have the championship tattoo and sixteen we don't know about."

"Sounds like I'll have my work cut out for me next week."

"I'm afraid so."

Amberlyn ended the call and headed back upstairs to her room as she debated her plan of attack for the day. She could take advantage of her time off and go to the national memorial service, or she could review the evidence gathered at Eli Duffy's house.

With no desire to suffer through the emotional turmoil of two memorial services in as many days, she headed for the shower. She'd get ready for the day and get up-to-date on everything the FBI had on this case. When she arrived in Pine Falls, she wanted to have every shred of information available, right down to the detailed description of the vehicle believed to house the second bomb.

Her cell phone vibrated with an incoming message. Ian sharing Luke's number with her.

Her phone vibrated again, another text from Ian. *Go to the memorial service. You have a seat in the reserved section at the front.*

Leave it to Ian to know she was avoiding and to push her to go. And to arrange for her to have special privileges.

With an air of resignation, she headed for the shower, texting Ian as she went. *I'm going.*

———

Luke had expected the president to broadcast the memorial service from the White House, especially after his quick trip to Turkey, but instead, they had all flown to Kansas City for a live event.

He took his place beside Parker in the wings of the stage as the Secret Service agents shifted into position in preparation for the president's speech. The college auditorium had been chosen for today's memorial to ensure all the friends and family members of the victims could attend while also allowing sufficient space to accommodate the portable metal detectors that had been brought in to ensure the president's safety.

Luke's cell phone buzzed with an incoming text, and he checked it to make sure it wasn't another update from the FBI. Ian had reached out an hour ago to let him know Amberlyn would be the agent standing in as his girlfriend. Luke hoped their fake relationship would be better than their dinner together had been.

He read the new message, which was nothing more than his mom sending a photo of his eighteen-month-old niece sitting on top of the kitchen table. The kid was seriously adorable.

He hit the heart symbol and pocketed his phone.

The last few stragglers made their way to their seats, and Luke caught sight of Amberlyn walking toward the front section. Her short blonde hair was perfectly styled, and she wore a black dress with a blazer over the top. With the temperature in the high seventies outside, he suspected the blazer was so she could conceal a shoulder holster. Of course, with the president here, it was highly likely the Secret Service had required her to turn in her weapon for the duration of the event.

Parker pointed in Amberlyn's direction. "Isn't that the girl from the FBI?"

"Yeah."

"I'm surprised the Secret Service has anyone from the FBI working this."

"I don't think they do," Luke said. "She knew one of the victims."

"Man, that's got to be tough."

"Yeah." He couldn't imagine trying to process that kind of grief while still working, but from everything he'd heard from Ian and Jeff, it sounded like Amberlyn had yet to take any time off.

His phone vibrated with another incoming message, this one from Ian. *FYI: Amberlyn will be attending a funeral tomorrow at 11, but she'll be back in time to drive with you to Pine Falls first thing Sunday morning.*

"What this time?" Parker asked.

Luke tilted his phone toward Parker so he could read the message.

"She has to board a plane right after a funeral?" Parker shook his head. "That girl has been through the wringer this week."

The service started with a song and a prayer. As a local preacher took a moment to talk about the lives lost, Luke considered his own schedule for the next twenty-four hours. The president would be attending a service for two of the high-level FEMA employees tomorrow before they would fly back to DC.

An idea formed, one that might begin to make up for his and Amberlyn's disastrous first meeting. A little juggling of schedules and an extra security check would be all he'd need to give Amberlyn a much more comfortable ride home.

CHAPTER 9

AMBERLYN BARELY MANAGED to keep her tears from falling as she spoke with the dozens of attendees at Chanelle's funeral service. So many of them needed to talk about their struggles with Chanelle's untimely death, from Chanelle's parents and two younger siblings to the students she had worked with over the past decade to the many colleagues Chanelle and Amberlyn had shared. It was like going back in time to the early days, after a student had been killed—only this time, Amberlyn didn't have Chanelle to lean on when she needed someone to counsel her.

And on top of the emotional upheaval the funeral had churned up inside her, Amberlyn had the added stress of a very tight timeline after the graveside service to return the car she had borrowed from the local FBI motor pool and catch her flight back to DC.

After the closing prayer, several more of Amberlyn's former students encircled her, each needing comfort, as though she could somehow help them make sense of Chanelle's premature death. Amberlyn spoke with each of them about how talking with each other would help them sort through their feelings, that they should rely on each other. With each word, her heart shriveled a little more. She needed someone she could rely on right now, someone beyond her friends from the bureau.

As soon as she was able, Amberlyn headed for the door. She made it as far as the parking lot when Heather, another former coworker, approached her. She hugged Amberlyn and held on tight. "I still can't believe she's gone."

"I know," Amberlyn said, drawing her strength to repeat this conversation for the thirtieth time today.

Just another hour, one more ritual to complete, and she would be able to step away from the crowd and grieve privately.

Out of the corner of her eye, she caught sight of two men approaching as Heather released her, one of the men wearing a suit and the other dressed in a military uniform.

"I don't know how you're able to keep it together." Heather wiped at the tears glistening in her eyes.

Amberlyn turned so she could identify the men. Her eyes widened when Ray and Luke stopped beside her.

"Sorry to interrupt," Luke said. "Can we talk to you for a minute?"

"Yes, of course." Amberlyn gave Heather's arm a squeeze. "Can we catch up later?"

Heather nodded, her eyes still teary.

Amberlyn waited for Heather to continue toward a cluster of other friends before she asked, "What are you two doing here?"

"If it's okay with you, Ray is going to take your vehicle so you don't have to return it after the service," Luke said. "I can go with you to the cemetery and drive you to the airport."

The relief of having that stress removed from her was instant, but she didn't miss the sacrifice Luke would be making to come with her to what was certain to be another emotional service. "Are you sure you don't mind coming?"

"It's fine." Luke's gaze met hers and held. "No one should have to go to a funeral alone."

And even though she had been surrounded by so many friends, Amberlyn had felt very much alone. "Thank you."

"No problem." Luke started toward the government vehicle she had borrowed. "Let's move your things into my car."

Amberlyn unlocked the car and passed the keys to Ray while Luke transferred her suitcase to the trunk of the identical SUV. He hesitated a minute, waiting for her to open the passenger door before he climbed behind the wheel.

Luke turned on his headlights and hazard lights. Then he waited for the funeral home personnel to direct him to fall in line with the other cars heading to the cemetery.

"What are you doing here in Kansas City?" Amberlyn asked.

"I came with the president."

"You were at the memorial service yesterday?"

"Yes." Luke glanced at her. "Sorry I didn't get the chance to talk to you. I had to leave as soon as the president finished speaking."

"Security protocols. I get it." She wasn't sure she would have wanted to talk to anyone after the president's tear-jerker speech anyway. She'd nearly run through a whole travel pack of tissues. "I assume you heard that I'm standing in as your plus one for your reunion."

"Yeah." Luke reddened slightly. "I guess I'm now your fake boyfriend. Sorry about that."

She wasn't sure what he was apologizing for: their first, less-than-favorable meeting or the fact that they were about to go on future dates together. Amberlyn chose to change the subject. "Are you on my flight back to DC? It leaves at 4:10."

"I think it's more accurate to say you're on my flight back to DC."

"What do you mean?"

"I didn't think you'd want to deal with airport security, especially since you're probably armed, so I cleared it with Secret Service for you to ride back on Air Force One."

Amberlyn's jaw dropped. "You're taking me on Air Force One?"

"If that's okay with you," Luke said quickly.

She would be flying home with the president. And even better, she wouldn't have to sit in the airport, waiting to board her flight. "Yes. That's okay with me."

———

The novelty of flying on Air Force One hadn't been lost on Luke, but he had to admit, he enjoyed seeing it through Amberlyn's eyes. They had reached the aircraft an hour before the president, so Luke had been able to give her a quick tour before settling into the seating area in the guest section beside the press corps seating.

Luke had offered to take over for Parker in carrying the nuclear codes for the president, but Parker had insisted Luke accompany his guest. Now ill at ease, Luke struggled to find something to say.

Thankfully, Amberlyn broke the silence. "I guess we should talk about our cover story."

"I assume you won't want me telling people you work for the FBI."

"No, and I'll be using Jones as my last name so no one will be able to find me online." She paused, clearly pondering. "Let's go with saying I'm a teacher. That's what I did before I joined the bureau."

"What subject did you teach?"

"Psychology."

"Okay. What about our first date?" Luke hoped she wouldn't insist on using their real first meeting as part of what they would tell people—assuming any of his former classmates spoke to him at the reunion.

"Well, we can't very well say our first date was you bringing me on Air Force One."

"No. That wouldn't be wise," Luke said. "It's probably best if people don't know I work at the White House."

"So, we need a cover story for you too."

"I guess so." He shrugged. "We can say I work at the Pentagon. It's close enough that it makes sense for me to live in Arlington."

"Where in Arlington do you live?"

"Rosslyn."

"Me too." Amberlyn repositioned herself in her seat as though she needed to see him from a different angle. "I didn't realize we were neighbors."

"That will make it easier for us to drive down together tomorrow." Luke pulled his cell phone from his pocket. Maybe while he was getting her address, he could finally get her correct phone number. He pulled up her contact info and held out his phone. "Can you put your address in there?"

"Sure." Amberlyn took the phone from him.

"And would you mind also checking the number I have for you? I don't think it's the right one."

"It's the same as when I met you the first time." Amberlyn read the number on his screen, and then her gaze shot up to meet his, a look of shock on her face. "This isn't my number."

"That's the one you gave me."

Her shock morphed into embarrassment. "I'm so sorry. I must have typed the last number in wrong." She held up his phone, and Luke could almost sense her opinion of him changing in that instant. "Did you try to call me after that dinner?"

Luke's cheeks heated, and he nodded. "Yeah. Unfortunately, by the time I realized I was texting some guy named Todd Hart, Kevin had already transferred to Okinawa, and he was the only person I knew who had your number."

"Why didn't you just text him?"

"Because he changed his number when he moved to Japan, and I didn't have his new one." And chasing Kevin down to a base halfway around the world, even if it was just searching for him online, had felt just a little too desperate.

"I'm so sorry. All this time, I assumed you'd ghosted me."

"No." Luke shook his head. "And I still owe you for your dry cleaning and another piece of cheesecake."

"I think this ride on Air Force One erases that debt."

The flight attendant approached. "Can I get either of you anything to drink?"

"Some orange juice if you have it," Amberlyn said.

"Yes, ma'am."

"Just some water for me. Thanks."

The flight attendant left them, and Amberlyn asked, "How long have we been dating? We should probably say it's recent so people don't expect us to know too much about each other, but it needs to be long enough that it makes sense for you to bring me to your reunion."

"I only moved to Arlington in June."

"How about we say we met at the fireworks show on the Fourth of July?"

"I didn't go to the show on the mall."

"Actually, I didn't either. I always watch from the Iwo Jima Memorial."

Luke furrowed his brow. "Me too."

Surprise lit her eyes. "We were both there, but we didn't see each other?"

"I guess so." Although Luke didn't know how he could have missed her. Amberlyn was a presence wherever she went. Just like today. She had clearly been struggling with her own emotions, yet so many people had clustered around her as though she could make their hurts go away despite her own pain.

"The easiest thing would be to change our story to say we met that day."

"Who were you with at the fireworks show?" Luke asked. "In case anyone asks."

"I went with a date, but for our story's sake, let's say I was there with a girlfriend from school." Her expression clouded, and Luke could only imagine she was thinking of the friend she had lost this week.

Focusing on the other part of her comment, he asked, "Do you have a real boyfriend?"

"No." Amberlyn shook her head. "That was a one-and-only date. I'm not seeing anyone right now."

"Except pretending to date me."

"Right. Except for you."

CHAPTER 10

AMBERLYN HIT THE snooze button and draped her arm over her eyes. She needed to get up, but her entire body felt like it had doubled in weight overnight. Exhaustion. She recognized the signs, but she didn't have time to listen to them.

Moments from the last week pressed to the forefront of her mind, from the interrupted phone call with Chanelle right up to her trip on Air Force One. She tried to concentrate on last night, on the surreal experience of flying on a plane only a select few would ever see the inside of. When the wash of memories from Chanelle's funeral played out, the tightness in Amberlyn's chest and the grief intensified.

She fought for calm. The man from the diner was out there somewhere. If he really did have a second bomb, he needed to be found. And clearly, if Ian had assigned her to this job, he knew as well as she did that working was therapeutic.

She forced herself out of bed, showered, and selected a simple cotton dress to wear. After packing the essentials for a week away, she set her suitcase by the front door of her condo and checked the time. Five minutes until Luke was supposed to get here.

Though she wanted nothing more than to sink into the soft cushions of her couch, she likely would fall right back asleep if she did so. With a sigh, she did a quick check of the lights, leaving the one in the living room on so it would look like someone was still home. Then she opened the door.

Luke stood in the hall, a narrow burgundy tie hanging against a crisp, white, collared shirt. She'd never seen him out of uniform, and the church-going version was every bit as attractive as the military one. Not that she was noticing. He hadn't been interested in her two years ago. There was no reason to think he would be interested in her now.

He was her fake boyfriend, not her real one.

She pulled her suitcase into the hall and adjusted the strap of her computer bag on her shoulder. "Did you just get here?"

"A few minutes ago."

Amberlyn furrowed her brow. "Why didn't you tell me you were here?"

"I didn't want to knock on your door before six."

"You could have texted."

"Yeah. I guess so." He reached for her bag. "Let me take that for you."

The independent side of her would have been annoyed that he assumed she needed help carrying her suitcase. The exhausted side of her silently thanked him. "Where are you parked?" Amberlyn asked.

"In one of the visitor parking spots in the garage."

They took the elevator downstairs and were nearly to his parking space when she remembered what kind of car he drove. She eyed the old Civic. "I hate to say it, but if we arrive in your car, we aren't going to get the kind of attention we want at your reunion."

"I was kind of hoping to not attract any attention when we're there."

Amberlyn pointed at his car. "That will attract attention." She studied his face, not sure if he had taken offense at her observation. "Maybe we should take my car."

"No one is going to care what I drive." Luke shook his head. "These guys probably won't remember me anyway."

"It would still be smart to blend in." She waved in the general direction of her midsized SUV. "Mine isn't anything fancy, but it won't look like you're still living in the past, and it also won't make it look like we're trying to impress anyone."

"Trust me. The last thing I want is to live in the past."

"Then, you'll let me drive?"

He studied her intently. "We can take your car, but I'm driving."

"Don't tell me you're embarrassed to have a woman drive you somewhere."

"You can drive all you want when we get to Pine Falls, but right now, you're too tired to drive."

She couldn't argue with that. She also was surprised he'd noticed.

"I'll pull out so you can park in my spot while we're gone." Amberlyn held up her keys. "Then you can drive."

Luke handed over her suitcase. "Deal."

Why had he said yes to this again? With every passing mile, Luke's stomach knotted and his body tensed a little more. He didn't want to see the people he'd gone to school with. He didn't want to associate with anyone in Pine Falls, except Pastor Mosley.

He glanced at Amberlyn. She had fallen asleep before they'd reached the interstate and had barely stirred.

He took the turn onto Main Street, memories flooding through him. The frozen yogurt place where he'd worked his senior year, where the football team had come in to try one sample after another, but never bought anything, inevitably getting him in trouble with his boss. The movie theater where he was supposed to meet Brad Shoemacher for a night out with the guys only to have Brad and his buddies drive by and drench him with water balloons. The grocery store where Russ Gibson had beaned him with a five-pound bag of flour, leaving him covered in white from head to toe.

The mortification of those days clogged his throat. Maybe he could turn around. Maybe Jeff or someone else with the FBI could pretend to be him. No one would remember him anyway unless it was to laugh at him.

Amberlyn stirred beside him, and her eyes fluttered open. "I'm sorry. I didn't mean to sleep the whole way," she said, looking embarrassed.

"It's okay. You needed it."

"More than I realized." She straightened in her seat, and pulled down the visor to check her reflection in the mirror. She raked her fingers through her hair before letting it fall into place. She then retrieved a tube of lipstick and applied it to her full lips.

As soon as she flipped the visor back into place, she glanced at the clock on the center display. "I know we're a bit early, but maybe we should go straight to the church. I doubt the hotel will let us check in yet."

Luke fought the urge to turn around and continued down Main Street until he reached the turn for the church.

"I haven't had the chance to catch up on the suspect list," Amberlyn said. "How many on it still live here in town?"

"Five. Cooper Bird, Brad Shoemacher, Gavin Pennington, Russ Gibson, and Owen Lester." Three of his water balloon bombers, his flour attacker, and one who was the king of free frozen yogurt. "Owen has a tattoo. The others are on the maybe list."

"That's great. With any luck, we'll be able to eliminate all of them while we're here this week."

"Yeah. Maybe." But only if he actually saw them. Or maybe he could let Amberlyn do some spying without him present. That would be even better.

He pulled into the parking lot and backed Amberlyn's SUV into one of the spaces a few spots from the door. He looked over his shoulder to make sure the vehicle was evenly spaced between the lines.

"You know, I do have a backup camera." Amberlyn pointed at the display on the center console.

"Yeah." He shrugged. "Habit."

Amberlyn opened her door and glanced at the line on her side. "Not bad."

The simple compliment caught him by surprise. It also emphasized the difference between his life now and the one he'd lived in high school. Aside from Pastor Mosley, his family, and an occasional teacher, compliments weren't commonplace here in Pine Falls, at least not for him.

Luke joined Amberlyn on the sidewalk and held out her keys.

"Go ahead and hold on to them. I kind of like not having to drive."

Luke slid the keys into the pocket of his slacks.

Amberlyn stepped beside him and hooked her hand through the crook of his elbow.

Luke stared down at her. Standing here in the sunlight, a beautiful woman at his side, he could almost pretend she was here because she wanted to be with him, that they were a real couple.

She leaned closer, and his mouth went dry.

"Do any of the guys we talked about go to church here?" she asked.

Her question brought him back to reality. There was a reason he was still single. He didn't know how to act around women, and except for one short-lived relationship during college, his dating experience was limited at best.

He focused on the information she wanted to know, digging into the frustrations of his past. "A few did." Gavin had been responsible for Luke's dislocated shoulder during what was supposed to have been a friendly basketball game in the church's sports center, and Russ had been the one who had stolen toilet paper out of the supply closet when the football team had toilet papered Coach Zabrowski's house. "I don't know if they still go now that their parents aren't making them."

Luke opened the door and waited for Amberlyn to pass into the church foyer before he followed. She gazed toward the large painting of Christ on the wall facing the entrance. "This is a lot like the church I went to growing up."

A door opened down the hall, and two men emerged. Pastor Mosley looked exactly the same as he had when Luke had been in high school. Tall, lean, looking like he could still take on the young men on the basketball court. His hairline had receded until only two inches of white hair encircled the base of his skull, but the joy on his face was every bit the same as when Luke had last seen him in DC six months ago.

"Glory be, it's a miracle." The pastor crossed to him. "Luke Steele is back in church. And he's brought an angel with him."

"It's good to see you." Luke started to offer his hand, but the pastor pulled him into a hug. Pastor Mosley thumped Luke's back twice before releasing him.

"Boy, you look good." He turned and offered his hand to Amberlyn. "Pastor Graham Mosley."

"I'm Amberlyn Jones," she said, offering her alias. "It's nice to meet you."

"You too." The pastor nodded at Luke. "You clearly have excellent taste if you're dating this one."

Amberlyn smiled. "Clearly."

"How long are you in town for?" Pastor Mosley asked.

"Through next weekend," Luke said. "We came back for the reunion."

The pastor's eyebrows lifted. "I can't say I would have expected that."

"Amberlyn wanted to see where I grew up."

"She must be something special if she managed to get you back here."

"That she is." And even though Luke barely knew her, based on the depth of strength he'd witnessed in her the past few days, he suspected he spoke the truth.

CHAPTER 11

AMBERLYN SAT BESIDE Luke in one of the narrow side pews at the back of the church and scanned the room. Two of Luke's former classmates were in attendance, or rather, two who were still on their suspect list. Russ Gibson had passed by them without glancing in their direction, a championship ring on his right hand and the ink of a tattoo peeking out from beneath his shirtsleeve.

The second suspect in attendance, Gavin Pennington, had taken a seat on the opposite side of the church, and Amberlyn hadn't been able to spot a tattoo when he'd walked in with his wife and two young children.

Amberlyn leaned closer to Luke and whispered, "Do you know either of their wives?"

"I don't know," he whispered back. "They look kind of familiar, but if I knew them in high school, I don't recognize them now."

"We can look through their social media accounts tonight at the hotel."

The sermon ended, and Luke stood. Based on the way his feet were already angled toward the door, Amberlyn suspected he planned to make a speedy exit.

She took his hand to keep him in place. "Let's walk over this way." She leaned close again. "I want to see if Gavin has a tattoo or is wearing his ring."

Luke squeezed her hand, but with the way his body tensed, she couldn't tell if that was his silent way of saying yes or simply a reflex as he prepared to face a new challenge.

She tugged on his hand, and he fell into step with her as they crossed to the spot where the aisle between two sets of pews intersected with the open space beside the door.

Amberlyn stopped and looked up at Luke. "You should introduce me to some of your friends."

The horrified look on Luke's face spoke volumes. Clearly, he had not been on friendly terms with Gavin. She'd have to fix that.

Gavin and his family were nearly to them. She needed to delay only another fifteen seconds to reach the doorway at the same time as them.

She released Luke's hand and lifted both hands to straighten his tie even though it was in no need of straightening.

Then, as though she had no clue anyone was behind her, she stepped back and bumped squarely into one of their top suspects.

She whirled around. "Oh, I'm so sorry. I didn't see you there."

"No problem." Gavin started to move past her.

"Wait. Aren't you Gavin Pennington?" Amberlyn asked. "You are. Luke has told me all about you." Amberlyn extended her right hand. "I'm Amberlyn Jones." She nodded at Luke. "I'm Luke's girlfriend."

Gavin shook her hand without hesitation, the metal of his championship ring cold against her palm. Then he looked up as though noticing Luke for the first time. His eyes widened. "Luke Steele?"

Luke gave a crisp nod. "Gavin."

Gavin looked from Luke to Amberlyn. "You're going out with him?"

The disbelief in the man's tone grated on principal. It also spoke volumes about why Luke had been so reluctant to greet him.

Amberlyn's gaze flicked down long enough to spot the tattoo on Gavin's wrist. She offered a bright smile and slid her arm around Luke, pleased that he lifted his hand to her waist. "I am."

The woman with Gavin stepped forward, two little boys following behind her. "I'm Felicia, Gavin's wife."

"Nice to meet you." Amberlyn shook Felicia's hand as well.

"Felicia, we should get going." Gavin looked down at their children. "Come on, boys."

Felicia offered a quick wave. "Enjoy the rest of your weekend."

"You too." Amberlyn kept her arm around Luke's waist and glanced toward where Russ had been sitting.

"He already left," Luke said, seeming to know whom she was looking for.

"Is there anyone else you want to talk to before we leave?"

Luke shook his head.

Amberlyn took a step toward the door on the opposite side of the church. "I guess we can see if there's any way we can check into our hotel early."

"It's worth a try." Luke walked with her toward the exit, the two of them sidestepping a family of six as they navigated their way along the back of the chapel.

When they reached the door, Pastor Mosley was waiting. "I was hoping to catch you before you left." Pastor Mosley put his hand on Luke's shoulder. "We have a dinner here tonight, mostly for some of the other religious leaders in the area. You should join us."

"I don't know—" Luke started.

Amberlyn put her hand on his arm. "We'd love to. That is, if we wouldn't be imposing."

"Not at all. You will both be welcome additions."

"I guess we'll be here, then," Luke said. "What time?"

"Five thirty."

"We'll see you then." Luke put his hand on Amberlyn's back and guided her to the exit. When they reached the car, he opened her door and waited for her to get in so he could close it for her as well. He didn't speak until he slid behind the wheel. "Do we have to go to dinner tonight?"

"It will give us great access to the people who will have their fingers on the pulse of the community," Amberlyn said. "It's perfect."

Luke turned on the engine. "If you say so."

A run-in with Gavin Pennington only an hour after arriving in town, a dinner Luke didn't want to go to. This girlfriend/boyfriend thing wasn't all it was cracked up to be.

Luke pulled into the long, narrow parking lot of the lodge, several paths leading off the main lot so the guests staying in cottages could park close to their rooms.

Amberlyn pointed at the covered entrance. "Want to drop me off so I can check us in?"

More than willing to avoid any more potential meet-ups with people from his past, he nodded. "That's fine."

He pulled up beside the main entrance.

Amberlyn hopped out and headed inside.

Luke rolled the windows down and turned off the engine. Emotionally exhausted after being in the same room as two of his childhood tormentors, he pulled his cell phone from his pocket in the hope of finding a distraction. He read through his messages, a general daily update from his office topping his inbox. The contents included the new schedule that had allowed Luke to take administrative leave to attend his reunion. He'd much prefer to be back at the White House, fulfilling his planned duties.

A car pulled into the lot, and Luke glanced up. Two women in their fifties climbed out of the luxury sedan and walked past him toward the lodge.

As soon as they disappeared inside, he turned his attention back to his phone. Luke read through the latest email from his sister, complete with photos of his two nieces, and started deleting the junk mail that had come in since yesterday. He was still filtering through his inbox when Amberlyn walked out, keys in hand.

She climbed into the passenger seat. "We're in one of the cottages. Number eight."

"We're sharing a cottage?" Luke asked. He hadn't expected that, nor was he sure how he felt about it. He rather liked having his own space, and he didn't want to think about what his mother would say if she found out he was living in close quarters with a woman he wasn't related to.

"Don't worry. We have separate bedrooms." Amberlyn handed him one of the keys along with a map to their cottage. "And it was either this or have rooms in the lodge for three days before having to move to a cottage anyway. I guess all the rooms are booked up for your reunion weekend."

"I guess we're staying in a cottage, then." He'd never been in one of the cottages. Then again, he'd never been in one of the rooms in the lodge either.

Luke pulled forward and followed Amberlyn's directions to the little wooden structure perched among the pine trees and dogwoods, the rumble of the falls in the distance carrying to them.

Luke climbed out of the car and pulled both suitcases from the trunk before retrieving his computer bag.

Amberlyn stepped beside him and raised the handle of her suitcase. After she slipped her backpack onto the top of it, she headed for the door.

Luke locked the car and walked inside with her.

An expansive room lay before him, encompassing the entire length of the structure. Just inside the door, a couch and two chairs were arranged to face the gas fireplace and the flat-screen television hanging above it. The kitchen spanned the left side of the back half of the house, a rectangular table and six chairs situated in front of the huge window that overlooked the falls.

"Oh wow." Amberlyn left her suitcase beside the couch and crossed to the window. "What a great view."

Luke closed the door behind him and flipped the lock. He dropped his computer bag on the nearest chair and joined Amberlyn by the window.

The wide waterfall wasn't more than twenty feet high, but they had the perfect view of it and the stream and walking path below.

"How far does that path go?" Amberlyn asked.

"About three miles." He had jogged that route more times than he could count while in high school, often using the peaceful setting to clear his thoughts after whatever teenage crisis he had endured on any particular day. Too bad he hadn't learned self-defense back then instead of waiting for the Marine Corps to teach him how to stop being a victim of whichever bully decided to target him.

Luke lifted his chin and turned away from the view and the memories. He peeked through one of the three doors positioned opposite the long island in the kitchen. "Which room do you want?"

"It doesn't matter."

Luke walked into the room closest to the kitchen to discover it had a private bathroom. He retrieved his suitcase and put his bag in the other bedroom, leaving the master for Amberlyn. She might have forgiven him for the cheesecake fiasco, but it wouldn't hurt to stay on her good side.

The furnishings in his room were simple—a bed, two night tables, and a closet that included a built-in dresser. A small desk occupied the space by the window, but the wooden chair didn't look like it would make the most comfortable workspace.

Luke set his suitcase on the bed and proceeded to hang up his uniform and unpack the rest of his belongings. With his shaving kit and his toothbrush in hand, he headed for the bathroom that connected both to his room and the living room. He set his toiletries on the counter and tried to pretend he was on vacation with his sister.

When he stepped back into the living room, Amberlyn was emerging from the other bedroom, her dark brown eyes meeting his. His stomach lurched, a sudden reminder that Amberlyn was most definitely not his sister.

"I'm starving. I say we find somewhere to eat, and then we can find a grocery store."

"The lodge has a restaurant."

"I know, but most of the people there will be from out of town." Amberlyn retrieved her service weapon from her backpack and tucked it into a medium-sized purse. "I'd rather go out where we might run into people you knew from high school."

Great. Though he wanted nothing to do with the people in town, he pulled her car keys from his pocket. "Do you like Mexican food?"

"I love Mexican food."

"Then, I know just the place."

CHAPTER 12

AMBERLYN STEPPED INTO the brightly decorated restaurant, a circular bar occupying the center of the large space. Adobe walls with large arches built into them sectioned off the two dining areas to the left and the right. The scents of sizzling meat and fried tortillas carried on the air.

A hostess, who appeared to be in her late teens, stood at the narrow counter in front of them. She picked up two menus. "Table for two?"

Amberlyn nodded. "Yes, please."

The hostess showed them to a booth situated halfway between the front door and the wall of windows. As soon as they were seated with menus in hand, Amberlyn did another quick analysis of the space. One main entrance, undoubtedly another exit at the rear. The only patrons in their section of the dining room were a young family several tables away and an older couple by the window.

Amberlyn skimmed the menu and confirmed they had her favorite—chicken flautas—before setting it aside.

As soon as Luke set his menu down, she asked, "What's the deal with you and Gavin?"

"Nothing."

She lifted both eyebrows.

Their waiter arrived and set a basket of chips and two small bowls of salsa on the table. A moment later, he returned with two glasses of water. After taking their order, he headed for the kitchen, and Amberlyn picked up the conversation where they'd left off.

"If we want people to believe we're dating, I need to know more about you, especially about your relationship with the people we're investigating."

"I didn't have a relationship with any of them." Luke picked up a chip and dipped it in the salsa nearest him. "I already told you that."

"That's not the impression I got." Amberlyn hated to press, but the only way they were going to successfully gather information was if the townspeople let their guard down around them, and the quickest way to get that to happen would be if they were a couple. "It's not hard to figure out that the two of you weren't friends."

"No. We weren't." Luke took a sip of his water. "I'm kind of surprised he even remembered me."

"Why's that?"

"The only time he spoke to me in high school was to tell me to get out of his way." The bitterness in Luke's voice was new, but Amberlyn suspected it only hinted at the depth of hurt inflicted upon him during his teenage years. And she couldn't deny that the raw vulnerability on his face tugged at her.

When she'd first met him, she'd assumed he was very much like Gavin or Russ, a former high school jock who was used to getting what he wanted and accustomed to women chasing him.

In her opinion, Luke was better looking than either of the men she'd seen at church, yet he didn't seem to have any awareness that he likely turned heads when he walked into a room. Quite the opposite. If her suspicions were correct, Luke preferred not being noticed.

"Were any of the football players kind to you?" Amberlyn asked.

"Kindness wasn't really their thing."

The lack of a personal connection between Luke and their suspects was going to complicate things. They needed people to want to talk to Luke, and she had just the way to make that happen, even though she doubted he'd be thrilled with her idea. "I know we talked about not letting people know where you work, but we may need to rethink that decision."

"Why?"

"What you do is impressive." Amberlyn took a chip from the basket and scooped up some salsa. "It will attract attention."

"The kind of attention I usually got here in town wasn't the kind I'd want to repeat."

Amberlyn guessed at the source of the problem. "Gavin was a bully."

"He was one of many."

Her heart went out to the boy Luke had once been. "I know sharing who you are now may not be comfortable for you, but we need answers, and this could help us find them."

"How do you figure?"

Amberlyn glanced at the nearby tables to make sure there weren't any new arrivals. Even though they were isolated from the other diners, she leaned forward. "If people know you work with the president, that will automatically make them want to spend time with you, to ask questions."

Luke leaned in. "Whoever blew up the FEMA building isn't going to be impressed that I work at the White House. It's more likely he'd avoid me."

"Which is another reason we should let people know what you do."

"I thought you wanted the bomber to interact with me."

"I did, but with nineteen suspects, it might help to see how people react when they find out what you do," Amberlyn said. "Besides, I'd think you would want to show these guys that you're a success."

"I'd rather they not think about me at all." Luke looked past her and shook his head. "You've got to be kidding me."

"What?"

"Gavin and his wife just walked in."

Amberlyn put her hand on his and leaned forward. "Don't hate me."

"For what?"

Amberlyn swiveled in her seat and waved at the new arrivals.

Felicia's eyes lit up when she spotted them. Gavin scowled.

The hostess saw the interaction and pointed in their direction. Gavin shook his head and pointed at the other side of the restaurant.

Luke's relief was instant. So was Amberlyn's frustration. If she was going to create a spin on Luke being someone everyone would want to socialize with, first she needed someone from the old championship football team to talk to them.

It was like getting a concentrated refresher course in dating. First, church with Amberlyn. Then lunch, and now dinner with the pastor and who knew how many other religious leaders from around town. Luke was exhausted from so much socializing. All he wanted was a comfortable couch and a remote control.

Amberlyn stepped beside him on the sidewalk leading to the multi-purpose room at the back of the church. "You ready for this?"

"If I say no, does that mean we can leave?"

"No." She took his hand. "Come on. Let's see if anyone here can give us some insight into our suspects."

He looked down at their joined hands, a little surprised by the naturalness of the gesture.

As though reading his thoughts, she whispered, "We're a couple, remember?"

"Right." He tilted his head toward the side entrance. "It's this way."

When they approached the door, Luke reached for it at the same time as Amberlyn. He got there first and pulled it open.

She remained beside him instead of walking inside. "You know, I can open my own doors."

"Sorry. It's habit," Luke said. "My mom was old-fashioned."

Apparently satisfied by his answer, Amberlyn passed through the door and stepped inside. Luke joined her in the already crowded space. Four round tables laden with white tablecloths took up the space beside a microphone that had been set up at the far side of the room. The scent of pot roast and potatoes carried from the serving tables that lined the wall to their right.

"It smells good," Amberlyn said.

Luke couldn't disagree. Anytime someone served potatoes, it was a good day.

A broad-shouldered man approached, his physique not unlike a linebacker, although he appeared to be well into his sixties. "Welcome, welcome." He offered his hand. "I'm Reverend Bowman. I don't think I've met the two of you before."

Luke shook the reverend's outstretched hand. "I'm Luke Steele. This is Amberlyn Jones."

"Good to meet you both." His gaze shifted from Luke to Amberlyn and back again. "Did you say Steele?"

Luke nodded.

"You're not Pamela Steele's boy, are you?"

"Yes, sir."

"Well, isn't that something. You've certainly grown up since I've seen you last."

Luke didn't remember the reverend, but with how many people passed through Pastor Mosley's doors, he could hardly expect to remember all of them.

"You be sure to tell your mom I said hello. We sure miss her around here."

"I'll pass that along."

Amberlyn squeezed his hand. "Where do you want to sit?"

"Come sit over here with me and my wife." The reverend escorted them to the table in the center. "Rebecca, you remember Luke Steele."

"Oh, yes. So good to see you again."

"Thank you."

Amberlyn stepped up and offered her hand to the reverend's wife. "I'm Luke's girlfriend, Amberlyn."

"Have a seat and chat a while."

More socializing with strangers. Not Luke's idea of a good time. With his luck, he'd be signed up for a half dozen service projects before the night was through, most of which would serve as yet another reminder that his only friend during his teenage years had been his pastor.

Amberlyn and Luke sat between Mrs. Bowman and the other couple already seated at the table.

"This is Chaplain Miller and her husband, Calvin." Mrs. Bowman gestured across the table.

"Good to meet you both," Amberlyn said.

Luke nodded a greeting.

The reverend also sat as Pastor Mosley joined them.

"Glad you made it." Pastor Mosley shook Luke's hand before taking the empty seat beside him.

One of the other pastors stood and welcomed everyone before offering a blessing on the food.

"Eat while it's hot." Pastor Mosley ushered them to the food table, insisting they serve themselves before him.

They joined the other twenty people in line, and Amberlyn immediately started talking to Mrs. Bowman again. "Have many other people already arrived for the high school reunion next weekend?"

"I don't know about that, but the lodge is going to be busting at the seams with both the reunion and the open house for the new youth center happening on the same weekend."

"Youth center?"

"It's an interfaith project we've all been working on," she explained.

"Instead of all the churches trying to run their own youth programs," her husband said, picking up where his wife left off, "we pooled our resources to create a central location where teens and preteens can spend time away from the pressures of everyday life."

"That's a noble objective." Amberlyn scooped potatoes, carrots, and pot roast onto her plate before passing the serving spoon to Luke. "When is the grand opening?"

Reverend Bowman picked up a plate and added a roll to it. "The celebration will be Sunday afternoon, and it will open to the public on Monday."

Pastor Mosley stepped behind them in line. "We'd hoped to have it open before school started, but the soundproofing took longer than we expected."

"Soundproofing?" Amberlyn asked.

"The neighbors were insistent," Pastor Mosley said. "They knew we would have concerts there as well as sporting events in the gym. Both can be a bit on the loud side."

"We're having a concert as part of the grand opening." Reverend Bowman scooped some pot roast and vegetables onto his plate. "If you're still in town, you should come. A few of your old schoolmates will be speaking at the grand opening."

Though Luke had no interest in socializing with the people of his past, he forced himself to ask the question. "Who?"

"Owen Lester and Brad Shoemacher will be there, and I'm sure Trevor Moran will come too," Reverend Bowman said.

"Who's Trevor Moran?" Amberlyn asked Luke. "I don't think I've heard you mention him before."

Pastor Mosley spared Luke from answering. "He graduated a couple years behind Luke."

They reached the end of the serving table and retrieved cups of punch before returning to their table.

They made it halfway through dinner before the pastor who had opened the meeting approached the podium again. "While we're finishing up, we'll go ahead and start our program for tonight."

Amberlyn leaned closer to Luke and whispered, "The program?"

"All the faith leaders will take a turn to share what's happening with their congregations, what struggles they might be having, and what help they need."

Amberlyn looked around the crowded room, and her eyes widened. "All of them?"

Luke nodded. "Just remember," he whispered back, "you're the one who wanted to come."

CHAPTER 13

LUKE COULD HAVE warned her. Last night, the program had lasted two hours and thirty-seven minutes. Amberlyn had timed it.

When the program had ended and they'd returned to their cottage, all she'd wanted was her bed.

Now it was six fifteen. Amberlyn slipped on her running shoes. She should have just enough time to put in a four- or five-mile run and shower before the phone calls from her office would start.

Dressed in a pair of spandex shorts and a baggy T-shirt, she opened her bedroom door. To her surprise, Luke was already up and sat at the kitchen table. He was leaning over, lacing up his shoes.

The oddity of seeing someone so early in the morning, especially since she typically didn't share living spaces with anyone, caught her off guard.

He glanced up as though seeing a woman in his kitchen were no big deal. "Morning."

"Good morning."

Luke stood, his faded blue T-shirt showcasing his lean physique and the fact that he clearly wasn't a stranger to exercise. He slipped the key to the cottage into his shorts and zipped the pocket.

"I was heading out for a run," Amberlyn said, stating what was probably obvious to Luke. "Did you want to join me?"

"Sure." He headed for the door and opened it. Following his usual pattern, he waited for her to walk through before following her outside.

They walked down the trail together toward the river's edge, Luke leading the way. He glanced back at her. "I'm afraid to ask, but what do you have planned for us today?"

"I'd like to set up run-ins with the other possible suspects who are here in town, especially the ones who we don't know if they have tattoos or not."

"You could do that without me."

"Maybe for some," Amberlyn said. Splitting up would let them cover more ground. "Brad Shoemacher works at the bank, so I might be able to see him without you there."

"Cooper Bird works construction." Luke reached the trail and glanced back at her. "There's no point catching up with him during working hours. Even if he usually wears his ring, he probably wouldn't while using power tools, and he'd likely wear long sleeves and work gloves that would cover his tattoo."

"That's true. We'd be better off trying to see him socially." Amberlyn grabbed her ankle to pull her leg up and stretch her quad. Luke stretched as well, but she didn't miss the pained expression on his face. "You're going to hate this, aren't you?"

"I'm only here to give you an in." He waved toward the falls. "It's beautiful here and everything, but when I left after graduation, I didn't ever plan to come back."

"Pastor Mosley is glad you're here."

"Yeah." The pained expression on Luke's face lessened. "It was good to see him again, even if we did have to suffer through one of their interfaith council meetings."

"I gather you went to a lot of those." Amberlyn headed down the path at an easy pace away from the falls.

Luke fell in beside her. "More than I care to remember. They've been talking about building this youth center since I was in high school."

"It sounds like it will give teenagers a safe place to spend their time."

"The faith leaders want it to be more than that," Luke said. "They'll have tutoring and college prep so people who don't want to work in the mines can create a new life away from Pine Falls."

"That's interesting that they're trying to help people move away."

"They're trying to give people options." Luke increased his speed, his shoes pounding against the paved trail. Amberlyn matched his pace.

"Did they help you find options when you were a teenager?" Amberlyn asked, her breathing now heavy.

"They didn't have to." Luke shrugged. "I had parents for that."

"Not everyone is that lucky."

"That's true." Luke fell silent.

They ran over a mile before the main part of town came into view. Above them, a few early risers sat on the deck of a restaurant overlooking the river. The majority of the patrons appeared to be businessmen and women grabbing an early morning cup of coffee. For a mining town, there appeared to be a good number of people working in other industries.

They passed by the central section of what she guessed was the backside of the Main Street businesses, finally turning around when they reached the end of the trail. Based on how long they'd been jogging, Amberlyn guessed they were around the two-mile mark.

They turned back and returned to where they had started.

Though his breathing was heavier now, Luke asked, "Did you want to put in another mile? We can head up to the falls. It's about another half mile until the trail ends on this side."

"Sure." They kept going, but when they reached the end of the trail this time, Amberlyn stopped and took in the view.

Evergreens mixed with maples, oaks, and aspens, the leaves already sporting their fall colors in stunning splendor. Amberlyn suspected that in a few weeks, the branches would be bare. Water misted the air, and the roar of the waterfall was louder than she expected, making it necessary to raise her voice to be heard.

"This is beautiful."

Luke simply nodded.

They stood there for a moment before turning back toward the cottage, this time walking instead of jogging.

A trickle of sweat dripped down the center of Amberlyn's back, and she wiped at her upper lip to erase evidence of moisture there.

"What do you want to do for breakfast?" Amberlyn asked. "That little restaurant up the way looked cute."

"We could go there." Luke turned onto the path leading to their cottage. "Or we could go to the grocery store and pick up a few things. We do have a kitchen."

"How about we do both?" Amberlyn trailed a half step behind him. "We can go to breakfast, see if we run into anyone there, and then we can go grocery shopping. That will give us options for our other meals."

"That works." They reached their cottage, and Luke unlocked the door.

Amberlyn waited for him to open it, then passed through. She was already inside before the simple gesture caught up with her. She'd been around Luke for only a day, and already, she expected him to open doors for her. Maybe this pretending-to-date thing wouldn't be as hard as she'd thought.

––––––––––––––

Eating out twice in two days. Even though Luke would receive a travel allowance from the government for meals, the economical side of him cringed as he read the prices on the menu. Eighteen dollars for avocado toast? He could make it himself for less than two. And four dollars for a glass of juice? He could buy the whole carton for that.

He and Amberlyn had opted for a table outside to take advantage of the clear October weather. The restaurant had changed ownership since Luke had lived here. Previously, it had been an Italian restaurant. Now it leaned more toward an eclectic mixture of American favorites with some European influences.

Luke set his menu aside and studied the woman across from him. The breeze tugged at her chin-length hair, the sunlight catching on the various shades of blonde. She tucked a lock behind her ear before she, too, set her menu aside and looked up.

Only she didn't focus on him. Rather, she scanned the other patrons sitting nearby.

Luke already knew who was beside them. Fred White had been working finance at the mine for the past twenty years. Luke's mom had done an interview with him about the mine's future when Luke was in tenth grade. Doctor Bernard, Fred's brother-in-law, sat across from him. The doctor had been one of the few people in town who hadn't thought there was something wrong with Luke. Just shy was his diagnosis. Well, that and dyslexia. Luke hoped he had overcome both by now. Or at least learned to deal with them.

At the table beside them, two of Luke's older sister's friends, both dressed in scrubs, chatted about the latest drama at the hospital. Two middle-aged couples sat at the only other occupied table, all of whom were clearly tourists. With their Texan drawls, they had spent the better part of the past few minutes debating whether visiting Montpelier, the former home of James Madison, was worth the forty-dollar entrance fee.

Their waitress approached and took their orders, both of them opting for eggs and pancakes.

Within minutes, their food was before them. Amberlyn ignored hers in order to look out over the edge of the deck at the view below. "It's so beautiful here. It's nothing like what I expected."

"The mine is a few miles out of town, and most of it is obscured by the trees." Luke's phone rang, and he pulled it from his pocket.

With her voice a little louder than Luke expected, Amberlyn said, "Don't tell me the president is calling you at this time of morning."

Luke read the name on his screen. "It's the chief of staff." He hit the button on his phone to accept the call. "Good morning, Mr. Ellis."

"Morning, Captain. Are you somewhere you can speak freely?"

Luke glanced around the deck, with the tables crowded far too closely together. "No, sir."

"Then I'll keep this brief. The president wants progress reports on the investigation as soon as they become available," the chief of staff said. "I want you to send me updates on the FBI's suspect list any time you have a change."

"I'll email you the latest as soon as I get back to my hotel room."

"Thank you, Captain."

As soon as the call ended, Luke pocketed his phone.

"Luke, was that really the White House chief of staff calling you?"

Luke's natural instinct was to downplay that part of his life, but he couldn't miss what Amberlyn was trying to do. Her use of his first name, the slightly-louder-than-necessary voice. She wanted rumors to start. About him.

"Mr. Ellis just wanted me to send him an updated report."

"I still can't get used to the idea of you working with the president of the United States every day." Amberlyn scooped a bite of eggs onto her fork. "It has to be so amazing to work at the White House."

He couldn't deny that. Trying to imagine what it would be like if they were really dating, he said, "Maybe you can come have lunch with me at the Navy Mess one day."

"The Navy Mess?"

"The Navy Mess, the White House Mess. Same thing." Luke bit into a piece of bacon. "It's kind of like the White House equivalent to an executive dining room."

"That sounds amazing," Amberlyn said. "I have a teacher workday a week from Monday. Maybe we could do it then."

His eyes narrowed fractionally before he remembered. This week, she was a high school teacher, not an FBI special agent. "That should work. I'm sure I'll be on duty after taking this week off, so as long as the president isn't traveling, we should be good."

"I'm excited," she said. The waitress approached and refilled their drinks, but Amberlyn didn't wait for her to serve them before she continued. "I'll get to meet your old high school friends this weekend. Then I'll get to meet your friends at the White House next week."

"Before the month is out, you'll know more about me than you ever thought possible," Luke said.

"I'm looking forward to it."

Luke wished he could say the same.

CHAPTER 14

AMBERLYN TOOK ANOTHER bite of her pancakes. She'd been disappointed that she hadn't found a way to slip Luke's professional success into the conversation last night, but this morning's call at breakfast would be even better. The two older men sitting at her five o'clock had perked up when she'd asked about the president, and the two women in their midthirties had paused their conversation to listen in while Amberlyn and Luke had made their date for lunch at the White House. Only the table full of tourists hadn't taken notice of them. Of course, at this point, their argument about entrance fees had gotten so tiresome that Amberlyn was nearly to the point of telling the woman with the white hat to just pay the forty bucks already if she wanted to visit Montpelier so badly.

The two women in scrubs paid their check and started toward the door leading into the restaurant. They paused when they reached Amberlyn and Luke's table.

"Are you Brianna Steele's brother?"

Luke nodded. "Yeah."

"I thought that was you," the woman said, her expression brightening. "The next time you talk to her, tell her Marissa said hello."

"I'll do that."

Amberlyn smiled inwardly. With any luck, news about Luke's job would circulate through town before the week was over.

The balding man at the table on the other side of them took a last sip of his coffee before standing and making a beeline for Luke. "Why, Luke Steele. It's been a long time."

"Hello, Dr. Bernard."

When Luke didn't introduce Amberlyn, she offered her hand. "I'm Amberlyn. Luke's girlfriend."

"Nice to meet you." Dr. Bernard clasped a hand on Luke's shoulder. "I watched this young man grow up. He was a careful one. Not nearly as many broken bones and stitches as the other boys his age."

Luke squirmed in his seat.

"I didn't mean to eavesdrop," the doctor continued, "but did I hear you're working at the White House?"

"Yes, sir."

When Luke didn't elaborate, Amberlyn satisfied the doctor's curiosity. "He's a military aide to the president."

"Well, that's something." The doctor nodded his approval. "I always knew you would make something of yourself. And I like it when people prove me right."

Again, Luke seemed like he was at a loss for words.

"How long have you lived here, Doctor?" Amberlyn asked.

"Better part of my life. My daddy worked the mines for more than forty years, but he wanted better for me. Sent me to Richmond to get a college education, and I came back a doctor."

"That's wonderful that you know the town so well," Amberlyn said. "We'd love to catch up with you while we're in town. Maybe we can get together for dinner later this week."

"That's a fine idea." The doctor pulled out his cell phone and handed it to Luke. "Here. Put your number in there, and we'll set something up. My wife would love to see you too."

Luke glanced at Amberlyn, a hint of accusation in his eyes, as though he couldn't believe she'd just deliberately connected him with someone from his past. He should know by now that this was her purpose for being here. Anyone in town who could provide information was worth talking to.

Luke finished putting his contact information in the doctor's phone and handed it back to him.

"I'll text you my number, and we'll set up that dinner."

"We'll be sure to reach out," Amberlyn said.

"You do that." The doctor gave a satisfied nod. "Luke, good to see you again."

"You too, Doctor." Luke signaled the waitress for the check.

As soon as he paid it, Amberlyn checked her watch. "It's already after nine. Let's swing by the bank on our way to the grocery store."

"How about you go into the bank while I wait in the car?"

She glanced behind her to make sure no one was still in earshot. "It'll look strange for us to walk in there without some kind of business to conduct," Amberlyn said, considering. "I don't suppose you still have an account there, do you?"

The truth flashed on his face, and he didn't deny it.

"Great. You can make a withdrawal while I check out Brad Shoemacher."

"Okay, but only if you promise we can stay in for dinner tonight. I need a break."

Amberlyn could relate to that. "Fine. We'll wait until tomorrow night to go out with the doctor."

"Or we could not go to dinner with the doctor."

"Am I correct in assuming that the doctor knows most people in town?"

"Yes."

"Then, sorry, Luke. We're going."

———

Luke spotted Brad Shoemacher the minute Luke walked through the door. The man's previously husky physique had softened over the past fifteen years, and he looked like he hadn't seen the inside of a weight room for some time. Judging from his private office, a glass wall separating him from the bank's main lobby, he must have had some success working for Mr. Fairburn, the bank manager who had been an institution since before Luke had left town.

Amberlyn put her hand on Luke's arm and leaned close. "Do you see him?"

"Center office on our left," Luke said, his voice low.

She kissed his cheek and kept her face close to his when she whispered, "You go make a withdrawal. I'll try to get a look at his hand."

The gesture could have been one his mom or sister would give him, but somehow, the simple kiss didn't make him feel brotherly. "Did you just get lipstick on me?"

Her smile was instant. "Maybe a little." She rubbed her thumb over his cheek. "I'll see you in a minute."

Luke nodded and moved to the small counter where deposit and withdrawal forms were located. He filled one out the best he could and got in line behind a man in his seventies. Only one teller was at the counter, a man around Luke's mom's age.

He finished with his current customer and waved the older man forward.

A moment later, a woman approached the other teller station. Luke struggled not to react when he identified her as the woman who had been with Russ Gibson at church.

She waved Luke forward. "I can help you here."

He approached the counter. "I need to make a withdrawal, but I don't have my account number. Can you look that up for me?"

"I just need some identification."

He pulled out his military ID and slid it across the counter.

She set it beside her keyboard and started typing. She was halfway through his name before she looked up, her eyes wide. "Luke Steele? Oh my gosh! I didn't even recognize you."

Luke didn't remember her at all.

When he didn't say anything, she pressed her hand to her chest. "I'm Julia White. Well, I'll be Julia Gibson soon. Russ and I got engaged a few months ago."

He still didn't remember her. "It's been a long time."

"It sure has." Julia's gaze strayed past him. "Is that your girlfriend?"

Luke glanced over his shoulder and spotted Amberlyn waiting by the door. "Yes."

"She looks like one of those famous actresses, all dressed up for a day out on the town."

With her trendy blouse and dress pants, Luke could see where Julia was coming from. Even though he was well aware that Julia was fishing for information, he forced himself to give it to her. "Actually, she's a teacher."

"She looks way too put together for standing in front of the class-room." She counted out his money and focused on Amberlyn again. "I guess it's true what they say. It's always the quiet ones."

Luke had no idea what she was talking about. He slid his ID and cash into his wallet. "Thank you."

"Wait. I'm sure Russ would love to see you. You should come out to dinner with us tonight. You and your girlfriend."

The word *no* burned on his tongue, but Luke could almost feel Amberlyn's stare. And he had no doubt what answer she would want him to give. "That would be great."

"Meet us at the Grandview at six."

"Sounds good," Luke lied.

He headed to the door and opened it for Amberlyn. As soon as they reached Amberlyn's car, she took him by the arm. "That was the woman with Russ at church, wasn't it?"

"Yeah."

"And you just set up a dinner date with them?"

"I figured you'd want me to say yes."

A look of wonder and approval illuminated her face. "I'm so proud."

Luke opened the passenger's side door, and Amberlyn climbed in while he circled to the driver's side. He'd already started the car when it dawned on him that Amberlyn had yet to take over driving duty. "I should have asked—Did you want to drive?"

She shook her head. "The folks around town are already getting used to seeing you drive my car. Might as well let them think it's yours."

"Just let me know if you want to take over." Luke put the car in gear and headed to the nearest grocery store.

"Sorry you won't get the quiet evening you hoped for."

"Maybe we can try for tomorrow night."

"That will work if the doctor can have dinner with us on Wednesday."

"Or your friends at the FBI could catch the second bomber, and we wouldn't have to go out to dinner with Dr. Bernard at all."

"As much as I'd love for that to happen, most cases don't get solved that quickly," Amberlyn said.

"Doesn't mean I'm going to stop hoping."

"You and me both."

CHAPTER 15

AMBERLYN HAD EXPECTED a short trip through the grab-and-go section of the grocery store and maybe a walk down the breakfast aisle. Luke clearly had different plans. Already, the cart was filled with fresh fruit and vegetables, a rotisserie chicken, a bag of rice, and a carton of eggs.

"You know we're only going to be here for a week, right?" Amberlyn asked as he added a gallon of milk to the cart. "And we'll be eating out for probably half of that."

"That doesn't mean we can't eat well the rest of the time." He turned down the international aisle. Tortillas, green chiles, and enchilada sauce came next.

"You know, most people like to go out to eat so they don't have to deal with cooking," she said.

"I like to cook." Luke gave her a pointed look. "And tomorrow night, no matter who invites us out, I'm eating in."

"Military aide to the president and he cooks. You better be careful, Captain Steele. You might not be a bachelor for long if you start bragging about your culinary skills. I mean, if someone cared about that." And it wasn't that Amberlyn couldn't cook. She just rarely had the time. When they turned down the baking aisle and he added a couple of spices to the cart, she spotted the premade pie crusts. "Do you like chocolate?"

"Yeah. Why?"

"If you're making dinner tomorrow night, I thought I could make dessert."

"I'm good with that."

Amberlyn gathered several needed ingredients from the baking aisle before heading back to the dairy section. "I'll be back in a minute."

"I'm almost done," Luke said. "I'll meet you up front."

Amberlyn went in search of the cream cheese and whipped cream she would need to make her no-bake chocolate mousse pie. She was nearly to the front of the ice cream aisle when she spotted a man in a deputy uniform.

Though technically Amberlyn should inform the local authorities that she was working in the area, she wasn't about to risk her cover being compromised.

She passed by him, but she didn't miss the way he glanced at her, his eyes sparking with interest.

Opening the last freezer case on her right, she grabbed a container of Cool Whip, then turned to find the deputy standing between her and the end of the aisle.

She started to move around him, but he shifted at the same time, blocking her path.

Amberlyn lifted her gaze to meet his. "Excuse me."

He didn't move. "I haven't seen you around here before."

"I'm here visiting with my boyfriend." Even though she kept her tone friendly, she sized up the man in front of her. His posturing and the way he stood a little too close for comfort made her think of the crooked cops portrayed on TV. She read his name tag. Deputy Lester.

"Who's your boyfriend?"

"Luke Steele."

"You're dating Luke Steele?" he asked, clearly surprised. "You?" he repeated, this time his utter disbelief carrying in his tone.

"That's right." She instinctively glanced down at the man's hands to check for rings. No wedding band, but his right hand sported a championship ring just like the one in the photo. The telltale lines of the championship tattoo were also visible.

Luke appeared behind the deputy with their cart.

"There you are." Luke eyed the man standing between them, his expression darkening.

Amberlyn took advantage of Luke's arrival to angle her body sideways and push past the deputy.

The deputy turned to face Luke. "Luke Steele." He shook his head. "Never thought I'd see you around here again."

Luke met the deputy's gaze. "Never thought I'd be back here again."

Even though she had no interest in knowing the obnoxious man in front of them, she asked, "Luke, are you going to introduce me?"

"Amberlyn Jones, Owen Lester."

"That's Deputy Lester now."

"Luke, we'd better go." She put the cream cheese and Cool Whip in the cart. "You'll want to get back to the lodge before you get another call from the White House."

Owen shot Luke a look of disbelief.

Amberlyn didn't expand on her comment. "Nice meeting you." She headed toward the checkout counter, Luke following behind her.

The woman at the checkout counter was in her early twenties, too young to have attended school with Luke. She rang them up, and Luke paid for their groceries.

Amberlyn started to pull her wallet out to offer to pay for her part of it but then decided to wait until they didn't have an audience.

She sensed someone staring at her and wasn't surprised to find Deputy Lester behind her.

Luke accepted his receipt from the cashier and pushed the cart outside.

Amberlyn helped him load the groceries. "That deputy gave me the creeps."

"Sorry about him. He was the sort who spent as much time trying to impress the popular crowd as he did tormenting anyone smaller than him."

Amberlyn glanced back toward the store. "He also had a championship ring on and a tattoo."

"That's one more name we can move from our possible to the suspect list," Luke said. "Although if he's working at the sheriff's office, it might be easy to check his work schedule."

"That's a good idea." She transferred the last two bags of groceries into the back of her car, and Luke pushed the cart to the cart return.

As soon as they were both in the car, Amberlyn continued the conversation. "If Owen Lester was working when that photo was taken in St. Louis, we'll know it wasn't him."

"Does the FBI already have people checking out the other suspect's work schedules?"

"Some of them."

Luke pulled out of the parking lot and headed toward the lodge. "Why not all of them? It would be a heck of a lot faster if we could eliminate people without having to check out their wrists and ring fingers."

Amberlyn didn't disagree, but she had also worked enough cases to know how quickly leads could dry up if they weren't careful. "We don't want to tip our hand that we're looking for someone from your hometown," she explained. "The investigative team will verify schedules for everyone who is with larger companies because they can do it without rousing suspicion."

"You're avoiding the small businesses here in town?"

"And the six people on our list who are self-employed," she said, although she suspected the FBI offices in the cities where the suspects lived were already doing what they could to help eliminate them.

"Maybe we need to spend more time looking for the missing car instead of who got a tattoo in high school."

"Trust me. We are."

Luke pulled up beside their cottage and circled to open the back. When he picked up the bag with the pie crust in it, he asked, "What are you making for dessert anyway?"

"Chocolate mousse pie."

"That sounds way better than anything we'd eat at the Grandview."

"It probably is."

When he shot her a hopeful look, she couldn't help but laugh. "Are we going to have a debate every time we're invited out to eat?"

"I'm a pretty good cook," Luke said. "We could stay in."

"I'll take that as a yes."

"Yes, as in we can stay in?"

"Yes, as in we're going to have a lot of debates this week about going out." Amberlyn grabbed several bags. "At least you can eat here for lunch."

Luke unlocked the door. "It's going to be a working lunch, isn't it?"

"Probably, but that doesn't mean we can't take a break before we go to dinner," Amberlyn said. "I'd love to check out more of the lodge."

"After running into people at literally every place we've stopped, maybe I'll let you go without me."

Amberlyn shook her head. "Where's the fun in that?"

The suspect list was shrinking but not nearly fast enough. Sitting at the kitchen table, Luke skimmed over the latest update, which indicated that one of the men on their maybe list had been in London when the photo was taken in St. Louis. The FBI had also confirmed alibis for four others, all of whom had been working that day.

Across from Luke, Amberlyn tapped on her laptop keyboard, making notes as they went through the intel. "With those five off the list and Brad Shoemacher not having a tattoo, that leaves us with thirteen people. Five who we know have tattoos and are still wearing their rings and eight left in the maybe category."

"Except for Cooper Bird, we won't be able to check on any of the others until the reunion activities start." The homecoming game on Friday night, which would include a special tribute to the football coach and the championship team, a tour of the high school on Saturday afternoon, and the actual reunion on Saturday night. Luke was already dreading it all.

"We've been assuming everyone coming for the reunion would wait until Friday to come in, but it's possible some could get here early,"

Amberlyn said. "I'll ask the investigating office to request a warrant to ping our suspects' cell phones. That will let us know when they arrive in town."

"And give us their locations so we can accidentally run into them." Luke took a sip from his water bottle. "Smart."

Amberlyn let out a sigh and looked up from her laptop. "They got the DNA results back from Eli Duffy's car. The only samples they found were from him and his girlfriend."

"That's a bummer." Luke leaned back in his seat. "It would have been too easy if we'd gotten a hit on that."

"We're due for some breaks to fall our way." Amberlyn motioned toward her screen. "I hoped someone would have something on the missing car by now, but so far, no one has seen any sign of it."

"Do you think they swapped out the license plates?"

"Probably. For all we know, they could have painted it too."

Luke stood and crossed to the sink to refill his water bottle. "Was there any sign of paint at Duffy's place?"

She shook her head. "Not that I saw."

"Then there's a good chance it's still white."

"Yes, but it's also one of the most popular cars and one of the most common colors."

Which was likely why they had chosen it. "Has your team had any luck figuring out where these guys might strike next?"

"No. This is the second incident attributed to Forever Freedom, but we haven't been able to determine a logical motive for either attack." Amberlyn's frustration was obvious. "I was working on the library incident during the week leading up to this bombing."

"You can't blame yourself for what happened," Luke said. "No one could have known the FEMA building was the target."

"I can't help but think that if I'd done a better job, Chanelle would still be alive."

"Survivor's guilt is normal." He'd seen the signs often enough among his fellow Marines.

Amberlyn narrowed her eyes. "Don't tell me you have a degree in psychology too."

"No. International relations, but I did get a minor in peace and conflict."

"There's a minor in peace and conflict?"

"Yep. Psychology played a part in a lot of those classes."

A shadow of grief crossed her face. "I'm learning quickly that no matter how many psychology classes someone takes, it doesn't prepare you for dealing with something like this."

"You need time."

She glanced down. "Speaking of time, we need to get going."

Luke swallowed his protest. He'd already figured out that Amberlyn would ignore any attempts he made to avoid socializing. He secured his laptop in his room and stepped into the shoes he'd kicked off after they'd returned from the store.

When he walked back into the living area, she was waiting, her purse in hand.

"Are you ready?" she asked.

"Ready to have dinner with a guy I don't even like?" Luke shook his head. "No."

"How does Russ Gibson feel about you?" Amberlyn asked.

"I'm sure he dislikes me as much as I dislike him." Otherwise, why would he have spent so much time tormenting Luke at lunchtime? He had no idea why Julia would think Russ would love to see him. Maybe she meant Russ would love to harass him. Just like old times.

"Sounds like tonight is going to be interesting."

"That's a nice word for it."

Amberlyn stood by the door and looked up at him, her expression unexpectedly serious. "I don't know if I've said this already, but I really appreciate your helping me with this."

"You've already thanked me." And Luke preferred to avoid a scenario where he didn't help and had to face the same survivor's guilt Amberlyn was already struggling against.

"I hope the older version of Russ is nicer than the one you went to high school with."

Luke crossed to the door and pulled it open. "I wouldn't count on it."

CHAPTER 16

THE CLINK OF glasses against wooden tables competed with the buzz of conversation in the restaurant Julia had chosen for dinner. Amberlyn inhaled the waft of freshly grilled steak, fried shrimp, and stale beer. The first two stirred her appetite. The last warranted a quick scan of the bar at the center of the restaurant.

Only three patrons sat on the line of stools, two men chatting. The third, a woman, appeared to be waiting for someone.

Amberlyn spotted Russ and Julia at a large, round table, another couple already seated with them.

"Did you know someone else was coming too?"

"No." Luke clenched his jaw briefly. "Knowing Russ, he invited Brad so they could run up the tab and stick me with the bill."

"Then, I guess we'll have to engage some preventative measures."

"Good luck with that."

Julia spotted them and waved.

Though Amberlyn wanted to ask Luke if he was ready for their interrogation session with Russ, she already knew his answer. She reached for his hand and gave it a squeeze.

He looked down at her and offered a subtle nod. Then he started forward, leading her to the empty seats at the table.

Russ stood as though he needed to demonstrate that he was taller and bulkier than Luke. With the way his eyes adjusted slightly to meet Luke's gaze, Amberlyn suspected Luke had gained a couple inches since graduating from high school.

"I didn't think you'd show up," Russ said.

Luke didn't respond.

Hoping to break the tension, Amberlyn offered her hand. "You must be Russ. I'm Amberlyn, Luke's girlfriend."

Russ shook her hand. "This is my fiancée, Julia. And this is Brad Shoemacher and his wife, Mikayla."

"It's nice to meet you all."

Amberlyn moved to sit down, and Luke pulled out her chair for her, helping her settle before taking the seat beside her.

"Brad, I think I saw you in the bank today," Amberlyn said.

"Yes. I'm the assistant manager."

"That's great," Amberlyn turned to Russ. "What about you? What do you do?"

"I work for Premier Homes," Russ said. "We're building a new development east of town."

Julia put her hand on her fiancé's arm. "Russ is the top salesman in this region."

"That's impressive."

"Word is Luke here is the one trying to impress people," Russ said.

Luke instantly stiffened.

"What makes you say that?" Amberlyn asked.

Brad hooked his arm around the back of his wife's chair. "Rumor has it that our old buddy here is working for the president."

Small towns really did have a communication network that defied logic.

"I'm not sure where you heard that," Luke said.

Julia held up her menu. "Uncle Max said he heard you talking on the phone this morning."

Amberlyn looked from Luke to Julia. "Your uncle?"

"Dr. Bernard," Julia said.

"Well, that explains where the rumors started." Amberlyn turned her attention to Luke. "Remember, he was sitting near us when the chief of staff called this morning."

Brad took a sip of his beer. "Are you sure Luke here isn't telling you stories?"

Amberlyn had had about enough of these men's cocky attitude. She eyed them coolly. "I might have thought so if I hadn't met him at the White House."

Brad nearly choked on his drink. "You two met at the White House?"

"Yes." Luke didn't expound on his answer.

"I was on a tour when we ran into each other. He came out of some restricted hallway when I was first walking into the executive mansion."

Russ let out a knowing chuckle. "You sure he wasn't on a tour too?"

"Positive." Amberlyn let her gaze hold Russ's for a long moment. "Tourists can't take their girlfriends on Air Force One."

"Wait." Brad set his beer down with enough force to send foam sloshing over the top of the glass. "Luke took you for a ride on Air Force One?"

"That was an unusual circumstance," Luke said. "Amberlyn was in Kansas City, visiting a friend after the bombing, and I was there with the president. The president was kind enough to let me bring her home with me instead of making her fly back commercial."

Amberlyn hadn't anticipated Luke to use the truth to introduce the bombing, but now that he had, she pushed forward. "I still can't believe the FEMA building is gone or why someone would go after it. I mean, Kansas City isn't exactly a likely target."

"That office covers a lot of area," Russ said, "even if it is only four states."

"True, but it's not like it's responding to hurricanes and earthquakes," Amberlyn said. "I'd bet that office deals mostly with tornadoes and maybe some flooding."

Brad lifted his stein again, tipping it toward Russ. "And snowstorms."

Snowstorms? Surely Chanelle's death hadn't been because someone was upset about a snowstorm in Kansas or Missouri.

Their waiter approached to take Amberlyn's and Luke's drink order. Though Amberlyn would have been content with water, she ordered a lemonade so the waiter would have to start a tab for them.

After Luke ordered his usual ice water, Amberlyn spoke to the waiter again. "We may need to leave early, so can you make sure you keep our check separate?"

"No problem."

The expressions on Russ's and Brad's faces suggested Luke's evaluation of the situation had been spot on.

Amberlyn opened her menu. "So, what's good here?"

Luke was in awe. Not only had Amberlyn headed off the inevitable awkwardness of who would pick up the check tonight, but she had also fabricated a late-night teleconference with his boss that had allowed them to leave after a mere fifty-one minutes of torture, the majority of which they'd spent listening to Brad brag about being next in line for branch manager and Russ brag about his Corvette. All the while, Amberlyn had tried to dig deeper into their backgrounds without sounding like a special agent.

He dropped Amberlyn's car keys on the kitchen counter and shrugged out of his jacket. "You are a master manipulator."

"Thank you." Amberlyn stepped out of her heels. "I think."

"It was a compliment." Luke moved to the sink and poured himself a glass of water. "The way you told the waiter to keep our check separate was genius."

"They really were going to stick you with the bill, weren't they?"

"Oh yeah." He nodded. "That was one of their favorite pastimes in high school. They'd order some big meal and then invite someone to join them at the last minute. Before you knew it, they were gone and the check was in front of you."

"How many times did they do that to you?"

"Just once, but I wasn't the only victim." Luke suspected just about every kid in school who wasn't part of the in crowd had fallen for the ruse at one point or another.

"I can see why you were dreading going out with them tonight." Amberlyn headed into her bedroom, returning a moment later with her laptop. "Let's hope the torture was worth it."

"What are you talking about?"

"Snowstorms." She set her laptop on the kitchen table.

"You think someone bombed the FEMA building because of a snowstorm?" Luke rounded the counter and joined her at the table.

"I don't know, but the fact that they had a possible motive is suspicious, don't you think?"

Luke felt another research project coming on. "Don't tell me we're about to search through the past fifteen years' worth of snowstorms in that region."

"Like Russ said, it's a lot of area but only four states."

"It's odd that Russ would know how many states the Kansas City office covers."

"I thought so too." Amberlyn opened up the FEMA website. "Kansas City is in Region 7, which includes Iowa, Kansas, Missouri, and Nebraska."

"Wasn't that first bombing by Forever Freedom in Nebraska?"

Amberlyn nodded. "Yes, it was."

"I'll grab my laptop." Luke disappeared and returned a moment later with it in hand. He settled at the table beside her. "Where do you want me to start?"

"Since Nebraska is in Region 7 and that's where the first bombing was, I say we start there."

"When was the Nebraska bombing?"

"Five months ago," Amberlyn said. "I'll start from there and work backward. You start from when you graduated and work forward."

"You don't really think someone has been holding a grudge for fifteen years, do you?"

"It's happened before, but usually, there's some sort of catalyst to push people into action."

Luke pondered for a moment. How long would it take for a group to organize themselves and stage an attack? "Maybe I should go five years back. That's probably a more logical time frame."

"Good idea," Amberlyn said. "We can always work backward from there if we need to."

Luke logged into his computer. "What exactly are we looking for?"

"For someone to strike out and kill so many people, there must have been some tragedy that was personal to the people involved."

"Maybe we should be digging into Eli Duffy's connection to the area."

"That's a good idea." Amberlyn looked at her watch as though she'd forgotten it was already well past working hours.

"How late do you want to work tonight?" Luke asked.

Amberlyn glanced at her watch again. "Maybe a couple hours, but you don't have to do this. You've been at it all day."

"So have you." And Luke wouldn't be able to relax if he knew she was still working.

"Yes, but this is my job."

"For now, it's my job too."

———————

This was getting ridiculous. Nearly every article about deaths that occurred during snowstorms in Nebraska required Amberlyn to subscribe to the newspaper in order to gain access. Even then, she had paid the dollar for the introductory offer for several of them only to find she couldn't read anything that had occurred before today.

She leaned back in her seat. "I'm striking out. Almost every article here is blocked unless you're already a subscriber."

Luke looked up. "I'm having the same problem."

"I'll email Jeff and Ian. Someone in my office should be able to get us access."

"It's only nine thirty. Is there anything else you want us to work on?"

"Maybe we should take a break." Amberlyn closed her laptop and crossed into the kitchen. "I'll make up that dessert for tomorrow night."

"Need any help?"

"Sure." Amberlyn motioned to the refrigerator. "We need the cream cheese and Cool Whip from the fridge."

Luke retrieved both and set them on the counter while Amberlyn rummaged through the cabinets until she came up with a saucepan.

Setting it on the stove, she retrieved a bar of baking chocolate and handed it to him. "Can you break this up and put the pieces in here?"

"Sure."

Amberlyn gathered the rest of her ingredients.

Luke unwrapped the chocolate and began breaking it into pieces. "Do you often cook when you're stressed?"

"Not often, but sometimes." She'd never really thought about it before. "It's nice to know that when I cook, I'll have something to show for my efforts when I'm done. That's not always the case in my day job."

"I know what you mean." He leaned against the counter beside the stove.

"How long have you been working at the White House?"

"Since April," Luke said. "It's a two-year assignment."

"Then what?"

"I don't know. Rumor has it that once you work as a mil aide, you can practically pick your next assignment." He shrugged a shoulder. "I guess we'll see if that's true."

Amberlyn turned on the burner so she could melt the chocolate. "What would your dream assignment be?"

"I'm not sure." A little line formed on his brow. "I like strategy, but people at my level don't often get to do a whole lot of that in the Marine Corps. At least, not without someone up the chain changing everything."

"That would be hard."

"I imagine it's like that in most jobs."

"Maybe." Though Amberlyn hadn't experienced that in her current position. More often than not, she and her coworkers operated as a team, no one worrying about who had what level of experience. They talked out ideas until they had the best possible analysis to present.

"Did you plan to go on a run again tomorrow?" Luke asked.

"Yeah. You?"

He nodded.

"What time should we go?"

"That depends on if you want to sleep in," Luke said.

"I'm not very good at sleeping in. How about we go around quarter after six?"

He nodded. "Anything else I can help with?"

"I think I've got it."

"Okay, then, I'm going to take a look around outside before I lock up."

"You aren't worried about Russ and Brad showing up, are you?"

"It's a small town." Luke stepped into his shoes. "By now, everyone knows we're here and where we're staying. And they might piece together that you knew one of the bombing victims."

"That's an unsettling thought." She shifted to face him. "Why did you mention that to your friends?"

"It was the only thing I could think of to see if they would react," Luke said. "And it was obvious that they weren't going to trust any kind of casual conversation, although you did a pretty good job of turning that around."

She hadn't planned to share any real information about herself, but she couldn't deny that it worked.

He moved to the door leading to their balcony. "I'll be back in a minute." He opened the sliding door and closed it behind him.

Amberlyn mixed the cream cheese with the chocolate, expecting Luke to walk back inside and cross to the front door. He didn't.

After she finished blending the last few ingredients, she spooned the chocolate mousse filling into the pie crust. After she covered it and put it into the freezer, she crossed to the balcony. When she didn't see Luke, she stepped outside and looked down at the eight-foot drop to the sloping hill below.

She scanned the woods and listened for any sound, but she couldn't distinguish any footsteps over the rumble of the waterfall.

She stepped back inside at the same time the front door unlocked and Luke walked inside. They closed their respective doors and locked them in unison.

"How did you—?" She broke off, not quite sure how to phrase her question.

"I climbed down the side of the deck. It has a trellis on one side."

"Why?" Amberlyn furrowed her brow. "You could have just walked back inside and left through the front door."

"Yes, but if anyone was planning to mess with us, that's where they would have been." Luke crossed to the sink and washed his hands. "They wouldn't expect me to approach from the side of the cottage."

"You know, you sound paranoid right now."

"Maybe, but I'd rather be paranoid and safe than reckless and dead."

"I don't think this group is the sort to go after people one at a time. They like to target large groups, and the use of explosive devices suggests the need for distance from the deaths they create."

"That may be how they operate as a group," Luke said, "but how they react as individuals may be completely different."

"That's true." And terrifying. "Are you sure you didn't take any psychology classes?"

"I didn't need psychology classes to understand these guys. Russ and Brad never had any trouble being on the front line when someone else experienced pain."

"Someone like you."

Luke lifted his left shoulder. "Like with their restaurant tricks, I was one of many."

CHAPTER 17

LUKE ONLY MADE it two steps out the door before he spotted the vandalism to Amberlyn's car. All four tires were flat, and shaving cream covered the windshield and windows.

Amberlyn gasped, her eyes wide.

"I'm so sorry." He shook his head. "They must have come over after we went to bed."

She clenched her jaw before lifting her chin. "You think Russ and Brad did this?"

"I can't think of anyone else who would have bothered." Luke pulled out his cell phone. "I assume you want to report it to the police."

"Oh yeah."

Luke dialed the nonemergency number and explained the situation while Amberlyn used her phone to take photos of her car from every angle.

When he hung up, she walked around the car again, but this time, she was looking away from it instead of toward it.

"What are you doing?" Luke asked.

"I was hoping there might be some security cameras on one of the cottages."

"Sorry. I'm afraid we're out of luck on that."

She headed up the gravel drive, her focus on the road. "It doesn't look like they drove down here."

"They probably parked up in the main lot and walked down." He pointed in the direction of the lodge. "It would help them make sure we didn't hear them drive up."

"In that case, let's go."

"Where?"

"To request the security tapes of the main parking lot," Amberlyn said.

"Maybe you should let the local authorities take care of that," Luke suggested. "You're not law enforcement right now, remember?"

She blew out a frustrated breath.

"I'm sorry, Amberlyn. They obviously thought your car belonged to me." Guilt welled up inside him. "I'll pay to fix any damage."

"Even if they thought this was your car, what was the purpose? It's not like either of us did anything to them."

"They planned to put me in my place last night," Luke said. "You didn't let them."

"So they messed with my car?" She narrowed her eyes. "Have they ever done this to you before?"

"I didn't have a car when I was in high school." He motioned to her SUV. "This is one of the reasons I didn't want one."

A police car approached and parked beside Amberlyn's SUV. The deputy climbed out, and Luke inwardly winced. Owen Lester. Not exactly the person who would take care of a problem members of the old in crowd caused.

"What seems to be the trouble here?" he asked as though he couldn't see the shaving cream dripping down the side of Amberlyn's car.

Amberlyn gestured to the vandalized vehicle. "I would think it's obvious."

"Looks like some kids having some fun."

"You call vandalism 'kids having fun'?" Amberlyn asked, her voice tense.

He leaned down and looked at the tires. "It looks like the tires have just lost their air, and a bucket of water will take care of the rest. You can hardly call that vandalism."

"We certainly can," Amberlyn insisted. "And I want to file a report."

"Now, there's no need for that."

"Deputy Lester, are you aware that if you refuse to report a crime, it could be considered obstruction of justice?"

Owen's eyes darkened. "Luke, maybe you should tell you girlfriend how things work around here."

"I think my girlfriend is perfectly capable of figuring that out for herself," Luke said. "And it seems to me that she has the legal right to have her statement put on file."

"Or I can simply speak with the sheriff and ask him why his deputy refused to report a crime," Amberlyn added.

"You want to make things hard on yourself? Fine." Owen went back to his car and returned to Amberlyn and Luke with a piece of paper. "Fill this out, but it's not like you'll be able to prove who did this."

"No, but you can." Amberlyn accepted the report sheet and began writing out her statement. "Whoever did this must have parked in the main lot of the lodge. I want the security footage pulled for the time period between eleven last night and six this morning."

"You want us to go to all this trouble for some shaving cream and someone letting the air out of your tires?"

"Yes." Amberlyn finished filling out the report. She took a photo of it and then handed it back to Owen. "Here you go. I'll be checking with your office later to ensure this was properly filed."

Owen's jaw tightened. He took a step back. "Have a nice day."

Luke waited until Owen climbed into his car and pulled away before he spoke. "If you have any friends who can request that security footage from the lodge, you might want to make a call."

"You don't think he'll do it?"

"Knowing him, he'll make sure it doesn't exist," Luke said. "He and Brad were pretty tight in high school. I doubt that's changed much."

Amberlyn dialed her phone.

Luke headed inside.

"Where are you going?" Amberlyn asked.

"To find a bucket." Luke waved at her SUV. "I'm going to wash your car."

A five-mile run, a workout in the lodge's exercise room, a long shower—none of those had helped Amberlyn dispel the anger simmering through her. And it wasn't just anger for her situation. Luke had clearly suffered at the hands of these bullies for years. The way he had washed her car as though it had been no big deal made her suspect that he was no stranger to helping others who had been victimized by the former high school football team.

Now dressed in a pair of jeans and a sweater—no need to dress up if they were staying in all day—she walked out of her room to find the living area empty. She peeked through Luke's open bedroom door. "Luke?"

No answer.

Not sure where he would have gone, especially since her car still had four flat tires, she grabbed her laptop and carried it to the couch. The kitchen chairs were not nearly comfortable enough to use the table for her workspace two days in a row.

After retrieving a notebook and pen from her bag, she checked her email. No updates from Jeff beyond a quick, *I'll look into it.*

Amberlyn pulled up her notes with the complete list of the championship football team, the names listed in three columns. Thanks to their efforts and the efforts of her coworkers, they had narrowed it down to five remaining suspects who definitely had championship tattoos, the three they were still uncertain about, and the fifty-four who either had an alibi or who had been identified as not having the wrist tattoo.

She zeroed in on Brad. He might not have had a tattoo, but he had been far from sympathetic to those who had lost friends and loved ones in the bombing. The possibility of more than one of Luke's former classmates being involved loomed in her mind, and she looked at the suspect list in a new light.

The front door opened, and Luke walked in, a smudge of black on his hand.

"Where were you at?"

"Putting air in your tires." He crossed to the kitchen sink and turned on the water. "Pastor Mosley came over with his air compressor so we could take care of it."

"That was sweet of you. And Pastor Mosley."

"I didn't think you'd want to be without transportation for long." He washed his hands and tipped his head toward the front door. "I mounted a camera out front, too, to make sure we know if anyone tries to cause problems again."

"You went out and bought a surveillance camera?"

"I should have thought to put one out when we first got here, but I didn't think anyone from the lodge would share which bungalow we were in."

"They could have driven around and looked for our car."

"Maybe."

Amberlyn looked back at her suspect list. "I don't know who I want arrested more, Russ and Brad or Deputy Lester."

"Owen Lester's a jerk, but he's just trying to avoid getting on Russ's and Brad's bad side." Luke turned off the water and dried his hands. "Even I was surprised last night when Russ and Brad were so callous about the bombing."

"I was thinking maybe more than one person from here is involved."

"It's possible, but before we kick that hornet's nest, I say we figure out who was in that photo." He grabbed his laptop from his room and sat on the couch beside her. "Where do you want me to start?"

"I don't have any updates from my office yet, but since they have more resources, we'll have them continue the search on the snowstorms. I'll keep going on the alibis, and you can make up a list of who was friends with whom."

"I already told you, I didn't hang out with any of those guys."

"I have a hard time believing everyone on the team spent their nights letting air out of people's tires."

"That's true."

"Maybe start by making a list of the guys people like us would avoid while in high school."

"People like us?" He looked up from his open laptop, his eyebrows raised. "I figured you for the cheerleader type."

She had no idea how he'd figured that out. "I was a cheerleader who also ran track, but that doesn't mean I'd want to hang out with guys like Brad and Russ."

Luke studied her for a moment, as though trying to figure out how to process this new information. Finally, he said, "Let me know if you need any help with the alibis."

"I will." But first, she was going to enlist Kiera's help. It was time to match cell phone locations to alibis. Somewhere, someone was lying, and it was time to find out who.

CHAPTER 18

LUKE HAD SURVIVED the trip down memory lane. Barely. He'd also muddled through the text message exchange with Dr. Bernard to set up dinner for tomorrow night, a dinner that would be at the doctor's home rather than in a restaurant. At least Luke wouldn't have to worry about someone sticking him with the bill.

Amberlyn had been on the phone with her coworkers on and off all day, but so far, it seemed like all she was getting was a dump of information rather than answers.

She hung up yet again.

"What's the latest from your office?"

"We're striking out on finding anyone with an electronic signature near St. Louis on the day that photo was taken. Same with Kansas City the day of the bombing," Amberlyn said. "Everyone was either where they said they were, or they left their cars and cell phones behind."

"I know I wouldn't drive my car if I were going to commit a crime."

"Me neither, but I was hoping we would finally catch a break. We are so due for one."

Luke agreed. Changing the subject to something they could control, he asked, "What time do you want to eat dinner?"

She checked her cell phone. "It's already four thirty?"

He nodded. "The enchiladas will only take about forty-five minutes to make."

"I'm good for whenever you are."

After only eating a sandwich for lunch, Luke was famished. "Are you hungry?"

She paused to consider his question. "Yeah. Actually, I am."

"I'll get started, then." He set his laptop aside and crossed to the kitchen. He pulled the rotisserie chicken out of the refrigerator and grabbed a bowl. Reverting back to their earlier conversation, Luke said, "Unfortunately, most people have watched enough TV to know the cops can use your cell phone to track you."

"That's true." Amberlyn pushed to her feet, her laptop still in hand. "I have the list of phones that were in the area when the photo was taken. Unfortunately, there's a truck stop right behind that diner."

After he washed his hands again, Luke used a fork and his fingers to pull the breast meat off the chicken, shredding it before putting it into the bowl. "How many phone numbers are there?"

"Fifty-three." She set her laptop on the serving counter and slid onto the stool opposite the stove. "We have names on forty-nine of them, but none of them have any obvious connection to Eli Duffy or this town."

"And the other four?" Luke asked.

"They're all prepaid phones we haven't identified."

"Were any of those names Eli Duffy?"

"No." She opened her laptop again. "But one of those burner phones was traced to Kansas City. It's likely the one used to detonate the bomb."

"Which takes us down to three possible phones to track." Luke added the chicken to the pan along with the cream cheese and green chiles. "Assuming our guy was carrying a phone."

"We'll find out soon enough." Amberlyn tapped on her keyboard. "The St. Louis office is tracking down the remaining three numbers. We'll check for connections between your high school or Eli Duffy."

"Or if any of them show up here in Pine Falls."

"That too." Amberlyn fell silent for a moment. "So far, it looks like all three of those phones have left the St. Louis area. One is in Los Angeles. Another is in Pittsburgh, and the other is in Austin."

"Could be terrorists, or they could all be truckers."

"With where they all ended up, I'm guessing truckers," Amberlyn said. "All three of those places would be logical destinations along the trucking route, but we'll have someone keep an eye on all of them regardless."

"That's good." Luke stirred the filling for the enchiladas and added some cumin and garlic powder.

Amberlyn peeked around the edge of her laptop screen. "Don't you need measuring spoons or a recipe?"

Luke shook his head. "I've been making this since high school."

"Who taught you how to cook?"

"This one was my mom, but my dad did most of the cooking in my house," Luke said. "He was home more often."

"What does your dad do?"

"He runs an accounting firm." Luke slid the pan off the burner and retrieved a baking dish and the tortillas. "Mom's schedule was a lot more chaotic. You never knew when she'd have to travel for some story."

"Was she a reporter?"

"A news anchor." He began spooning filling into the tortillas. "She worked out of a local station in Richmond."

"She commuted to Richmond from here?" Amberlyn thought DC commutes were bad. "That has to be a two-hour drive."

"She only went into the station once a month or so. Her cameraman lived down the street from us. The two of them handled this region of the state."

"Is she still working in the news industry?"

"Yes. My parents live in New York now."

Amberlyn's eyes widened. It didn't take a genius to figure out she'd put two and two together. "Your mom is Pamela Steele with News Tonight?"

He nodded.

She shook her head as though trying to realign her image of him. "Let me get this straight. You grew up with a celebrity for a mom, and those guys still treated you like dirt?"

"Yep." Luke finished making the enchiladas and slid the pan into the oven. "They didn't want me to think I was better than they were."

"You are better than they are. You're nice."

Warmth rushed through Luke that had nothing to do with the heat emanating from the oven. He closed the oven door and looked up. "Thanks."

"How long do those need to cook?" Amberlyn asked.

"About twenty minutes."

"Great. That should be just enough time."

"Time for what?"

"For you to call your mom to see if she can pull the research on the snowstorms in Nebraska."

"I thought your office was working on that."

"They are, but it's slow going through every newspaper and station one at a time," Amberlyn said. "I'll bet your mom would have access through her work to get it all in one shot."

"You're probably right." He pulled out his phone and checked the time. Almost five. His mother would most certainly be in makeup about now. He dialed her number, and she answered after the second ring.

"Hey, honey," his mom said. "I only have a minute. I have to be on camera soon."

"I know, but I wondered if you could do me a favor."

"Of course. What do you need?"

"First, we need to keep this confidential, but I need some research I'm having trouble finding." Luke explained the basics of what he needed. "Do you think your research department can help us with this?"

"Us?"

Luke muted his phone. "Can I tell her this is for the investigation?"

"As long as she doesn't share that with anyone."

He hit the Unmute button. "Off the record, I'm helping a friend with the FBI. These stories could narrow down the suspect list for the Kansas City bombing."

"And I can't share that with anyone?"

"No, but I suspect the FBI would be willing to share the story with you as soon as an arrest is made." He lifted his eyebrows in question.

Amberlyn nodded.

"I'll put Roslyn on that, but it'll take some time. She probably won't be able to pull it together until morning."

"That'll work. Thanks, Mom."

"Where are you, anyway?" she asked. "I thought you were flying to Europe this week."

"I was, but plans changed. I'm still in Virginia." He wasn't about to tell her where in Virginia, not right before she went on camera. The shock might be too much for her. "Call or text me when you send the info, okay?"

"I will. Love you, sweetie."

"Love you, too, Mom." Luke hung up. "She's having her assistant pull the info, but we probably won't have it until tomorrow."

"You know what we should do?" Amberlyn asked.

"What?"

Amberlyn waved at the flat-screen TV hanging above the fireplace. "We should watch a movie tonight."

"I thought you'd want to keep working after dinner."

"I want answers, but we could both use some downtime."

Luke retrieved two dinner plates from the cabinet. "I can't argue with that."

———

Amberlyn stretched her legs out, her feet propped on the coffee table in front of her, Luke's body mirroring her own. Her idea to watch a movie had quickly been hijacked when they discovered the playoff game was on between the Braves and the Dodgers.

Thankfully, they had both chosen to cheer for the Braves. Unfortunately, their team was down three to one.

"They need to switch out the pitcher." Luke motioned to the TV. "McKay doesn't have anything left."

"Who do they have available in the bullpen?" Amberlyn asked.

The words were barely out of her mouth when the television announcer said, "It looks like McKay may be on his last batter."

The commentator then ran through the different options in the bullpen.

Amberlyn gestured toward the TV. "It's like they were listening to us."

"It's common sense. If they let any more runs score, it's going to be tough coming back to win."

The batter popped the ball up to the first baseman, and the manager immediately signaled a pitching change.

The commentator's voice filled the room. "Looks like that'll do it for McKay."

"It's a smart move," the other commentator said. "They can't afford to drop any more runs, or it will be hard for them to stage a comeback."

Luke narrowed his eyes. "Okay, that was weird."

Amberlyn pushed to a stand. "I'm going to get a piece of pie. Do you want some?"

"Yeah, that sounds great. Thanks."

Amberlyn set the pie on the counter and went in search of a knife to cut it with. "Did you play baseball in high school?"

"No."

"Any sports?"

"No."

"Really?" She unearthed a pie server in the utensil drawer and held it up. "I figured that since you run every day, you would have run track."

"Russ and Owen were both on the track team. So were a lot of their buddies," Luke said. "It wasn't worth the frustration."

"Did you ever think they would have been lucky to have you on the team?" Amberlyn asked. "You look like you could give any of them a run for their money."

"That was the problem. They don't like to lose, and it would have been miserable for me to win." He shifted on the couch so he was facing her more fully. "You saw what they did to your car, and all you did was save me from paying the bill."

"They really are bullies."

"Yeah."

Amberlyn cut the pie into eight slices and transferred two onto plates. She put the leftovers away and carried the two plates to the couch.

Luke reached out his hand. "Thanks."

"You're welcome." She set hers down on the coffee table and returned to the kitchen. "Do you want something to drink?"

"You don't have to wait on me." He started to rise.

"It's fine. You cooked dinner. It's the least I can do."

Luke lowered back into his seat. "If you're sure, a glass of water would be great."

She poured water for both of them and returned to her seat as the game came back on. "If they don't win tonight, I don't know how they'll be able to take the series." Amberlyn propped her feet on the coffee table. "Not with them already down by a game and heading on the road tomorrow."

"It's crunch time now," the commentator said. "If they don't win tonight, it's going to be tough coming back, especially since they go on the road for the next two games."

Amberlyn and Luke both laughed.

"Okay, seriously." Amberlyn lifted her fork. "Where's the listening device?"

"You know, if this FBI thing doesn't work out, you may have a future in sports broadcasting."

"Only if you do it with me," she said. "We make a good team."

"Yeah." His expression turned thoughtful. "We do."

CHAPTER 19

LUKE SNUCK A peek at Amberlyn as they reached the end of the trail and turned back toward the lodge. This morning had been incident free, allowing them to go for their run as planned.

"I still can't believe the Braves came back to win it last night," Amberlyn said as she matched her pace to his.

"Home-field advantage."

"It worked for them last night."

"Yeah, it did." A walk-off home run in the bottom of the ninth had put the Braves back even with the Dodgers in the series.

"You know, it's a good thing we set up dinner with Dr. Bernard for tonight instead of tomorrow, or we'd both be wishing we could get back home to watch the game."

Luke latched on to her comment. "Does that mean you won't try to set up dinner with anyone for tomorrow night?"

"No guarantees, but the probability is leaning in your favor."

"Good." He was a little surprised at how much he had enjoyed their time together last night. It had been like a date but without the pressure. Too bad he hadn't known she was a baseball fan two years ago when he'd met her. Maybe then he would have been able to talk to her over dinner.

They fell into a comfortable silence until they reached the falls and both came to a walk. Amberlyn linked both hands behind her head as she caught her breath.

Luke bent his knee and grabbed his ankle to stretch out his quad. He silently counted to ten before he switched sides.

Amberlyn let both hands drop to her sides, and she took a step closer to the edge of the trail. "The falls really are stunning."

"It's always been one of my favorite places."

"I'm surprised we haven't seen anyone else running down here in the mornings."

"Tourist season has passed, and with school in session, mornings aren't a popular time to be down here."

"I imagine it's going to be strange for you to visit your old school."

"Yeah." They headed back toward their cottage.

Halfway up the trail, he heard a distinctive rattle. Luke grabbed Amberlyn's arm to stop her right before he spotted the rattlesnake coiled and ready to strike.

She gasped and took a step back. "Where did that come from?"

Luke had his guess, but he wouldn't be able to confirm it until he checked the feed from the surveillance camera. "Back away. Nice and slow."

Amberlyn took another step back, but Luke remained where he was until she had cleared the snake's range.

She tugged on his sleeve. "Luke, come on."

He eased back slowly, keeping his focus on the snake until they reached the bottom of the hill.

Amberlyn breathed out a sigh of relief. "That was scary. Thank goodness you saw it when you did."

"This is a new low for them."

Amberlyn pulled on his arm until he turned to face her. "You think Russ and Brad planted that snake?"

"Oh yeah. You don't find rattlers down here by the river," Luke said.

"We need to check the camera you set up."

"Already planned on it." Luke guided her to the path that led to the neighboring cottage.

As soon as they reached their cottage, Luke pulled up the security program on his laptop and rewound the surveillance feed until it showed them leaving. Within minutes of their departure, a figure appeared at the edge of the image, a thick canvas bag in his hand. With the way the bag jerked back and forth, there was little doubt that a snake was trapped inside. "Looks like Russ."

As soon as Russ came closer, Luke hit the button to capture a screenshot of him.

"See if you can catch a shot of him leaving too. If his bag is empty, it will prove he planted the snake," Amberlyn said.

Luke sped up the security feed. When Russ didn't reappear within the first couple of minutes, Luke increased the speed. It was nearly forty-five minutes later when he came back into view.

"He must have waited until he saw us coming to let the snake go." Luke shook his head. "He wanted to make sure it didn't disappear before we had the chance to stumble onto it."

Fury flashed in Amberlyn's eyes. "We need to call the sheriff." She pulled out her phone. "And I mean the sheriff. I'm not dealing with his deputy again."

Though Luke would love nothing more than to see those guys held accountable for their actions, he hesitated. "Maybe we should hold off on that."

"Why?"

"I have to imagine what they did is against the law somehow, but it might be good to have something to hold over them if you end up hauling them in for an interrogation."

"I doubt they'll be worried about a misdemeanor compared to facing a murder charge."

"Maybe not, but if they weren't involved and they do know something, it might give you some leverage," Luke said. "As it is, hauling them into the sheriff's office is only going to rile them up."

"Right now, I'm the one who's riled up."

"I can see that." His phone chimed with an incoming text.

He read the message from his mother. *Check your inbox. I sent you the info you asked for.*

"Looks like we have that research we wanted." He opened his email and downloaded the attachments.

"Can you forward that to me? We can split them up."

"Yeah." Luke hit the Forward button and pulled up her email address.

As soon as he hit Send, Amberlyn asked, "Ready to get to work?"

Luke nodded toward the bathroom. "I'm going to grab a shower first."

"I guess I should do that, too, before I get too distracted."

"What about Russ?" Luke slipped both hands into the pockets of his sweatpants. "Are you going to wait on turning him in to the sheriff's office?"

"For now," Amberlyn said. "But only because we'll learn more if he isn't locked up."

"Please tell me you'll press charges after all this is over," Luke said. It was childish, he knew, but he couldn't resist adding, "I'd love to see him behind bars."

"After seeing a demonstration of what these guys like to do for fun, so would I."

———

Amberlyn couldn't remember ever being in a town she wanted to leave more than this one. No wonder Luke had been so resistant to the idea of coming to his reunion.

Sitting on the couch, her computer on her lap, she scanned through the third article Luke's mom had sent them. A family of three had broken down along the highway during a storm and had been found dead in their car. According to the article, the severe snowstorm had prevented emergency personnel from venturing out onto the roads until the whiteout conditions had passed.

Amberlyn did a crosscheck of the family with Eli Duffy. When she found none, she expanded her search to potential relatives in Pine Falls.

From his spot on the couch beside her, Luke straightened. "I think I found something."

"What is it?" Amberlyn set her laptop on the coffee table and leaned closer.

"A huge storm three years ago. Ninety-four people died, most of them from freezing to death in their cars." Luke angled his laptop toward her. "According to this, a lot of people blamed the governor for not closing down the freeway before the conditions worsened."

"That could give some motivation to the bombing of the election location in Nebraska," Amberlyn said. "The governor was running for reelection on the day of the bombing."

"Not only that. This article mentions that a bond referendum from the year before the blizzard was for an upgrade to the county's emergency communication system."

That was something. "I gather it was voted down."

"You got it." Luke nodded. "Unfortunately, the list of victims isn't in here."

"They were probably still notifying families when the article was printed." Hope rose inside her. "But if we narrowed down our search parameters to this incident for now, we should be able to search through obituaries and funeral records. Most of those are available without having to subscribe to the different papers."

"I'll start looking."

"And I'm going to enlist some help." Amberlyn forwarded the information to the rest of her team and the St. Louis FBI office to ask for assistance in pulling the death records and searching through the obituaries. She added a brief summary of their conversation with Russ and Brad on Monday night along with a request that a thorough background check be conducted on both men.

As soon as she pressed Send, she texted Ian to let him know to look for her email.

She set her phone down at the same time Luke looked up from his laptop.

"I think I found it." He gestured to his screen.

"You only started looking two minutes ago."

"Yeah, but I jumped straight to the local newspaper here so I didn't have much to sort through." Luke zoomed in on the obituary on his screen. "Kyle Moran died on the same day as that storm."

Amberlyn had anticipated searching through obituaries in Nebraska, but Luke's logic to look closer to home was sound.

"He was one of the team members who died, right?"

Luke nodded. "Not only that, but he died in the same county as the bombing. He was only about thirty miles from there."

Finally, they had a possible motive. Adrenaline rushed through her. "Maybe someone was upset enough about his death that they got involved with this Forever Freedom group." She thought for a moment. "Or this group was founded by people who were affected by the tragedy."

"That gives us ninety-four possibilities."

"It gives us ninety-four places to start," Amberlyn corrected. "All those people had family and friends. We need to know which of them were connected to Eli Duffy."

"We've already narrowed the suspect list here in town to the old championship team," Luke said. "Knowing Kyle Moran may have been the reason for the bomber's actions doesn't bring us any closer to knowing who it is."

"It might." Amberlyn slid closer. "Pull up your list of the team. Tell me who Kyle hung out with. I assume Russ and Brad were friends of his."

"Yeah. He was part of the crowd I avoided."

"Then, that's who we focus on. The people you avoided."

"It's still a pretty long list."

"How many of them are ones who have the championship tattoo and are still wearing their championship ring?"

"Three. Owen Lester, Russ Gibson, and Gavin Pennington." Luke pointed at the next column. "And Cooper Bird is on our maybe list."

Amberlyn opened a new email. "Give me those names again. I'm going to forward them to my office and have them run background checks on all of them."

Luke repeated the names slowly, giving her time to type each as he did so.

"How long will it take for them to pull that information?"

"Not long. We should have it well before lunchtime." She caught the hopeful expression on his face. "Sorry. Even if we narrow our suspect pool down to one, we're still going to dinner with the doctor tonight."

"I'd rather go back out and deal with the rattlesnake."

"Eating with the doctor can't be nearly as bad as sharing a meal with Russ and Brad."

"I sure hope not."

CHAPTER 20

READING OBITUARIES WAS not how Luke had planned to spend his day. He set his laptop on the couch between him and Amberlyn. "I say we give this a break until your office sends us the complete list of victims."

She rolled her shoulders. "I could use a break."

Taking the opening she'd given him, he stood. "Where do you want to go?" He held his hand up. "Anywhere but trying to run into my old classmates."

"I'd say we could go for a walk, but I'd rather not have a second meeting with a rattlesnake in one day." She closed her laptop. "Is there a shooting range around here?"

That wasn't what he'd expected. "There used to be." He unlocked his phone and did a quick search. "Yep. It's still there."

"Are you up for some target practice?" Amberlyn asked.

"I would be, but I didn't bring a gun with me."

"You can use my backup."

He lifted his eyebrows. "You brought two guns with you?"

"I was coming to an unfamiliar area more than two hours from the closest FBI office. Of course I brought a spare." She stood. "I'm surprised you didn't bring a weapon. You knew what we'd be walking into."

Luke pushed to his feet and shrugged. "I'm not authorized to carry on military bases or at the White House, so I didn't even think of it."

"You do know how to shoot, though, right?"

Luke cocked an eyebrow. "I'm a Marine."

She shook her head. "How could I forget?" With her laptop in hand, she headed for her bedroom. "I'll be right back."

Luke secured his laptop in his room and grabbed his shoes. When he returned to the living room, Amberlyn was waiting for him with her purse over her shoulder and a gun case in her hand.

"Maybe we should grab some lunch while we're out." Amberlyn gave him a pointed look. "Since someone finished off the enchiladas for breakfast."

"Don't give me that look. You had some too."

"Only because I knew they'd be gone by lunchtime," Amberlyn said. "And after the rattlesnake incident, I needed comfort food."

"My enchiladas rank among your comfort foods?" He kind of liked that.

"They are pretty good." She shrugged. "Anyway, I doubt we'll have much time today for either of us to spend preparing food."

She was right. As soon as her office sent her the complete list of victims, she would undoubtedly want them to search for connections to the bombers and possibly someone in town beyond Kyle Moran.

"How about we order something for takeout after we finish at the shooting range?" Luke opened the door. "That way, we don't have to cook, and we also won't have to sit through a meal with people watching us eat."

"Sounds like a fair compromise." Amberlyn walked outside.

He locked the door behind him and did a quick check underneath the vehicle and beneath the hood. The possibility of someone planting a car bomb was highly unlikely, but after their recent string of incidents, he wasn't taking any chances.

As soon as they were both settled in the car, he opened the security app on his phone to turn on the motion-sensor alarm.

"I'm kind of surprised there's a shooting range in a town this size," Amberlyn said, not commenting on his extra security precautions.

"It's nothing fancy," Luke said. "Just a big field with old Mr. Quick sitting in the shade to make sure no one does anything stupid."

"You think this Mr. Quick is still running it?"

"With all the development going on around here, I guarantee it. If he weren't, I'm sure the property would have been sold off long ago. It's only about five minutes from here."

Luke drove the familiar roads to the expansive property where his grandfather had taught him to shoot. "Who taught you to shoot?" he asked Amberlyn.

"The instructors at the FBI Academy," she said. "I never planned to go into this kind of career, and my family wasn't into hunting or anything."

Curious, he asked, "How did you end up in the FBI?"

"One of my students was killed."

That was the last thing he'd expected to hear. "I'm sorry. That couldn't have been easy."

She kept her eyes on the road. "He was into drugs and was hanging with a rough crowd. Those decisions led to him being in the wrong place at the wrong time."

"And that made you want to join the FBI?"

"My involvement with finding his killer put me on the FBI's radar. I was invited to interview, and a year later, I graduated from the FBI Academy."

"Wow. That's not a typical path into law enforcement."

"One thing I've learned in my time with the bureau is there is no typical path for law enforcement or for criminals."

"Isn't that your job though? Figuring out the patterns?"

"It's more studying the patterns of human behavior, what motivates people to do what they do."

"Like blowing up a government building."

"Yes." Now she turned to face him. "Like that."

Amberlyn squeezed the trigger one time after another until she emptied her magazine. She may have been late to learn about guns, but she was a quick study, and she had a good eye.

The shooting range was little more than an open field behind a house, with targets arranged at various distances. As Luke had predicted, an older gentleman sat on the back porch in the shade. A glass of lemonade rested on the table beside him along with a pair of binoculars.

At the station beside her, Luke lowered his gun. "You're a good shot."

"I've been practicing almost every day for four years."

"Looks like your practice has paid off."

"Thanks. You clearly know your way around guns too."

"In my family, knowing how to shoot is considered a basic life skill."

Amberlyn retreated from the firing line to a bench a short distance away and proceeded to clean her weapon.

Luke joined her and did the same.

"How old were you when you learned to shoot?" Amberlyn asked.

"About eight. I'm not much into hunting, but my dad and grandad are."

An alert sounded on Luke's phone. He placed her weapon in its case and pulled his cell from his pocket. Then he stood abruptly. "We have to go."

She secured her weapon in her purse. "What's wrong?"

"Someone just broke into our cottage." He jogged toward her car, and Amberlyn sprinted to keep up.

"What do you mean, someone broke into our cottage?" Realizing her question served no useful purpose, she rephrased. "Who is it?"

"Can't tell." He climbed behind the wheel and handed her his phone.

She took it, quickly buckling her seat belt as he sped out of the parking lot. Gravel spewed into the air behind them, and the tires squealed when he made the turn onto the paved road.

Amberlyn put her hand on the dashboard to keep herself steady as the car fishtailed slightly before straightening. She focused on Luke's cell phone screen, only the front porch and the space in front of their cottage visible.

"I don't see anything. Any chance he already left?"

"I doubt it." Luke shook his head. "I caught a glimpse of someone walking in right after the sensor went off."

Amberlyn debated whether she should back up the surveillance feed to see who it was or let it keep going so they would know if the intruder had left. She kept it on the live feed.

"See anything?" Luke asked.

"Nothing yet."

"It's probably Russ or Brad planning another surprise for us." Luke cast her a quick glance. "In case you haven't caught on, I think they're hoping we'll leave town."

"I caught that."

Following protocol, she retrieved her cell phone from her pocket and dialed 9-1-1.

"Are you calling the cops?"

"Yeah."

A woman's voice came over the line. "Nine-one-one operator. What's your emergency?"

"We have a break-in at the Pine Falls Lodge, bungalow eight."

"Is anyone inside?"

"No. We're heading back now."

"Ma'am, I recommend against that. I'm dispatching a deputy now."

"ETA?"

"One moment."

Amberlyn angled the phone away from her mouth. "How close are we?"

"A minute. Maybe two."

The 9-1-1 operator's voice came back on the line. "A deputy is on his way. He should be there in four to five minutes."

"Advise the deputy that a law enforcement officer will be on the premises when he arrives."

"Ma'am?"

Not willing to explain further, Amberlyn hung up the phone.

"How do you want to play this when we get there?" Luke asked.

Amberlyn balanced Luke's phone on her lap and pulled her gun from her purse. She slid a new magazine into place. "I'll take the front. You take the back."

"Just don't shoot me when I come through the balcony door." Luke turned the car into the lodge parking lot, only slowing enough to maintain control. Then he sped down the gravel road to their cottage. He slowed when the cottage came into view, the door slightly ajar.

Luke parked behind a large oak tree, partially shielding Amberlyn's car from view while also giving them the woods to use for cover. "I don't see another vehicle."

"Me neither." Without taking her eyes off the cottage, she passed her spare weapon to Luke.

The click of the case opening was followed by the sound of a magazine sliding into place.

Luke opened the door. "Give me a minute's head start. I don't want you going in there until I'm on the back deck."

Amberlyn nodded and climbed out of the car.

Luke disappeared into the trees, and she counted off the seconds in her head.

With her weapon aimed at the ground, she crept forward until she reached a tree opposite the front porch, only fifteen feet of open space between her and the door.

She reached the count of sixty in her head, drew a deep breath, and exhaled as she rushed forward.

Pressing her body to the side of the entrance, she pushed the door open before settling her free hand on her weapon to steady it. She then peered into the empty living room.

Luke appeared at the back door, and for the first time, it dawned on her that his key might not work on the balcony door.

She was debating whether she should cross through the living room and kitchen to let him in before clearing the bedrooms when the sliding door opened, relieving her of that decision.

Luke stepped inside, leaving the door open behind him. With his gun gripped in his left hand, he held up his right and signaled that he would search the bedroom closest to him—her room. She nodded as he disappeared from sight, then she headed for Luke's room.

Her second step caught a creaky floorboard at the same time a siren sounded in the distance. Before she could continue forward, a hooded figure rushed out of Luke's room, a gun in hand.

"FBI! Freeze!" Amberlyn called out, but she already knew the warning wouldn't be heeded. Adrenaline pumping through her, Amberlyn ducked behind the living room chair at the same moment the gunman fired two shots in rapid succession.

Amberlyn tried to pretend this was a training scenario in Hogan's Alley at the FBI Academy. But it wasn't. This was a real person with a real gun, shooting real bullets.

Amberlyn slid around the far side of the chair and popped up long enough to squeeze off a shot of her own.

The bullet caught the gunman in the shoulder, and he lifted his gun again. Or rather, she. The gunman was a woman.

"Drop it!" Amberlyn called out.

"You heard her," Luke said from where he now stood in her bedroom doorway.

The assailant shook her head and fired again.

Luke and Amberlyn fired in unison, and the woman collapsed onto the floor.

Amberlyn rushed forward and stepped on the woman's wrist, kicking the gun free of her hand with her other foot.

Luke scooped up the woman's weapon and flipped the safety on.

Amberlyn pulled her phone from her pocket and handed it to Luke. "Call an ambulance."

She leaned down to check the woman's injuries. "Who are you? Why are you here?"

The woman gasped for air but didn't speak.

As soon as Luke made the 9-1-1 call and requested an ambulance, Amberlyn asked, "Do you know her?"

He looked at the woman's face and shook his head. "I don't think so."

The sirens grew louder and then stopped, the flash of blue lighting the front window.

"Better check out your room to see if you can tell what she was doing in there." Amberlyn nodded toward his doorway. "I'll deal with the deputy."

Luke didn't argue. He disappeared into his room.

Deputy Lester walked into the cottage, his gun still in the holster, his posture that of someone who expected to find a stray dog rather than a gunman inside.

He spotted Amberlyn, gun in hand, with the gunshot victim on the floor. He fumbled for his weapon.

In the same moment, Luke rushed out of his room, a gun in each hand. "Bryn, run!" he shouted, shortening her name as though he didn't have time to say the whole of it.

Amberlyn didn't ask questions. She sprinted toward the door.

Deputy Lester now had his gun in hand, but he clearly sensed danger and raced after them.

The three of them stumbled onto the porch. They made it only a few steps before the ground rumbled beneath their feet. The force of the explosion lifted Amberlyn into the air and knocked her to the ground.

CHAPTER 21

LUKE IGNORED THE pain from his body impacting the hard ground as he scrambled to Amberlyn's side. He'd dropped the two weapons when he'd used his hands to brace his fall, and he left them where they lay in the dirt. He didn't know if the gas line had already ignited. If it hadn't, another blast was imminent.

Amberlyn tried to sit up, but Luke stretched his arm over the top of her back to keep her down as the second explosion sent flames spearing through the air and intense heat blasting over them. A sharp pain pierced his neck, but he ignored it. He stayed low, his hand on Amberlyn's head to protect her from the flying debris.

A wave of guilt washed over him that he hadn't tried to haul the woman outside with him, but with only nine seconds left on the detonator, he'd had to choose. And he'd easily chosen Amberlyn.

The crackle of flames competed with the ringing in his ears, and a new set of approaching sirens.

Luke eased off Amberlyn and took his first look at the remains of the cottage. The glass from the windows had shattered, and smoke and flames spilled through them. More flames licked at what was left of the front porch and the tree closest to the cottage.

Amberlyn sat up, her expression dazed. "Someone just tried to kill us."

That fact pierced through him. "Yeah." Someone *had* tried to kill them.

Luke spotted Owen Lester lying motionless a short distance away.

He focused again on Amberlyn. "Are you okay?"

"Yeah." She looked around until she spotted where her gun had fallen beside her.

Luke managed to stand and stumbled to Owen's side. A shard of wood protruded from his back, and he lay motionless. He put his fingers on the side of the deputy's throat, relieved to find a pulse beating there. Luke might not want to spend time with Owen, but that didn't mean he wanted him dead.

The ambulance pulled up, and the paramedic on the passenger side immediately grabbed a medic bag. The other picked up the radio, undoubtedly giving their status.

"What happened?" the one with the bag asked.

"A bomb went off." Luke motioned to Owen. "He was the closest to the cottage when the device detonated."

The paramedic knelt. "Have you moved him?"

"No," Luke said. The other paramedic approached, and Luke asked, "Did you already call in the fire?"

"A fire truck is on the way." The second paramedic leaned down on the other side of Owen.

Luke stepped back and returned to Amberlyn's side. She was standing, but she still didn't look quite steady. Then again, he was pretty sure the ground wasn't supposed to look like it was moving. He spotted the two weapons he'd dropped and retrieved both.

"We need to secure her gun," Amberlyn said. "I have an evidence bag in my car."

Luke turned to where he'd parked. Thankfully, the trees seemed to have shielded the car from the worst of the blast.

"I need to secure our weapons too," Amberlyn continued. "The local sheriff will need to take ballistics samples from both of our guns. Procedure."

"Sorry, but I'm not a fan of you being unarmed, not after what just happened."

"Me neither." She led the way to her car. "Maybe we should drive to Richmond." Amberlyn opened the trunk. "We can turn our weapons in there, and I can get a replacement."

"Or two. I'd rather stay armed until we know who's behind this."

"I'll see what I can do." She retrieved an evidence bag from a tote on one side. She opened it and held it out for Luke to put the shooter's gun into it. After she sealed it, she grabbed a Sharpie from the same bag and marked it as the unidentified woman's weapon.

"Let's hope forensics can pull her fingerprints from her weapon and that they're on file. Otherwise, identifying her now isn't going to be easy."

Another set of sirens pierced the air as a fire truck rumbled down the narrow road. It moved past the ambulance, and four firefighters jumped out and began unraveling hoses.

"Maybe we should move your car before we get trapped down here," Luke suggested.

Another siren sounded, and a police car raced toward them. It pulled to the side of the road right behind Amberlyn's car, and the sheriff climbed out.

Luke looked at her. "Or maybe not."

———

A dozen scenarios raced through Amberlyn's mind on how to handle the next few minutes. If she flashed her badge and admitted she was FBI, word was bound to spread. On the other hand, she'd hardly be able to deny her involvement once the coroner discovered the bullet wounds in the corpse.

Amberlyn tried not to think about how the bullet wounds might have killed the woman had the bomb not ended her life or how she had played a part in the woman's death.

The sheriff pointed at her and Luke. "Stay there." He then continued to where the paramedics were still working on Owen. "How is he?"

"Looks like he has a concussion, and he took some debris in the back. We're preparing to transport him to the hospital now."

"Keep me informed."

"Yes, Sheriff." The paramedic moved to the back of the ambulance and retrieved a stretcher.

The sheriff returned to where Amberlyn and Luke waited. "Who wants to tell me what happened here?"

Amberlyn started with the basics. "Someone broke into our cottage while we were out. When we came back, we found out she'd planted a bomb."

"A bomb?" the sheriff repeated. "Here in Pine Falls?"

"I'm afraid so."

"Why would anyone do that?" Sheriff Mapleton looked from Amberlyn to Luke, accusation in his eyes. "What are the two of you involved in that would draw this kind of thing here?"

"We're only here for my high school reunion," Luke said.

"Trouble obviously followed you here."

"Or it was already waiting for us," she countered. "Deputy Lester might have a better idea of who's been causing problems for us. He's the one who took the report about my car getting vandalized yesterday morning."

"I didn't hear anything about that."

Amberlyn pulled out her phone and opened one of the photos she had taken of her car. She turned it toward him.

"That looks like a couple of kids pulling a prank."

"And that?" Amberlyn pointed at the burning remains of the bungalow. "Is that a prank too?"

"No." His tone grew more serious. "You said there was a bomb. Did you see it?"

"I did." Luke lifted his hand. "It was an old-fashioned suitcase bomb. C4, single detonator. It was handcuffed to the bed, or I would have thrown it out the window."

"Where did you learn about explosives?" Sheriff Mapleton asked.

"I'm a Marine. It was part of my training."

"And this woman who planted this bomb, where is she now?"

"Still inside the cottage." Amberlyn motioned toward the cottage. "I suggest you call the coroner and your arson investigator."

"We don't have an arson investigator, but the fire chief is right over there." The sheriff motioned to a fireman in his forties who stood at the back of the fire truck. "Dispatch said one of you was law enforcement."

"I'm the one who said that," Luke said. "After our run-in with Deputy Lester, I didn't want to take a chance that he'd come in and mistake us for a criminal."

"So, you aren't law enforcement?"

"Not exactly."

Amberlyn jumped on the chance to protect her identity. "He works for the president."

"The president of what?"

Amberlyn nodded at Luke, signaling him to answer.

He lifted his chin slightly. "Of the United States."

"You work for the president?"

"Yes, sir."

"Is there anyone who can verify that?"

"If you call the White House switchboard, they can put you through to my boss. Mitchell Hobbs is the deputy director of the White House Military Office," Luke said. "Would you like the number?"

"I'll look it up. Not that I don't trust you, but under the circumstances, I'd rather find it myself."

The ambulance pulled away, and one of the firefighters approached. "You two should get checked out at the hospital."

"We're fine."

"Get checked out anyway," Sheriff Mapleton insisted. "I'll drive you over there."

"We can drive ourselves," Luke said. "I don't want to leave our car here."

The sheriff took another look at the fire. "Fine. I'll follow you over."

As soon as the sheriff retreated to his car, Amberlyn asked, "Are you okay to drive?"

"Yeah." He climbed behind the wheel.

Amberlyn took her seat and debated their next move. "We have a bit of an issue though. Since these weapons will be part of a criminal investigation, I need to keep them with me. I have to maintain the chain of evidence."

"I know." He furrowed his brow. "There aren't any metal detectors going into the hospital. We can put them in that emergency-kit bag you have in the back and take them in with us."

The same bag the weapons were already hidden in. "I guess that's the best we can do."

"You might want to call the lodge and let them know we need new rooms."

"All of our clothes, our computers, everything is gone," Amberlyn said, the reality of their situation hitting her. "We literally only have the clothes on our backs."

"And transportation," Luke said. "You can decide if you want to get out of town or go shopping."

"I'd rather leave town, but we clearly have someone rattled. We need to figure out who."

"Yeah." He fell silent as he drove through the center of town. "I'm sorry I didn't grab the woman who shot at us. She might have survived if I'd hauled her out of there."

"Had you tried, we'd all be dead." She reached over and put her hand on his. "You saved my life. Thank you."

"I didn't do much." He pulled up to a red light and stopped behind an old pickup truck.

"Yes, you did." One simple truth pushed to the forefront of her mind. "You showed me I could trust you. If I hadn't known that, I might not have reacted fast enough to get out of there in time."

Luke glanced at her hand on his before lifting his gaze to hers. "I trust you too."

"I'm glad." She squeezed his hand before she released him and held up her phone. "But I think we need a few more people we can trust."

"Like whom?"

"I'm putting in a call to the Richmond office. I need someone to come get these weapons from us and issue us new ones."

The light turned, and Luke pulled forward. "No longer planning to drive there yourself?"

"With the sheriff insisting we go to the hospital, I doubt we'll have time to drive over there before the office closes for the day."

"If you're getting someone to come over here, any chance you can have them arrange for us to have a rental car?"

"Why would we need a second vehicle?"

"Because everyone knows what yours looks like. We're sitting ducks any time we drive it."

"You want to use my car as a decoy?"

"Yeah."

"That's not a bad idea," Amberlyn said. "But I'm having them bring some surveillance cameras too. I like my car."

"I like your car too. I even washed it, remember?"

CHAPTER 22

LUKE WASN'T CRAZY about being separated from Amberlyn, but he could hardly expect to be in the room while the doctor examined her. Then again, he couldn't say he'd be thrilled to have her sitting next to him now that he'd been forced into a hospital gown with nothing but his underwear underneath.

They had arrived at the hospital too quickly for Amberlyn to call the lodge after finishing her conversation with one of her counterparts at the FBI. Instead, their focus had been on Luke shielding her while she'd gathered her things—the three handguns included—from the trunk of her car.

Now that he'd had time to sit around with nothing left to do but try to ignore the pain from whatever had embedded in the back of his neck, his mind was racing. Who would want to kill them? No one here knew Amberlyn was FBI, and no matter how much his old classmates might not like him, he didn't think they would go to the extreme of trying to blow him up. And the woman. Who was she, and how was she tied into all of this?

The door to the examination room opened, and Dr. Bernard walked in.

"Dr. Bernard, I didn't expect to see you here," Luke said. "I thought you only worked private practice."

"I work the emergency room a few times a month to help out. The hospital's been short staffed for a while now."

"Any chance you can sign whatever paper you need to so I can get out of here?"

"We'll see what I can do." Dr. Bernard proceeded to ask him a series of questions, undoubtedly to check for a concussion. He then conducted a physical exam much like when Luke had been a child and his mom had forced him to go in for a checkup every year.

Dr. Bernard reached the spot on Luke's leg that had earned him his purple heart. "What's this?"

"An old wound."

"That looks like a bullet hole."

"I spent some time overseas when I first joined the Marines."

"I see." The doctor continued his examination. "Looks like you've got some glass embedded in the back of your neck. Let's get that out of there." The doctor moved to stand behind him.

Luke clenched his teeth as the doctor went to work on him with a pair of tweezers and who knew what else. After five minutes of torture, the doctor finally moved back to the front of the examination table.

"All in all, you got off very lucky."

"We all did," Luke said. "Well, almost all of us."

"I heard someone didn't make it out," Dr. Bernard said. "Any idea who it was?"

"No. I've never seen her before."

"I'm sure the coroner will identify her sooner or later." Dr. Bernard stepped back. "You can get dressed, and I'll start the paperwork to release you."

"Thanks, Doctor."

"I know you've been through a lot today, but I'd still love to have you come by my house for dinner tonight. You have to eat anyway, and it'll give me a chance to make sure you're doing okay."

"I don't know—"

"I'll feel better if I can check on you after you've had some time to rest," he interrupted before Luke could manage an excuse.

"I'll talk to Amberlyn," Luke said. "How is she?"

"Dr. Anderson is with her now." Dr. Bernard headed for the door. "I'll let him know you want to see her."

"Thanks."

"Assuming all is well with your girlfriend, I'll plan to see you tonight, six o'clock."

As soon as the doctor left, Luke changed back into his clothes. The collar of his polo shirt caught on the bandages on the back of his neck, and he winced. Moving more slowly, he adjusted his shirt and put on his shoes.

He opened the door and peeked into the busy corridor outside his room. Two nurses stood behind a desk, their voices low. The younger of the two looked familiar, but Luke couldn't place her.

A man wearing a business suit approached, a soft-sided briefcase hanging from his shoulder. He looked at the room number beside Luke's door before addressing him. "Are you Luke Steele?"

"Yes, sir."

"I'm Special Agent Whitley, with the FBI." He showed Luke his badge and ID. "Can I ask you a few questions about the bombing today?"

"Yeah. Sure." He stepped back into his room and leaned against the examination table. "What office are you from?"

"Richmond." Special Agent Whitley closed the door behind him. "This is highly unusual, but I have something for you."

He opened his briefcase and retrieved a clipboard. "I need you to sign here."

"What's this for?"

"To acknowledge the receipt of your weapon." Special Agent Whitley reached in his bag again, this time producing a pistol, complete with a belt holster. He set it on the table along with a spare magazine of ammunition. "I understand the president wasn't happy when he learned one of his aides had nearly died in an explosion."

"The president knows what happened?" Luke hadn't thought to call his office after the bombing. He'd been more concerned with Amberlyn and keeping her safe.

"Our office informed the director of the FBI, who informed the director of Homeland Security."

"Who informed Chief of Staff Ellis, who then told the president," Luke finished for him. He might still be relatively new in this job, but he'd been around the White House long enough to know how things worked. "Have you already seen Amberlyn?"

"Yes. The doctor is stitching up a cut on her arm, but she should be released soon."

Luke picked up the weapon, storing the extra magazines in the holster before attaching the holster to his belt. "Does she already have one of these?"

"She does. After you're released, I'll drive the two of you to the sheriff's department to make your statements. Then I'll take you back to the lodge. Your rental car is waiting for you in the parking lot there. I secured new laptops and surveillance cameras in the trunk for you." He reached into his pocket and handed over a set of keys. "Assuming the room was charged to a government credit card, you can put in a claim for any personal losses."

"Thanks."

Someone knocked on the door, and Special Agent Whitley opened it.

Amberlyn stood on the other side, her short hair slightly tousled and a fresh bandage on her forearm. "Are you ready to get out of here?"

"More than ready." Luke nearly resisted the urge to cross to her and pull her into his arms. Then he reminded himself that they were supposed to be boyfriend/girlfriend. Such behavior would be expected, right?

He slid his arms around her and pulled her into an embrace. "I'm glad you're all right."

Her arms encircled his waist. "I'm glad you're all right too."

———

Amberlyn wasn't crazy about leaving her car at the hospital, but she supposed that was as safe a place as any. Security cameras covered the parking lot, and she had every intention of pressing charges if someone else vandalized her car. The fact that Deputy Lester would be in the hospital until tomorrow also meant there would likely be someone from the sheriff's office nearby for the next day or two.

Luke offered her the front seat of Special Agent Whitley's car and took the spot behind her.

"Now that we don't have to worry about being overheard, can you tell me what really happened at the lodge?" Special Agent Whitley asked.

"Luke set up a surveillance camera at the front of the cottage," Amberlyn explained. "The motion detector went off while were gone, and when we got back there, a woman was still inside."

"And she's the one who planted the bomb?"

"It had to be," Luke said. "Amberlyn was watching the security feed the whole way back. No one else went inside."

"I'll put a rush on the fingerprints on the gun, assuming we can find any."

"She wasn't wearing gloves." That oddity hadn't registered with Amberlyn before now. "She must have assumed the bomb would hide any evidence of her presence."

"I want to know how she knew to come after us in the first place," Luke said. "I can see Brad and Russ wanting me to leave town. With the way Dr. Bernard was talking about my job, they wouldn't want me to take any attention away from them, but that doesn't mean they'd try to kill us."

"Unless they're involved with Forever Freedom and they know you're FBI," Special Agent Whitley said to Amberlyn.

"I don't know how they would figure that out." Amberlyn shook her head. "I've been using a different last name, and Luke doesn't have any official tie to the investigation."

"What about your statement to the police when your car was vandalized?" Luke asked. "Did you use your real name, then?"

"No." Amberlyn swiveled in her seat so she could see him. "But if the deputy added my license plate to the report, the registration would have popped up."

Special Agent Whitley's eyebrows lifted. "You think the deputy is involved?"

"No." Amberlyn shook her head. "He never would have come into the cottage if he'd known someone was going to plant a bomb."

"Want to bet he spread it around town that I was driving your car?" Luke asked. "He could have easily said something to one of his buddies. If he mentioned the car being under a different last name, that could have caused all sorts of rumors."

"And if those rumors made it to someone in town with Forever Freedom, he or she could have easily googled my name and found me listed on the FBI's website." Which was probably what had happened.

"If your cover is blown, we need to pull you out of here," Whitley said. "There's no way to be sure if the woman in your cottage was running the show or if she was one of many involved with Forever Freedom."

Whitley was right. And following his advice would be the smart thing to do, especially since she might have already spooked the man in the photo. But by staying, she could determine if anyone on the football team didn't show up. They needed to find the man from the photo because if they didn't learn who was behind the Forever Freedom movement, more people were going to die. More people like Chanelle.

A deep ache welled up inside her. "I can't leave. Not until we have answers. For all we know, the woman in the cottage was the person behind the FEMA bombing. Eli Duffy and the man with the tattoo could have been hired hands."

"Maybe. Maybe not. There's no way to be sure," Whitley said. "Captain Steele, what about you?"

"If Amberlyn's willing to stay, so am I." He leaned forward. "Any chance you heard how Owen was doing?"

"Yeah. He's going to be fine. They're keeping him overnight for observation, but it's likely he'll be able to go to the game on Friday night."

"I'm glad he's okay," Amberlyn said.

Whitley nodded. "I'll make sure I stress to the deputy that he needs to keep his knowledge about your involvement with the bombing confidential," he said.

"You can tell him to keep quiet," Luke said, "but by now, the news has already spread around town. Everyone will know the cottage that blew up was the one Amberlyn and I were staying in."

"Yes, but the deputy is the only person who knows that the bomber was shot before the bomb went off and that Amberlyn's the one who shot her."

"True," Luke conceded.

"As soon as I get the weapons turned in, I'll head back out here," Whitley said. "You may need some backup."

"That would be great, but how are you going to explain what you're doing here?" Amberlyn asked.

"I'm going to take the direct approach. I'm a federal officer investigating a bombing."

Luke shook his head. "The sheriff isn't going to like that."

Special Agent Whitley cast a glance at him. "I don't care."

CHAPTER 23

LUKE COULDN'T BELIEVE he was doing this. He and Amberlyn had nearly died in a bombing, for heaven's sake, and they hadn't even had the chance to buy new clothes to change into. Surely that was sufficient reason to bow out of dinner with the Bernards. And if not that, the fact that they didn't have a place to sleep tonight was cause enough not to spend the next hour or two socializing.

No room at the lodge. That had been the manager's claim when he and Amberlyn had asked for new accommodations. Whether they really were booked up or the manager simply didn't want the kind of trouble Luke and Amberlyn had brought with them, Luke couldn't be sure.

Yet despite the challenges of the day, here Luke was, walking two blocks down the sidewalk beside Amberlyn to make sure no one spotted the new rental car they were driving.

Their pace was slower than normal, another sign that neither of them was quite themselves.

"Are you sure you're up to this?" Luke asked. They were already ten minutes late. Maybe they could still bow out.

"I'm sure I'm not, but we don't have a lot of time to fish for information, especially if Forever Freedom has identified us as a threat."

Luke couldn't help but admire her determination.

"How far do you think we'll have to drive to find a hotel tonight?" she asked.

"There are a few along the freeway," Luke said. "Best guess, about thirty minutes."

"Not ideal, but it's no worse than my morning commute."

Though the thought of driving a half hour to and from town seemed like so much farther than driving to work. "If we were in DC right now, both of our bosses would be insisting we stay home tomorrow."

"Instead, they're both hoping and praying we find answers."

They reached the doctor's house, a stately colonial with several cars parked in front.

Amberlyn stopped beside the driveway. "It looks like we aren't the doctor's only dinner guests."

"If Russ is here, we're not staying."

"Agreed." Amberlyn tucked her hand into the crook of Luke's elbow. "Shall we?"

He'd rather put pins in his eyes. Straightening his shoulders, he walked with her to the front door and rang the bell.

Dr. Bernard answered a moment later. "I was starting to worry about you two."

"Sorry. We got held up at the sheriff's office," Luke said.

"I thought it might be something like that." The doctor stepped aside. "Come on in."

Luke waited for Amberlyn to walk in first before entering. They all walked into the living room, where Mrs. Bernard stood talking to Pastor Mosley and a couple in their forties.

Pastor Mosley crossed to Luke and pulled him into a bear hug. "I heard what happened. Thank the Lord you're okay."

"Oh, I have," Luke said.

The pastor released him, and his gaze dropped to the bandage on Amberlyn's arm. "How are you?"

"They were both very lucky," Dr. Bernard said, reiterating what he had said in the hospital. He motioned to his wife. "Luke, you remember my wife. And this is Miguel and Abby Gomez."

Luke couldn't say he remembered the doctor's wife, but Mrs. Gomez was a familiar enough face. She'd been the history teacher who had refused to let him take her AP class because she'd been convinced he couldn't keep up.

"It's nice to meet you." Luke shook Miguel's hand. Playing the boy-friend role, he put his arm around Amberlyn. "This is my girlfriend, Amberlyn Jones."

"It's nice to meet you," Mrs. Bernard said.

Everyone exchanged greetings, and within minutes, they were all seated at the dining room table.

"Luke, I understand you work at the White House," Mr. Gomez said.

"Yes, sir. I'm one of the military aides."

"That must be so exciting, walking the same halls as the president." Excitement filled Mrs. Gomez's voice.

Though Luke would have preferred the conversation be directed elsewhere, at least they weren't pumping him about the bombing. "I've enjoyed my time there."

"I don't know if Doc Bernard told you, but I teach history at the high school."

Her comment proved she didn't remember him. "No, ma'am. He didn't mention it." Nor did Luke know why it would matter.

"It would be so great for my students if they could see the White House firsthand."

"I'm sure it would."

Her face lit up. "Do you think you can arrange it?"

Luke paused in the middle of scooping mashed potatoes onto his plate and looked up. "Arrange it?"

"Yes. A tour for my students." She lifted her fork, a slice of carrot attached to the end of it. "It would only be about two hundred of them."

Someone in the town tried to kill them, and this woman wanted him to set up a tour of the White House. For two hundred people. Luke fought to keep a straight face. "I'm afraid I don't know much about how the tours work."

"But surely you know someone."

Amberlyn put her hand on his arm. "Luke's only been working in this assignment for a few months. I'm sure it takes time to learn all those ins and outs of who does what." Before Mrs. Gomez could press Luke further, Amberlyn asked, "Are you involved with the tour at the high school on Saturday?"

"Yes. They've asked all the faculty who was teaching fifteen years ago to be there."

"That's great that you'll get to see the students," Amberlyn said. "I understand there's also going to be a tribute at the game Friday to honor the old championship team."

"Yes. That will be bittersweet."

"Why's that?" Luke asked as though he hadn't heard about Kyle Moran's death.

"For one thing, it will be hard to see Coach Zabrowski retire, but I'm sure you also heard about Kyle Moran," Mrs. Gomez said. "He was killed during a blizzard in the Midwest a few years ago."

"I heard a rumor about that when I got to town," Luke said.

"That must have been so hard on his friends," Amberlyn prompted.

"It was hard on everyone, but especially his old teammates," Dr. Bernard said.

"I still feel guilty about Kyle." Mrs. Gomez shook her head. "If I hadn't encouraged him to apply for Iowa State, he never would have ended up in Nebraska."

"We all had a hand in him going out of state for college," Mr. Gomez said. "Doc helped him recover from his knee injury his sophomore year. Reverend Bowman provided him with tutors all through high school. I wrote him a glowing letter of recommendation."

"And none of our efforts had anything to do with his death." Pastor Mosley lifted his fork in front of him. "When the Lord wants to call someone home, He makes it happen."

"The pastor is right." Dr. Bernard took a bite of his roll. "And there's plenty of guilt to spread around. I know Russ, Brad, Owen, and Gavin had been planning to visit him in Nebraska, but they never got the chance. They regret not making the effort sooner."

"I'm sure everyone getting together with be therapeutic." Pastor Mosley took a roll from the breadbasket and passed it to Luke. "It helps to share memories when you lose someone you love."

"I can't remember who Kyle hung out with in high school besides Owen Lester," Luke said.

"Oh, there was quite a group of them," Mrs. Gomez said. "Kyle was the glue that held that group together."

More like, he was the instigator who identified who to pick on next.

"Enough talk about sad things," Mrs. Bernard said. "I want to hear more about Luke's job. Do you get to work directly with the president?"

Luke scooped some mashed potatoes onto his fork and braced himself for another hour of sheer torture.

CHAPTER 24

A DULL ACHE throbbed in Amberlyn's forehead, and Mrs. Gomez's persistence about Luke setting up a field trip for her students had gotten old the second time she'd brought it up. Now that she was making her fourth attempt, Amberlyn's patience was at its breaking point.

They'd moved from the dining room to the living room after dinner, but instead of gaining new information, Amberlyn and Luke had become the subject of the Gomezes' and Bernards' constant questions about life in DC.

Amberlyn put her hand on Luke's knee. "Honey, I'm sorry to cut this short, but I think I need to get some rest."

Gratitude flashed in his eyes. "I'm a little worn out myself." He stood, and Amberlyn followed suit. "Mrs. Bernard, thank you for dinner."

"Yes, thank you," Amberlyn said.

"You're welcome." Mrs. Bernard put her hand on Amberlyn's shoulder. "I hope we get the chance to see you again before you leave town."

Amberlyn hoped quite the opposite. "Thank you again."

"I should get going too." Pastor Mosley shook hands with Dr. Bernard and Mr. Gomez. "I'll see you all on Sunday." Amberlyn headed for the door and moved outside, Luke and the pastor right behind her. As soon as the door closed, Pastor Mosley put a hand on each of their shoulders. "Patience is a virtue. You two were very virtuous tonight."

Amberlyn's lips twitched into a smile. "Thank you."

The pastor released them and moved toward a white SUV that appeared to be brand-new. He looked around. "Where are the two of you parked?"

"Down the street." Luke waved in the general direction of their car.

The pastor gazed down the street. As though enlightened by a new awareness, he asked, "And where are you staying tonight?"

"We'll head out to one of the hotels along the freeway."

"What about the lodge?"

"They're booked up," Luke said. "Apparently, a lot of people came in for the reunion."

"Luke, we should get going." And even though Amberlyn wanted nothing more than to find a soft bed to lay her head, she added, "We still need to pick up some clothes from the store before it gets too late."

"You go do your shopping," Pastor Mosley said. "And then you come to my house. I have plenty of spare rooms. You can have your pick of them."

"We don't want to impose," Amberlyn said quickly.

"It's not an imposition." Pastor Mosley's determination lit his eyes. "And when you get there, you can tell me what I can do to help."

"Help?"

"You two are on a quest," Pastor Mosley said. "I trust it's a worthy one."

Amberlyn didn't know how to respond.

For a moment, Luke didn't speak either. Then he nodded. "Yes. It's a worthy one."

"I thought so."

———————

Luke pushed the cart out of Walmart to the side parking lot. The two of them had split up inside the store, gathering the essentials for the next few days. He'd added a duffel bag to his purchases, and Amberlyn had opted for a new suitcase.

They reached their rental car, and Amberlyn checked the area around them. "Did you recognize anyone in there?"

"The cashier in your line looked familiar, but I don't know if she knew me. I think she was too busy trying to figure out who you are."

"It's not easy to hide in a small town, is it?"

"No, but I do have a few tricks I learned over the years." Luke opened the trunk. He unzipped the new duffel bag, pulled out the paper that had been stuffed inside, and replaced it with the bags carrying his belongings. Amberlyn loaded her purchases into her new carry-on bag.

As soon as they had stored everything in the trunk, Luke pushed their cart to the cart return on the opposite side of the narrow parking area.

His phone chimed with an incoming text, and he read the message from Pastor Mosley. *Park in the garage. I'll leave the garage door open.*

Did the pastor know they were trying to keep their car out of sight?

Amberlyn was already seated in the passenger seat when he walked back to the car.

He climbed behind the wheel. "Are you okay with staying at the pastor's house?"

"You trust him, don't you?"

"Yes."

"It's not ideal," Amberlyn said, "but it'll be way easier on both of us if we can stay in town."

Luke glanced at her. "I'll take that as a yes."

"It's a yes."

Luke started the car and headed around the back of the store to keep from driving through the main parking lot. He'd used this trick often enough to avoid people from school as a teenager. He'd never thought he'd use those evasive maneuvers to ensure his physical safety.

As soon as he circled to the side exit, he asked, "How would you feel about letting Pastor Mosley know what we're really doing here?"

"Rule number one in undercover work is not telling anyone who you really are."

"Someone already knows who you really are." He glanced at her. "If they didn't, we wouldn't have had someone try to kill us."

"True," Amberlyn conceded. "And maybe if the pastor knows what we're trying to accomplish, he can help us narrow our suspect field."

Luke headed toward Main Street. "Even though it's hard to believe those guys would go to such extremes, Russ and Brad are still at the top of my list."

"They did put a lot of effort into making us want to leave, but we need proof."

"The FBI gave us new laptops. We could do some more digging tonight," Luke said. "Maybe the latest cell phone traces will show us who was near our cabin."

"That could help us identify the woman."

"And maybe who she was working with. Assuming we can pull her call and text logs."

"I'll put in a request for the Richmond office to pull what they can for the cottage today." Amberlyn sent a text message.

"Do you think they're working tonight?"

"I doubt it, but we should have something tomorrow by midmorning."

Luke turned into the pastor's neighborhood and drove by the typical two-story colonials that were about half the size of the doctor's home. The pastor's house was on the corner, a large cherry tree in the yard and azalea bushes lining the front porch. The garage door was open, the light on inside.

Luke pulled into the spot beside the pastor's car.

"Is it okay for us to park in the garage?" Amberlyn asked.

"He texted and told me to." Luke climbed out and retrieved their bags from the trunk.

"I'll get the laptops." She grabbed both and closed the trunk.

"Thanks." He moved to the door leading into the house and knocked before turning the knob.

"Want me to close the garage door?"

"Yeah, and can you turn off the light?"

Amberlyn did so and followed him inside.

Pastor Mosley was waiting for them in the kitchen. "Let's get the two of you settled."

He walked through the dining room and to the stairs. When they reached the top, he motioned to his right. "You'll have to share a bathroom, but you can use any of the three spare bedrooms."

"Thanks." Luke waited until Amberlyn peeked into the two closest rooms and set her laptop bag down in the one on her left. Luke traded her suitcase for the other laptop and set his belongings in the room across the hall from her.

"Take a minute and settle in." Pastor Mosley pointed down the hall. "The laundry room is next to the bathroom in case you want to wash your new clothes."

"Actually, that would be great," Amberlyn said.

"I'll meet you down in the living room when you're ready to chat."

"Thanks, Pastor Mosley."

He simply nodded. "Happy to help."

CHAPTER 25

WITH THEIR FIRST load of laundry in the wash, Amberlyn and Luke walked downstairs to where Pastor Mosley sat in a recliner, a large book open in his hand. He gestured to the couch across from him. "Have a seat."

The furnishings were dated but well kept, and floor-to-ceiling bookshelves lined the far wall, all of them filled to overflowing.

He closed the book in his hand and extended it to Amberlyn. "You might want to take a look at this."

She took it from him before settling it back onto the couch. The hardback book was none other than the yearbook from Luke's senior year. "It might help with your investigation."

Amberlyn's gaze shot up to meet the pastor's. His awareness was unmistakable. "How did you know?"

"It didn't help you any that Owen Lester ran your plates and found out you were using a different last name," Pastor Mosley said. "He was spouting off all sorts of theories in the diner yesterday."

"What kind of theories?" Luke asked.

"Nonsense about you hiring Amberlyn to pretend to be your girlfriend." Pastor Mosley shook his head. "Unfortunately for you, he shared your real last name. He didn't know you're FBI, but if anyone cared enough to dig deeper, it wouldn't have taken much effort to find out who you really work for. I found you out in less than fifteen seconds."

Like recognized like. "Were you law enforcement before you went into the ministry?" Amberlyn asked.

"CIA. Twenty-seven years."

Luke's eyes widened. "I never knew that."

"Not many people do. Most folks assumed I transferred from another church when I moved here." Pastor Mosley focused on Luke. "Your mom was one of the few who knew better. That investigative reporter in her has always made her more aware than most."

"She never told me anything."

"That's another skill she's always used well—her ability to keep a secret." Pastor Mosley smiled. "You've always been good at that too."

"I never knew any secrets worth telling."

"You have plenty now," the pastor said. "What is it you're investigating here? It must be something big if someone is trying to get rid of you."

Amberlyn had only this man's word that he was former CIA, but Luke trusted him, and they needed answers. "We're investigating the bombing in Kansas City."

"Kansas City? How did that lead you here?"

"One of our suspects was photographed a few days before the bombing. He was wearing a championship ring from the year the Pineview football team won state."

"I didn't see that coming," Pastor Mosley said. "A few of those boys had no idea what the golden rule was, much less a desire to follow it, but terrorism?" Pastor Mosley shook his head. "That's quite a leap."

"Unfortunately, the evidence continues to point in this direction," Amberlyn said.

"There was a woman in our cottage." Luke leaned forward and rested his forearms on his thighs. "Brown hair, about shoulder length, probably late twenties. Have you seen anyone like that around?"

Pastor Mosley furrowed his brow. "You didn't know her?"

"I didn't recognize her, anyway."

"Was she pretty?" the pastor asked.

"She wasn't very pretty when she was trying to shoot Amberlyn, but I guess she was attractive enough. Why?"

"There was a woman who stopped in at the diner this morning who fits that description."

"Do you spend all your time at the diner?" Luke asked.

"Most mealtimes." The pastor's eyes lit up like a teenager about to go on a first date. "Cynthia worries I'm not eating right."

"Is there a new Mrs. Mosley in your future?" Luke asked.

"I'm considering it."

"If you get serious about that idea, you let me know," Luke said. "You getting married would be reason for me to come back here, even if it does mean seeing all the jerks around here again."

"Before we think about Cynthia walking down the aisle, we'd best take care of your current problem."

Amberlyn couldn't agree more. "Who all was at the diner when you heard Deputy Lester talking?"

"Oh, there was a whole lot of them."

"Was Russ there?" Luke asked. "Or Brad?"

"Yes. They were both there. So was Cooper Bird and Gavin Pennington, along with a few of their wives," Pastor Mosley said.

"Any chance you noticed if Cooper was wearing his championship ring?" Luke asked.

"He wasn't," Pastor Mosley said with certainty. "He doesn't wear any jewelry because of work, not even his wedding ring."

"Do you know if he has a tattoo on his wrist?" Amberlyn asked. "Likely the one that a bunch of the football players got after they won the state championship?"

Pastor Mosley shook his head. "Cooper isn't the sort to get a tattoo. He's never been fond of any kind of needles."

One more suspect down. "Knowing that will save us from tracking him down."

"So, the others are at the top of your suspect list?" Pastor Mosley asked.

"Maybe not at the top, but they're on it," Luke said. "Russ left a rattler on the trail by the cottage yesterday, and we're pretty sure Russ and Brad were behind the shaving cream all over Amberlyn's car."

"As much as I hate to say it, I wouldn't put it past Russ. He sits out at that model home most days and gloats as though he's better than everyone else in town because he's got money in his pocket and he drives a Corvette," the pastor said. "Although I have no idea what he does at work now that they sold the last unit."

"His development is sold out?" A burst of adrenaline shot through Amberlyn. She looked at Luke. "Then he could have been in Missouri last week."

"Do you remember seeing him around town last Friday or on Monday?" Luke asked.

"Not that I recall, but I can ask Cynthia. The diner window looks right over Main Street. It's hard to miss Russ when he drives by."

"I'll take another look at his cell phone activity on that day," Amberlyn said. "If it wasn't used, it's possible he left it at home."

The pastor pushed to his feet, using his hands to help him make the transition from sitting to standing. "I'll get you the password for the Wi-Fi."

"Thanks," Amberlyn said, even though they didn't need it. Their new remote access cards that came with their laptops would give them secure access to the government servers.

"I do have one more question." He pointed his finger at Luke and then Amberlyn. "Are the two of you dating?"

Amberlyn glanced at Luke before answering. "No."

"You should be." Pastor Mosley looked from Luke to Amberlyn. "You make a good couple."

Not a cute couple. A good couple. Amberlyn wasn't sure why that distinction caught in her mind.

"I'll be right back." Pastor Mosley headed for the small office on the opposite side of the staircase.

"Do you want to try to do some work tonight?" Luke asked.

"We need to wait for our laundry to finish anyway," Amberlyn said. "We might as well."

"I'll get our new laptops."

Amberlyn put her hand on his to stop him. "I don't know that we should be accessing classified material with someone else around."

"Want to work in one of our rooms?"

Amberlyn nodded. "I think that would be best."

Pastor Mosley. Former CIA. So many moments from Luke's teenage years now made so much more sense.

Luke sat on the padded chair in the corner of Amberlyn's room, his laptop resting on his legs, while she used the desk beside him.

"Pastor Mosley was telling the truth about being a former agency employee," Amberlyn said.

"I should have known you would check out his story."

"We're staying in his house, and he knows who I work for."

"I hate to break it to you, but everyone in town probably knows who you really are."

"I don't think so." Amberlyn shook her head. "If I wanted to stay inconspicuous, I wouldn't tell everyone that I knew someone was a federal agent, especially if that person were clearly undercover."

He could see her point. He also didn't have a lot of faith in Russ's or Brad's common sense. "We could have Pastor Mosley ask his friend at the diner what she's heard. Most rumors circle through there about six times before they die."

"That's a good idea. It would be useful to know what people are saying before we walk into your reunion on Saturday night."

"If you're right about everyone not knowing who you are, they'll believe the story that I hired you as my date." Luke cringed inwardly. "They probably think I'm lying about working at the White House too."

"I guess we'll have to make sure we're a convincing couple."

"How do you plan to do that?" Luke asked. "Everyone is going to believe what they want to believe."

"I'm going to start by ordering a new dress. Walmart's selection didn't extend to cocktail gowns." She started searching online. "Do you think the pastor will mind if I have one shipped to his house?"

"I'm sure that will be fine, but do you think it would get here in time?" he asked. "We can always make a drive to Roanoke or Richmond."

"I'll have it expressed."

Luke supposed he'd have to find something at either Walmart or the men's shop in town to wear on Saturday. Not interested in dealing with that particular task right now, he opened the cell phone records Amberlyn had given him access to.

"According to this, Russ didn't have any movement over the weekend," Luke said. "Not on his cell phone anyway. His car had quite a bit of movement, but it was all around here."

"That's odd that he didn't take his phone with him."

"Unless he was trying to make it look like he wasn't out," Luke said. "Could be he let someone track him on one of those Find My Friends apps, and he wanted it to look like he was home."

"I don't know. With him driving a Corvette, it's not like he wouldn't get noticed wherever he goes."

"True."

Amberlyn tapped on her mouse pad, still scrolling through dresses. After several minutes, she turned the laptop toward him. "What do you think of this one?"

Luke didn't know much about dresses, but the fitted dress with the angled hemline was something he could see his sister snatching off the rack. "I'm sure you'll look great in that."

"What color?" She scrolled over the color palette to display the four choices: a deep blue, gold, red, and black.

"I doubt you have a bad color."

She looked over at him and smiled. "You're sweet. You also really don't care, do you?"

"Nope."

"In that case, I'm going with the blue. It's classy without making it look like I'm trying to catch everyone's attention."

"We already have everyone's attention." Especially whoever had bombed the FEMA building. Luke kept that thought to himself. Amberlyn didn't need another reminder of her friend's death.

"This does complicate our investigation," Amberlyn said.

"We should probably drive your car when we go to any events," Luke said. "That will give us the chance to keep a low profile if we need to go anywhere else in town when we don't want to be noticed."

"That's a good idea. We can just park the rental at the hospital when we pick up mine and swap vehicles again on our way back here."

Amberlyn's phone chimed with an incoming message. She read it and shook her head. "We came up empty on the fingerprints. The woman at the cottage isn't in the system."

"That's a bummer. Maybe we'll get lucky and the DNA results will give us something."

"Maybe." She held up her phone. "Jeff also said they managed to track down those last three unidentified cell phone numbers. As we suspected, they all belong to truckers."

A knock sounded on Amberlyn's open door, and Pastor Mosley stepped into the doorway. "Sorry to interrupt, but I just got off the phone with Cynthia."

"And?"

"She remembers seeing Russ's car drive by the diner several times last weekend."

Luke deflated. He'd been so sure Russ had been the man they were looking for.

"Is she sure?" Amberlyn asked.

"Oh, she's sure," Pastor Mosley said. "It stood out to her because when the car passed by, it wasn't Russ driving. It was Brad."

CHAPTER 26

MORNING COULDN'T COME soon enough. Amberlyn wanted a warrant, and she wanted Russ behind bars once and for all. To think she'd eaten dinner with the man who had helped plant the bomb that had killed Chanelle. He might not have been the actual bomber, but if they were right about Russ being the man in the photograph with Eli Duffy, he was involved. And at dinner, he'd acted as though life were just the way he wanted it. He was in for a rude awakening.

Proof. They still needed proof, like tying Russ to Eli Duffy or the woman who had planted the bomb at their cottage. And from there, they needed to place him in Kansas City or St. Louis.

Amberlyn managed to stay in bed until nearly six before she gave up on sleep. The pain in her arm from where the gash had been stitched tugged uncomfortably, and her entire body ached. She nearly put her new tennis shoes on before she thought better of it. Her body needed to heal, and she and Luke needed to stay out of sight.

She retrieved a change of clothes and headed for the shower. It wasn't until she was dressed in her new clothes that she realized she'd forgotten to buy a hair dryer. A quick peek beneath the sink revealed the pastor's guest bathroom didn't include such amenities. Since the pastor was nearly bald, she doubted he owned one at all. Apparently, she was going with a natural look today.

Running her fingers through her damp hair, she gathered her pajamas and makeup and opened the door. Luke stood in his doorway across the hall.

"I'm sorry. Have you been waiting long?" she asked.

"No. I was debating whether to go for a run, but being seen out in the neighborhood probably isn't a good idea."

"I had the same thought." Amberlyn rolled her shoulders. "Are you feeling as stiff as I am?"

"I've had better mornings."

"I'll bet." She stepped aside. "The bathroom's all yours."

"Thanks."

Amberlyn returned to her room and searched for any updates that had come in overnight. Nothing.

She pulled up the basic background information on Eli Duffy to see if she could find any ties between the two men.

Twenty minutes later, Luke knocked on her open door. "Do you want to grab something to eat before we dig into Russ's information?"

"I probably should." She motioned to her laptop. "Once we get a search warrant for him, things will get crazy."

Luke headed for the stairs. "Do they need a search warrant before they bring him in for questioning?"

"It's best if we have it first." She walked with Luke downstairs. "If he is working with anyone else here in town, we don't want someone destroying evidence when they find out Russ has been taken into the sheriff's office."

"I thought the FBI would do the honors."

"Oh, we will," Amberlyn said. "But we'll use the sheriff's office to conduct the interrogation."

"I guess that makes sense."

They reached the kitchen, and Luke opened the door to what turned out to be the pantry. He looked over his shoulder. "Pancakes?"

"That sounds great."

Luke retrieved a bag of pancake mix and set it on the counter.

"Will Pastor Mosley mind us using his kitchen?"

"Not at all." Luke leaned down and opened a cabinet. A moment later, he stood and put an electric griddle on the counter.

"I gather you've cooked in this kitchen before."

"The pastor let me hang around here a lot when my folks were working." Luke plugged in the griddle and fished a bowl out of the corner cabinet. "What's our plan for today? Do you want to follow up on the guys still on our maybe list? Or are we going to assume Russ is our one and only guy?"

Amberlyn wanted Russ to be their one and only guy, but Luke's question brought to the forefront the possibility that he wasn't. "I think our best course of action is to have Whitley bring Russ and Brad in for questioning. That keeps us away from rumors about me being law enforcement."

Luke grimaced. "I think I'd prefer those rumors over the ones about me hiring you as my date."

She couldn't blame him there.

He mixed the batter and spooned it onto the oversized griddle in eight equal portions. "What are the chances we can skip the reunion?"

"I guess that depends on what Russ and Brad say in the interrogation."

"I'd love to be a fly on the wall for that."

"Maybe we can be." Amberlyn considered their options for the day. "We can ask Whitley to set up a feed that we can tap into so we can watch from here. That would also let us feed him questions if we need to."

"That's a great idea." Luke flipped the first pancake. "What about the other guys we wanted to check out?"

"I'd love to finish off our list, but I'm not thrilled about taking the chance of people knowing where we are."

The pastor's voice sounded from behind her. "What are you trying to find out?"

Amberlyn swiveled to face him. She had to remind herself that this man had spent twenty-seven years working intelligence for this country. "We're trying to find out who on the championship football team has a wrist tattoo from when they won the championship. Ideally, we'd also like to know who is still wearing their ring. We still have seven whom we haven't been able to check out."

"How about I check them out?" Pastor Mosley asked. "No one will think twice about me driving around town and visiting people."

"He's right," Luke said, spatula in hand. "And most people have no idea we're still staying in town. Staying out of sight could be to our advantage."

"That's true."

"Then, it's settled." The pastor opened the refrigerator and pulled out the milk. "Give me a list of whom you still need, and I'll track them down. If you can ping their locations on their cell phones, so much the better."

"You really were intel." Luke shook his head as though he still hadn't quite wrapped his mind around it. He transferred the first two pancakes onto a plate. "I can't believe I never knew that about you."

"It's not the sort of thing you want to share in a small town, especially when you're in my line of work."

"Why?" Amberlyn asked. "Were you afraid everyone would think you were spying on them?"

"Yes, especially since that's exactly what I was doing when I first moved here."

"What?" Luke turned so he was facing the pastor. "Who?"

"An Iranian national who was hiding out." He shrugged before pouring milk into a glass. "The situation was resolved after a few months, but I liked it here. Since I was close to retirement anyway, I decided to keep my cover story as a pastor and make this my real life."

"That's incredible."

"That assignment was the best thing that ever happened to me," Pastor Mosley said. "I love this town, but I'm also not going to sit around and let someone from here cause terror somewhere else."

"Are you sure you have time to do our spying for us?" Luke asked.

"I need to stop by the new youth center, but that will only take me a few minutes," Pastor Mosley said. "And when it comes to situations like this, I'll make the time."

Luke shouldn't find happiness in someone else's misfortune, but it was hard not to enjoy seeing Russ and Brad in a situation out of their control.

He and Amberlyn currently sat at the pastor's kitchen table, both of their laptops in front of them. On Luke's screen, Brad paced restlessly across the otherwise empty interrogation room. On Amberlyn's, Whitley sat across from Russ, a file on the table between them.

"Can you tell me where you were on October 2?"

"I was at home."

"All day?"

"Yes, all day."

Luke wasn't sure what to think about Russ's casual air, as though being hauled into the sheriff's office were no big deal. "Do you find it odd that he hasn't asked why he's being questioned?" Luke asked.

"I was just thinking the same thing."

On her screen, Whitley shifted a paper in his file. "What about on October 5?"

"Same thing."

Amberlyn pointed at the screen. "He's also answering without any need to check his calendar."

Whitley pressed on. "Did you go to work or out to eat? Maybe take a drive somewhere?"

"No. I was off that day." Russ leaned back in his chair. "I was retiling my bathroom."

"Did you have anyone helping you?"

"I didn't need anyone to help me."

"What about someone who might have stopped by?" Whitley pressed. "A friend or girlfriend?"

"Sure. My fiancée hung out at my place on Friday night," Russ said. "Then Brad stopped by that Monday to return my car."

"Your car?"

"Yeah. I let him drive it so I could borrow his truck to haul supplies. I couldn't exactly fit a tile saw into my convertible."

"I see."

Luke let out a sigh. If Russ was telling the truth, he was only guilty of being a jerk. "Do you believe him?"

"He's not showing any signs of lying," Amberlyn said, "but he looks like the sort who might have mastered that skill."

Whitley flipped to a new page in his file. "Can you explain why you planted a rattlesnake on the trail outside the cottage where Luke Steele and Amberlyn Jones were staying?"

Russ's face flushed slightly. "I don't know what you're talking about."

Whitley slid two photos across the table. "This is you on Wednesday morning. The time stamp on the surveillance video shows you returning only moments before Captain Steele and his girlfriend came across the snake you planted."

"You can't prove I did anything." Russ shoved the photos back across the table.

"Where were you on Tuesday morning between 4:00 and 6:00 a.m.?"

"Sleeping, like any other sane person in this town."

Luke gestured toward the screen. "We figured it was Brad who messed with your car."

"Yes, but by asking that question, he just eliminated Russ as a potential alibi for Brad."

"Smart."

After a few more questions that didn't reveal anything beyond Russ's cocky attitude and stubborn silence, Whitley finally stood. "I may have some more questions for you, but for now, wait here. The sheriff will be in shortly to read you your rights."

"My rights? You're arresting me?" Russ pushed back from the table with enough force to send his chair toppling over. "I didn't do anything."

Special Agent Whitley took a step forward, his posture threatening. "You endangered a Marine Corps officer, one who has daily interaction with the president of the United States." Whitley took another step forward. "We take that sort of threat very seriously." Whitley pointed at the upended chair. "Now, sit down, and wait here."

Russ's jaw clenched, but he righted his chair and followed the FBI special agent's orders.

Amberlyn let out a sigh. "As much as I hate to say it, I don't think he was involved in the bombing. He wasn't the man in the photo in St. Louis anyway."

"How can you be so sure?"

"His skin tone changed when he lied about planting the rattlesnake. That makes me think he was telling the truth about where he was last weekend."

"Which means we're back to the drawing board." Luke let out a sigh. "We know Brad was in town. Plus, he doesn't have a wrist tattoo, and he isn't wearing his championship ring. I doubt it still fits him."

"Hopefully, Pastor Mosley can narrow down our maybe list," Amberlyn said. "I think we should focus on who the woman was in our cottage."

"How long will it take for the DNA results to come back?" Luke asked.

"The quickest I've ever seen is twenty-four hours."

Luke did the math in his head. He had no idea where the body had been taken for the autopsy, but he had to guess the FBI would make sure someone with crime-scene experience conducted it. That would definitely mean they would transport the body to one of the neighboring cities. "We probably won't hear back until this evening at the earliest."

"I'll put in a request for the coroner to cc me on the autopsy report."

"So, what do we do now?" Luke asked.

Amberlyn opened a new tab on her laptop. Within moments, she had the locations on the football team members who still remained on their suspect list. One appeared to be en route to Pine Falls, still more than four hours away, but two from their maybe list were currently together at the lodge.

"What do you say we pick up my car from the hospital and go have some lunch at the lodge?"

"You already know my answer to that question." Luke stood. "But I'll get my shoes anyway."

CHAPTER 27

AMBERLYN PUT HER hand in Luke's as they walked toward the lodge restaurant.

Luke shot her a puzzled look, and she leaned closer. "People are more likely to believe we're a couple when we act like one when we think no one is looking."

"Not that I'm complaining, but no one is looking."

"Maybe, maybe not." And she rather liked it when Luke held her hand. Though there was an entrance to the restaurant directly from the parking lot, she nodded toward the main entrance. "Let's walk through the lobby in case they're in there."

Luke adjusted to their new direction. He opened the door for her, releasing her hand as she passed through. As soon as they were inside, he took her hand in his again.

The desk clerk spotted them, and the man's stress was instant.

With a new destination in mind, Amberlyn gave Luke's hand a squeeze to signal to him she was deviating from her original plan. She approached the reception desk. "I'm sorry to bother you, but we wanted to see if you've had any cancellations."

"No, ma'am. I'm sorry."

"Would it be possible for us to leave our phone number in case you do have any?" Amberlyn pressed. "It's quite a drive coming in from the hotel by the freeway."

"If you'd like." The clerk passed her a small notepad and a pen.

"Thanks." Amberlyn jotted down Luke's phone number and passed it back to the clerk. She turned her attention back to Luke. "Since we're here, do you want to get something to eat?"

"Might as well." Luke released her to put his hand on her back, as though to guide her forward.

They reached the wide opening into the restaurant and stopped just inside. A quick scan of the nearby tables didn't give Amberlyn the desired results.

Luke leaned close and whispered, "At the bar."

She took a step to her left so she could see past the pillar at the entrance. Sure enough, two men sat at the bar, each of them with a beer in front of him.

The host approached. "Two?"

"Yes." Luke gestured toward the two men. "Can we sit over on that side?"

"No problem." He retrieved two menus from the podium by the door. "This way."

Amberlyn and Luke walked past the bar, but neither of the men so much as glanced in their direction.

"Is this okay?" The host motioned to a table a few yards from where the men sat.

"This is great," Luke said. "Thanks."

He waited for Amberlyn to sit before he claimed the spot across from her.

After spending so much time studying the photos of their various suspects, it took only a moment for Amberlyn to identify the man closest to her as Alex Harper, one of Luke's former classmates.

The other man, who she was pretty sure was Zachary Upton, tipped his beer toward the television that hung over the bar. "It was a mistake to trade Henderson. That may very well cost them the World Series."

Baseball. They were talking about baseball. Amberlyn supposed it would have been too easy if the men had been sitting in an open bar, chatting about where they had been the past week and a half.

She opened her menu and skimmed over it. Luke barely glanced at his.

"Do you already know what you want?" she asked. Though she was torn between a burger and fries or a salad after eating three pancakes this morning, she supposed she should go for something on the lighter side. "I'm just going to have the cobb salad."

"When you change your mind, I'll let you steal some of my fries."

And she would steal some. If french fries were in front of her, she wouldn't be able to resist.

Their waiter approached, and Luke ordered for both of them.

At the bar, Zachary Upton and Alex Harper debated over the starting lineup for the Braves.

In the hopes of getting their attention, Amberlyn said, "Is it going to be weird visiting your old high school on Saturday?"

"That's an understatement," Luke said.

"It was nice of the president to let you have leave so you could come back for the reunion."

"Technically, I report to the White House Military Office," Luke said.

"Still, I'm sure with your work schedule, it wasn't easy to take off."

"The other mil aides were good to step in and cover for me."

The two men fell silent, and Amberlyn sensed their attention had shifted to her and Luke. "I look forward to meeting the rest of them."

"Everyone will be at the Christmas tree lighting. That's always a big event."

"I look forward to it." Amberlyn slid her chair back. "Do you know where the restrooms are?"

"The back corner." Luke pointed toward the clearly marked restrooms.

She was at the wrong angle to walk past the men at the bar. She should have taken Luke's seat.

An unlikely option popped into her head. Hoping Luke would play along, she stood and circled the table so she was standing right beside him.

He looked up, his eyebrows furrowed, then his eyes widened when she put her hand on his shoulder and leaned in.

She pressed her lips to his in what was intended to be a brief kiss, but the moment her lips were on his, she couldn't help but let the kiss linger. An unexpected shiver worked through her, and she had to remind herself that the kiss had been intended to give her a better view of the men at the bar, not remind her of her growing attraction to the man she was currently calling her boyfriend.

She straightened. "I'll be right back."

A glance at the bar gave her the view she needed. Zachary Upton's right hand was currently curled around his drink, both his championship ring and football tattoo visible. Alex Harper's hand rested on his thigh, his hand void of jewelry, and the unblemished skin on his wrist exposed.

One more suspect eliminated, another one added. And a tingle on her lips that served as a reminder that her pretend boyfriend was a very attractive man.

———————

Amberlyn had kissed him, and Luke wanted her to do it again.

The gesture had been simple enough, but it had sparked the simmering attraction he'd been fighting since he'd shown her around Air Force One.

Even though he knew the show of affection had been for Zach's and Alex's benefit, Luke hadn't missed the slight flush in Amberlyn's cheeks when she'd drawn away or the little flash of surprise illuminating her eyes. Was it possible his feelings weren't one-sided?

Beside him, the conversation between Zach and Alex had started up again about the playoffs.

The waiter headed toward his table, bringing with him the smell of his burger and fries. The waiter was still setting their food on the table when Amberlyn returned from the restroom.

Following the etiquette lessons his mother had drilled into his head, Luke stood as Amberlyn approached. As soon as she reclaimed her seat and their food was before them, she picked up their conversation where she'd left off. "Do you think a lot of people will come back for the reunion?"

His gaze dropped briefly to her lips, and he could imagine all too easily what it would be like to kiss her when they didn't have an audience. With a good deal of effort, he tried to step back into their conversation as seamlessly as she had. "It's hard to say, but if the lodge is really booked up, there must be a lot of people in from out of town."

"It's too bad they couldn't find another room for us." Amberlyn speared a piece of lettuce with her fork and eyed his plate.

Luke smiled and nudged his plate closer to her. "Yes, you can have some of my fries."

She plucked one off his plate. "Thanks."

Luke squirted some ketchup onto his plate, and Amberlyn made use of it before biting into her french fry.

They ate in companionable silence as the conversation at the bar continued, the bartender now weighing in with his opinions.

A man around Luke's age approached the hostess and motioned toward the bar. Though the guy was vaguely familiar, Luke couldn't connect the face to a name.

After a brief conversation, he continued forward. Luke's gaze dropped to the man's right hand and the championship ring that gleamed beneath the bright overhead lights.

Luke put his hand on Amberlyn's and leaned forward so he could whisper in her ear. "Another one." He tapped his finger rather than speak the word *ring*.

She nodded her understanding.

Zach and Alex stood when the other man reached them. Greetings were exchanged, but instead of the newcomer ordering a drink for himself, the other two settled their tabs. Within minutes, the three left the bar, Zach and Alex both casting glances in Luke's direction as they headed for the exit.

As soon as they left, Amberlyn asked, "Do you know who that other guy was? I didn't recognize him."

"No. Whoever it was, he must have changed a lot since high school."

"It has been fifteen years. A lot of people have changed," Amberlyn said. "Including you, I'm sure."

"That's true." He caught the way her gaze dropped to his plate again. "You don't have to ask. Take as many as you want."

"It's the smell that gets me." She took another fry.

"Me too," Luke said. "Then again, I don't think I've met a version of potatoes I don't like."

"Have you ever been to The Old Europe in Georgetown?" she asked. "They have the best potato pancakes."

Luke's mouth watered despite the food before him. "I haven't, but I may have to check it out."

"We'll have to go when we get back to DC."

Luke didn't have to look around to know there weren't other diners sitting near them. Had she just said she'd go out with him again after this whole investigation was over? Hope needled through him. "I'd like that."

CHAPTER 28

AMBERLYN SETTLED INTO the passenger seat and didn't bother to reach for the door. As expected, Luke closed it.

She watched him as he circled to the driver's side. He really was nothing like her first impression of him. She suspected that the night they'd met, when he'd come off as arrogant, he'd been nothing more than shy. Now that she'd spent so much time with him, she recognized that he simply needed the chance to get used to people before he felt comfortable enough to initiate conversation.

She glanced at him as he buckled in and started the car. Did she need to explain why she'd kissed him, or should she pretend it had never happened? Surely he'd already figured out that it had been part of their cover and her need to maneuver for a better angle to see the men at the bar. She could explain it had meant nothing . . . but it had. And she wasn't sure how she felt about the connection she had experienced.

"Where to now?" he asked.

"You still need something to wear for the reunion."

Luke shot her a horrified look. "You want to go shopping? Here in town?"

Amberlyn nearly laughed at his expression and was proud of herself for keeping a straight face. She glanced at her watch. "It's almost two. With any luck, by the time we're done shopping, we'll have the DNA results back."

"Fine, but I'm not braving Walmart again."

"You're driving. You pick the place."

He pulled onto the road and headed toward the main part of town.

When Luke didn't continue their conversation, she asked, "How well did you know Alex and Zach?"

"Not very. They weren't part of the crowd that made life miserable for everyone."

"That would explain why they listened to our conversation but didn't talk to us."

"I'm not sure I've ever talked to either of them since Alex asked to borrow my markers in third grade."

"That was quite a while ago."

"Yeah." He turned onto a side street and parked beside a menswear store one building away from Main Street. "Looks like it's still in business."

"Did you shop here often?"

"My dad brought me here right before I left for college. He was convinced every man needs to own at least one good suit."

"It's true. You never know when you'll need it." She thought of Luke standing at Chanelle's funeral, dressed in uniform, and a twinge of grief that still hadn't gone away rolled through her. "I imagine being in the military, you wear your dress uniform more than you wear a suit."

"More now than I used to." Luke climbed out of the car.

By the time Amberlyn reached the front door of the shop, Luke was already holding it open. She walked inside and breathed in the scent of cedar and wool. The expected racks of men's pants and suit jackets dominated the main part of the store, but a smaller women's section was arranged in the area to her left.

Luke entered behind her, and a bell chimed overhead as the door closed.

An older gentleman emerged from a doorway in the back. It took only a moment for Amberlyn to recognize him from the dinner at the church a few nights ago.

"Well, hello there." He closed the distance between them and shook both of their hands. "It's good to see you both again."

"You, too, Mr. Cline." Luke motioned to a rack of slacks. "I hope you can help me find a new suit. I'm afraid mine didn't survive the fire at our cottage."

"I heard about that. A bomb." He shook his head. "Who would have ever thought such a thing would happen here?"

"Not me," Luke said.

"Well, thank goodness you're both okay." He moved to the nearest rack of suit jackets. "Any updates on who did it?"

"The person who set the bomb was killed in the explosion," Amberlyn said. "We still haven't heard anything about who she was or why she was there."

"You don't think she was after Luke because of his job at the White House, do you?" Mr. Cline asked.

"I doubt it," Luke said.

"Probably just a case of mistaken identity," Amberlyn added, her eye drawn to a white blazer on a nearby display.

"I hope that's all it was, but you two be careful." He took three suit jackets from the rack. "You make a handsome couple. We don't want anything happening to either of you."

Luke lifted his hand to Amberlyn's waist in a gesture so natural, it was like they were a real couple. "I appreciate that," he said.

"Now, let's get you taken care of." Mr. Cline selected pants that matched the jackets he'd already taken of the rack. "Follow me."

———

Luke used the spare remote to open Pastor Mosley's currently empty garage. He and Amberlyn had switched cars again in the hospital parking lot after he'd bought his suit and a couple of dress shirts. Mr. Cline had been kind enough to give him a discount, bringing the cost down to mostly reasonable.

Amberlyn had also purchased several items, including the white blazer she'd been eyeing from the moment they'd walked into the store.

"Do you want to work in your room?" Luke asked.

"I vote for the living room. More comfortable."

"I thought you didn't want to work down here in case the pastor came in."

"He's former CIA, and he's already helping us. We know he can be trusted," Amberlyn said.

"Okay then, I'll grab our laptops." He motioned to her garment bag. "Want me to put that upstairs for you?"

"That would be great. Thanks." She handed it over. "I'll see if we have any updates from Whitley."

Luke carried his new suit, still wrapped in a plastic bag, upstairs and hung it in the closet in his current bedroom. After he laid Amberlyn's purchases on her bed, he retrieved their laptops and headed back downstairs to the sound of Amberlyn's voice.

"I had a feeling you were going to tell me that," she said into her cell phone. "I have to update the suspect list anyway, so I'll put the notes in on Russ and Brad."

Amberlyn fell silent as she moved to the couch. After another brief exchange, she ended the call and hung up.

Luke set both of their laptops on the coffee table. "Whitley?"

"Yeah. He was giving me the update on his second interrogation session with Russ."

"And?"

"He came to the same conclusion we did. Russ doesn't lie well. It looks like he really was at his house all weekend." She opened her laptop and pulled up their suspect list.

"We can knock Alex Harper off our list," Luke said.

"And put Zach Upton on."

"That gives us four still on our list who we don't have an alibi for and five possibles." He settled onto the couch beside her.

"Let's hope Pastor Mosley can help us reduce our list further." Amberlyn turned her laptop toward Luke. "Look at these names. Let's see if we can figure out who that other guy was at the lodge."

Luke scanned through them, mentally checking off the ones he had researched on social media and focusing on the ones whom Amberlyn and her coworkers had checked out. "It's got to be Hayden Barry."

Amberlyn pulled up Hayden Barry's driver's license. A younger version of the man they'd seen today stared back at them. "Looks like you're right. He's already on our list of people we knew about."

"Yes, but now we know for sure that he's wearing his ring."

"Too bad we couldn't tell if he had a tattoo," Amberlyn said. "We'll have to make a point of talking to him at the reunion. If he shakes hands with anyone, we should be able to see if he has one."

Luke's cell phone chimed with an incoming text. A request from the chief of staff for an update. Luke messaged him back with the latest, keeping it brief that they had eliminated three more suspects.

He set his phone down as Amberlyn's phone buzzed.

She glanced at the screen, and her face lit up. "The DNA results are in." Amberlyn grabbed her computer and pull it onto her lap.

Luke shifted closer so he could see her screen. She opened up the email that included the report and pulled the file up. The face of the woman from the cottage stared back at them, her eyes bright, a smile on her face.

"Who is she?"

"Hallie Norris, twenty-nine years old. Last known address was Des Moines, where she worked as a waitress."

"What was a waitress doing carrying a gun and planting a bomb?" Luke asked.

"I have no idea." Amberlyn scrolled down. "Looks like she grew up on a farm. The first change of address on her driver's license was shortly after she turned twenty. Then there was another one five years ago when she renewed, but she's never lived outside of Iowa."

Iowa. "Kyle Moran went to Iowa State. Maybe she was connected to him." Luke grabbed his laptop and opened several tabs to check social media.

Amberlyn opened a new tab on her screen as well.

Luke accessed Hallie Norris's Instagram account. Images of her at restaurants with friends were mixed in with pictures of her dressed in camo with a rifle in her hand. In one, she extended her left hand toward the camera, a diamond ring sparkling on a significant finger. The next showed her kissing a man, but his face was mostly hidden.

He checked the date on the image. Just over three years ago.

"I found something." Amberlyn motioned toward her screen. "She and Kyle Moran lived in the same apartment building."

"It's possible they shared more than the same address." Luke showed her his laptop. "Looks like she got engaged a few weeks before Kyle died. Do you think this could be him in this photo?"

"It's hard to tell." Amberlyn leaned closer. "Are there any photos of her fiancé?"

Luke scrolled through several posts, but in the few that showed her with a man, the man's face was hidden. "None that show his face."

Amberlyn pulled up a new tab and started typing.

"What are you doing?" Luke asked.

"Checking to see what Kyle did for a living." She nodded toward his computer. "If someone is that good about staying off social media, it's probably on purpose."

"All I know is this account has been inactive since Kyle Moran died. The last post was three days before that."

"Here it is." She nodded with satisfaction. "He was working as a police officer in Des Moines. If the department had a policy against having their officers on social media, this would make sense."

"So, this not only ties back to the blizzard but also to Kyle Moran specifically." Luke wasn't sure what to think about that.

"You said they're honoring the championship team this weekend. It could be that she came for it."

"Yes, but who is she working with? Someone tipped her off that we're a threat."

Amberlyn put her hand on his arm and squeezed. "It has to be someone who is already here in town."

"There were only three people who fell into that category who have championship tattoos, and we already eliminated Russ."

The garage door rumbled open.

A moment later, Pastor Mosley strode into the room. "I may have hit the jackpot."

"How so?"

"Turns out a bunch of the guys happened to be at the diner today."

"And?"

Pastor Mosley waved at their laptops. "Do you have your list of suspects?"

"Yeah."

"Read them off, and I'll tell you who had tattoos."

Luke read him their remaining suspect list.

"They were all there except Tony Bachelli. As for the rest, only Danny Mahoney had a tattoo. He was also wearing his ring."

"But he isn't local," Luke pointed out.

"Which means the only person left on our suspect list who could have figured out that I'm FBI is Gavin Pennington," Amberlyn said.

"Any chance you remember if Gavin was at church a week ago Sunday?" Luke asked.

An intense sadness clouded the pastor's expression. "I'm sure he wasn't." He let out a sigh. "His wife and kids were there, but she said he was out of town on business."

A member of the championship team, wearing his ring, sporting a tattoo, and without an alibi. "Sounds like we have a new prime suspect," Luke said.

"Let's hope he's the right one." Amberlyn spoke with an air of professionalism, but Luke didn't miss the flash of grief that appeared on her face. "What can you tell us about him?"

"He's not someone I would have expected to put at the top of your list, but he and Kyle Moran were the best of friends," Pastor Mosley said. "Funny thing is, it was Kyle's death that brought him back to church. Before then, I hadn't seen him since he'd graduated from high school."

"Not what I would expect of a bomber," Luke said.

Amberlyn put her hand on Luke's arm. "No, but people who do things like this often think their actions are for the better good."

"Fanatics." Pastor Mosley shook his head. "The scariest kind of criminal."

"I agree," Amberlyn said.

Luke glanced at his laptop again. "On a different subject, do you know if Kyle was engaged when he died?"

"Come to think of it, I think he was. Pretty girl. He brought her home the Christmas before the accident. They came to one of our dinners so she could meet everyone."

"Reverend Bowman mentioned that he and Kyle were close," Amberlyn said.

"He was like a second father to Kyle," Pastor Mosley said.

Amberlyn stood and picked up her laptop. "I should check in with the investigative team."

"I'll keep looking into Hallie Norris's social media," Luke said.

"Thanks, Luke," she said.

"I'll help you." The pastor retrieved his laptop from his office and settled into his chair. "Who is Hallie Norris?"

"She's the one who tried to kill us."

CHAPTER 29

AMBERLYN HURRIED INTO the guestroom and closed the door behind her. She wanted privacy for her phone call, but she also needed a moment to calm her emotions. For the second time in two days, they had a solid suspect, and this time, there weren't any others. Maybe, finally, they had found the second person from the diner. And if they identified him, they would be able to determine everyone who was responsible for the Kansas City bombing.

Amberlyn pulled out her cell phone, automatically clicking on her favorites. She nearly pressed the button beside Chanelle's name to tell her the news before she remembered—they were investigating Chanelle's death and the deaths of the others killed at the FEMA building. Chanelle wasn't there to answer her phone, and she never would be again.

Grief welled up inside Amberlyn, clawing at her throat and stinging her eyes. She battled both sensations with determination. Every detail, every iota of proof, had to be handled perfectly. Gavin Pennington may have been acting out as a result of a personal loss, but he had no right to inflict his pain on others.

Needing a moment to settle her emotions, Amberlyn wiped away the lingering moisture in her eyes. Then she set her laptop on her desk and went over her notes on Gavin. He'd been one of the names mentioned in connection to those who were supposed to have visited Kyle in Iowa. His phone records indicated that Gavin hadn't left town, but if his wife had been telling the truth, logically, he should have had his cell with him on his business trip.

Amberlyn pulled up the records for Gavin as well as the other numbers listed on his account. She scanned through the second number listed, which was also under his name.

She sucked in a quick breath when she noted three of the phone numbers called during the days leading up to the bombing had a 660 area code. One of the area codes for Missouri.

Even though she was certain the investigating officer in Missouri would want the latest information, she dialed Whitley first. He'd have the best resources to get a search warrant here in Virginia. When Whitley didn't answer, she called Ian.

"Please tell me you've got something," Ian said in lieu of a greeting. "I'm so tired of telling the White House that we're still narrowing down suspects."

"If we're right, we've narrowed our suspect pool down to one."

"Details."

Amberlyn related the pertinent information, including the calls from what they had thought was his wife's cell phone number.

"That should be enough for a search warrant," Ian said.

"I already tried calling my contact in Richmond, but he didn't pick up."

"Keep trying," Ian said. "I'll coordinate with the investigating officer to make sure they loop in the Richmond office."

"Thanks, Ian. It will be nice to have this case closed."

"We've still got a ways to go for that. We still haven't located the missing car from Eli Duffy's house."

The mere thought of another bomb going off caused acid to rise up in her throat. "Someone had to catch it on a traffic camera somewhere."

"We still have people looking, but it's such a common car that without the license plate matching, we're searching for a needle in a haystack."

"Kind of like searching for championship rings and wrist tattoos." Amberlyn suspected if Luke hadn't been in the Situation Room the day of the bombing, they would still be searching for which school the ring had come from. "Has anyone connected Kyle Moran and Eli Duffy yet?"

"Just barely. Kiera found out Kyle Moran and Eli's brother were both on the police force together. They were together when they died."

"Which would definitely connect the two families."

"That's our thought," Ian said. "Kiera will keep looking into others who were close to the men who died, but so far, you've had the best leads. You're doing good work."

"It's only good work if the arrest sticks."

"And we have the right guy."

"We've got the right guy."

———

Gavin Pennington. Luke had plenty of memories of the teenager Gavin had been, but he'd rather hoped that after seeing Gavin in church with his family, the guy had grown into a responsible citizen and a caring person. If the clues they'd uncovered so far were correct, he was anything but responsible, and he was far from caring.

Luke glanced at the entryway. More than an hour had passed since Amberlyn had disappeared up the stairs. Could it really take that long to make a phone call or two?

From his seat across the room, Pastor Mosley said, "Maybe you should go check on her."

Luke didn't want to impose, but despite his natural inclination to let others alone, he hadn't lost sight of the fact that Amberlyn's best friend had died less than two weeks ago. He rose to his feet. "Maybe I should." He headed upstairs and knocked on her closed door.

The shuffle of a chair was followed by footsteps. Amberlyn opened the door, her eyelashes damp from recent tears.

"Hey." Though he wasn't quite sure what to say, he decided to try. "I was worried about you."

"I'm fine." She contradicted her words when she lifted both hands to wipe away the moisture still glistening beneath her eyes.

He couldn't relate to her pain, but the desire to soothe her grief rose within him. He reached for her hand. "You've been amazing through all this. I don't know how you've managed it."

She sniffled, and new tears formed. "I came up here to make some calls, and I started to call Chanelle—"

"And you remembered she wasn't there."

She pressed her lips together and nodded as tears spilled over.

Unable to resist, Luke released her hand and opened his arms.

She accepted the offered hug instantly, wrapping her arms around his waist as a sob broke from her.

Luke rubbed his hand over her back, trying not to be distracted by how well she fit into his arms. "It's okay to let it out."

The dam on her emotions broke, and Amberlyn's body trembled as another sob escaped from her. Tears continued to fall, dampening his shirt.

He wasn't sure how long they stood there in her doorway, but slowly, Amberlyn's sobs faded, and her body stilled.

She stepped back and lifted her gaze to his, her eyes filled with embarrassment. "I'm sorry. I didn't mean—"

"Don't apologize. This hasn't been an easy couple of weeks on either of us, but especially you."

"It could be over soon, assuming we can find the missing car."

"We'll find it."

Amberlyn retreated into her room long enough to grab a tissue. "I'm a mess."

"You're always beautiful." He was surprised when a blush rose to her cheeks. Uncomfortable, both with the words he'd spoken and her unexpected reaction to them, he changed the subject. "What's our next move?"

"The warrants should be in any minute. I want to watch the interrogation, but this time, I want to be there for the search."

"I'll come with you, but maybe we should wait until Gavin is taken into custody before we go over there," Luke said. "I'm not sure you'll want to see him right now."

"I already planned on waiting."

"Let me know when you're ready to leave."

"I need to fix my makeup, but I'll be down in a minute."

Luke took a step back. "I'll be waiting."

———————

Amberlyn drew a deep breath to fight against the lingering emotions that hadn't fully dissipated. The arrest and search warrants had come through only minutes after Luke had left her alone upstairs. Whitley must have already been in town, waiting for them, because five minutes later, he'd called to let Amberlyn know they had taken Gavin into custody.

Now she sat beside Luke in their rental car in front of the modest colonial house, a bicycle in the yard and a basketball hoop set up beside the driveway.

"You ready for this?" Luke asked, looking at her like he always did, like it was no big deal that she'd had a complete meltdown in front of him.

Oddly enough, the embarrassment she'd expected didn't come. "As ready as I'm going to get." She opened her car door and made her way inside.

A framed sign affixed to the entryway wall in front of her declared Friends Welcome. Amberlyn doubted she and Luke qualified. She moved forward anyway.

A member of the FBI's forensics team searched through drawers of a desk in the office to her right. Another dusted for prints, likely to determine whether Hallie Norris or Eli Duffy had been here.

Whitley descended the stairs. "The wife and kids are in one of the kids' rooms. The sheriff is driving Gavin over to the station."

"Have you checked the garage yet?" Amberlyn asked.

Whitley shook his head. "Not yet."

"We'll take a look." Luke headed down the hall. He turned the corner into a short hallway off the kitchen and opened the door to the garage.

"How did you know where it was?" Amberlyn asked.

"This house has the same floor plan as the one I grew up in." He flipped on the light.

Amberlyn pressed the button to open the garage door. A small SUV occupied the space closest to them, but the far side was empty, except for the workbench that stretched along the back wall. Power tools cluttered the space on top, and more tools lined the shelves above the workbench. In the corner, a large bin was filled with plastic sheeting that appeared to be streaked with blue.

Amberlyn circled what was likely the wife's car. More streaks of blue lined the garage floor. "Someone's been painting in here."

Luke walked the length of the garage and knelt beside the paint markings by the garage door. "The outline of the paint looks like it could be the size of a small to midsize car."

"You don't think the missing Camry was here in Virginia, do you?" Amberlyn asked.

"If the target is in this part of the country, it's possible," Luke said. "DC is only four hours from here."

Amberlyn's blood ran cold. If the members of Forever Freedom blamed the local government and FEMA for the death of the people lost in the Nebraska blizzard, it wasn't a far stretch for the blame to extend to policymakers in the nation's capital.

Safeguards were in place at all federal buildings, but after what happened in Kansas City, Amberlyn no longer trusted them. And the possible targets ranged from the FEMA headquarters building in DC to the various tourist sites. Regardless of which target they chose, the death count could rival or exceed that in Kansas City.

With a renewed sense of urgency, Amberlyn said, "We need to get to the sheriff's department."

The words were no sooner out of her mouth when Whitley entered the garage from the driveway. "Is that paint?"

"Yes. It's possible our second vehicle got a new color right here," Amberlyn said.

"I'll let the guys know to take samples," Whitley said. "After I do that, I'm heading over to question Gavin Pennington. Do you want to come, or would you rather stay here with the forensics team?"

Amberlyn headed for the car. "We're coming."

CHAPTER 30

SHE WAS AMAZING. Luke sat in the booth behind the two-way mirror as Amberlyn and Special Agent Whitley entered the interrogation room at the police station. Less than two hours ago, she'd been sobbing, but looking at her now, he never would have guessed it. Her crisp teal blouse contrasted with her newly purchased white slacks and blazer, and her expression could be described only as serious.

Gavin looked up from where he was seated at the table. "Why am I here?"

"We need to ask you a few questions," Whitley said. "I'm Special Agent Whitley, and this is my associate, Special Agent Reiner."

Luke cringed inwardly. Everyone would know Amberlyn's real identity now. He'd suspected that would be the case when Amberlyn and Special Agent Whitley had discussed having her involved in the interrogation, but he didn't look forward to facing his former classmates with the rumors buzzing, especially now that they would all know Amberlyn was FBI and he was simply her ticket of admission into their community.

It was too bad, really. Sometime over the past few days, he'd warmed to the idea of walking into his reunion with Amberlyn at his side.

She took her seat at the interrogation table. Special Agent Whitley remained standing. The two had already interviewed Gavin's supervisor at his office, and they were armed and ready with the truth.

"I understand you were out of town recently," she began.

"Yeah. So?" Gavin said.

"Where were you?" Amberlyn asked.

The typical belligerence Luke remembered from their teenage years emerged when Gavin asked, "Why do you want to know?"

In a surprisingly calm voice, Amberlyn said, "We believe you may have critical information regarding a recent crime."

Instantly, Gavin shook his head. "I didn't do anything wrong."

If Luke didn't know better, he'd guess that beneath that wall of belligerence was a healthy dose of fear.

As though Gavin were the most accommodating of people, Amberlyn continued. "I understand you are acquainted with Hallie Norris."

Gavin's eyebrows furrowed. "She was supposed to marry a friend of mine before he died."

"Kyle Moran."

"Yeah."

"When did you last speak to her?" Amberlyn asked.

"I don't know." He shrugged and leaned back in his chair. "It's been a while."

"And this trip you went on recently. It was for work?" Amberlyn asked, changing topics.

"Yeah."

In a conversational tone, Special Agent Whitley asked, "What do you do for a living?"

"I'm a computer programmer."

"What was the trip for?" Amberlyn asked.

"Training," Gavin said without hesitation.

"Where was it?"

Something flashed in Gavin's expression, a new show of arrogance. "You still haven't told me why you want to know."

Special Agent Whitley sat beside Amberlyn. "Like Special Agent Reiner said, we're investigating an incident, and we believe you may be a material witness."

"The only thing I'm a material witness to is how bad the room service was at my hotel."

Amberlyn jumped on the opening Gavin had given her. "Which hotel were you at?"

"What incident are you investigating?" Gavin asked, once more evading the question about his whereabouts.

Luke might not be a trained interrogator, but even he could tell Gavin didn't want to answer the question.

Amberlyn opened the file in front of her. "Is your phone number 540-555-9237?"

"Yeah. Why?"

"And your wife's phone number is 540-555-9743?"

Luke could almost see Amberlyn casting the line to reel him in.

"Why are you asking about our phone numbers?"

"We found it odd that both phones were at your home two weekends ago, yet your wife mentioned that you went out of town," Special Agent Whitley said.

Amberlyn tapped a manicured fingernail on the table. "And we checked with your boss. You weren't scheduled for training or any business trip. However, Mr. Simmons did mention that you were on leave from October 1 through October 6."

The arrogance magnified. Gavin jerked a shoulder. "Okay, so I went out of town to meet a friend."

"And you left your phone so no one would know where you were?"

"Yeah. My wife put one of the friend finder apps on my cell, and it would have been awkward if she'd come looking for me."

An affair? Was that the best alibi this guy could come up with? Luke shook his head. Gavin might have been popular in high school, but he was proving now that he wasn't the sort of person worth spending time with.

"How about telling us the truth about Hallie Norris," Amberlyn said. "You talked to her the day before you left town."

"So she called me," Gavin said, clearly unrepentant that he had exaggerated the truth. "What's the big deal?"

Amberlyn leaned in, for the first time taking an authoritative stance. "The big deal is that she tried to kill two people here in Pine Falls."

His eyes widened, and he leaned back as though he needed more distance between himself and Amberlyn's words. "What?" He shook his head. "No. There must be some mistake."

"There's no mistake. I'm one of the people she tried to kill."

"She didn't tell me what she was planning." He lifted both hands. "She called asking for the schedule of everything going on this weekend. We all knew she wanted to be here for the ceremony."

Luke assumed he was talking about the ceremony honoring the football team.

"Can you provide us with any kind of proof of where you were?" Amberlyn asked. "A credit card charge? A hotel receipt?"

"My friend put the hotel on her card, and I paid cash for everything else." He jerked his shoulder again. "I couldn't really make it look like I was in training in Richmond if my credit card put me somewhere else."

"I see," Amberlyn said, subtle disapproval in her tone. "What about the name of your friend? Can you give us that?"

"I'm not bringing her into this." Gavin lifted his arms. "I don't even know what 'this' is."

Amberlyn leaned back in her chair and glanced at Special Agent Whitley.

As though a silent baton had been passed, Whitley asked, "We noticed some paint on the floor of you garage that appeared to be fresh."

"So?"

"What were you painting?"

"A car. I have a side business to do car detailing and custom paint jobs."

"A side business," Special Agent Whitley repeated.

"Yeah. Do you have any idea how much it costs to put a kid in braces?"

"I can't say that I do," Special Agent Whitley said. "Did you do one of these custom paint jobs for Hallie Norris?"

"What if I did?"

"Then, we'd like the license plate number of the car or any other information you can give us on it," Amberlyn said.

"Why?"

Amberlyn waited until Gavin made eye contact with her before she spoke. "Because we believe that car is going to be used to house a bomb."

"Whoa!" Gavin lifted both hands again. "I don't know anything about that."

Special Agent Whitley leaned in. "Tell us what you do know."

"I know I have the right to a lawyer." Gavin folded his arms. "I'm not saying another thing without one."

Maybe Gavin was smarter than he looked.

"That's your right." Amberlyn stood and planted both hands on the table, leaning forward so Gavin had to look up to see her face. "I will tell you that if another bomb goes off, if more people die, you'll be facing the death penalty."

"Another bomb? I didn't have anything to do with the one at the lodge."

But he knew there had been a bomb. Interesting.

"We know Hallie Norris planted that one," Amberlyn said with steel in her voice. "And we suspect you're the one who planted the one in Kansas City."

CHAPTER 31

GAVIN'S SPUTTERED PROTESTS and demands to be released fell on deaf ears. Amberlyn kept her chin up and turned toward the observation room, where Luke waited. Special Agent Whitley followed.

Luke stepped into the hall as they approached. "He's on a rant in there."

Amberlyn had heard enough claims of innocence during her first two years with the FBI to fill in the gaps of what was being said inside the interrogation room.

Gavin pounded his fists against the door as he continued his outburst.

"I hope his lawyer can settle him down," Special Agent Whitley said.

Luke shook his head. "Don't count on it."

Amberlyn tried to visualize going through another round of questioning with the man responsible for Chanelle's death. Her insides withered. "Are you okay with handling the next session?" She motioned toward the viewing room. "I can analyze this interrogation to see if he has any tells we missed while we were in there. It's possible the video will help me find some nuances in his expressions that will indicate when he's lying and when he's telling the truth."

"That's a good idea," Whitley said. "I didn't catch anything obvious when he lied about how long it had been since he'd talked to Hallie Norris."

"Neither did I." And that worried her. If this guy was a compulsive liar, it would be harder to discern what was true and what wasn't.

Luke glanced at her, his concern for her evident. He nodded toward the room he had just emerged from. "I'll ask for the recording. That way we can work back at the house."

Though part of her wanted to be here when they finally broke Gavin, the thought of sitting around the sheriff's department and begging for a place to work along with the resources to get her job done didn't sound appealing.

"That would be great. Can you also let them know we'll need remote access to the future interrogation sessions?"

"No problem." Luke walked into the viewing room.

"I'll get a BOLO out on the car with the updated color," Whitley said. "It's got to be close by."

"Let's hope our initial analysis of Forever Freedom is correct, that this is a small, isolated movement," Amberlyn said.

"We can hope." But skepticism flooded his eyes. And anchored deep in Amberlyn's gut.

The bombings thus far may have been directly related to Kyle Moran's and Eli Duffy's brother, but so far, everyone identified within the group appeared to be living paycheck to paycheck. None of them had the resources to buy the car used in the bombing and the one the FBI was currently searching for, much less the supplies used to create the explosives. They needed to find who was at the head of Forever Freedom, or it was far too likely that the leader would continue wreaking havoc and find new followers to take the blame.

Luke reemerged from the viewing room. "We're all set. He emailed us the feed, and he's sending a link for the next time Special Agent Whitley wants to go at it with him again."

"I'll have the deputy arrange for Gavin to make a phone call," Whitley said. "Maybe his lawyer can convince him to cough up his alibi."

"Somehow, I doubt he has one," Amberlyn said.

Luke furrowed his brow. "Gavin's phone and car were here that whole weekend, right?"

"Yes."

"Then, someone here in town had to pick him up. Maybe we can find out who."

"Call Pastor Mosley to see if he can ask his friend at the diner if she remembers anything," Amberlyn said. "And also, ask if he or his friend knows anything about Gavin seeing someone on the side."

Luke made the call. He was on the phone for less than two minutes before he hung up. "He's going to ask Cynthia if she noticed anything," Luke said. "He'll fill us in on what he knows about Gavin when we get back to the house."

Amberlyn took a step toward the exit before another thought struck her. She turned back to Whitley. "Can you do me another favor?"

"What's that?" Whitley asked.

"Contact the wife. Find out if she can tell us when Gavin left and who picked him up."

"I'll call right now."

"Thanks." Amberlyn continued to the exit. They had found the bomber. She should feel some level of satisfaction, some sense of justice. She experienced neither.

Chanelle was gone, and finding her killer wasn't going to bring her back. A hollowness expanded inside Amberlyn, pain radiating from the very center of her being.

Luke opened the door for her and escorted her outside. "You were amazing in there."

"We didn't get nearly as much from him as I hoped."

"You caught him in a lie. That has to count for something."

"I caught him in an exaggeration," Amberlyn said. "I suspect he's the sort who tells people what he thinks they want to hear."

"Sounds about right," Luke said. "He was full of excuses when he burned down the storage shed at the high school because the football team wanted new equipment."

"He did what?"

"Like I told you before, I didn't hang out with the football team."

"I can see why," Amberlyn said. "Tomorrow night should be interesting."

Luke reached their rental car and opened her door. "I wasn't sure you'd still want to go to everything."

"We still have a lot of questions, and finding out what Gavin's friends know about him could help fill in some of the gaps." She offered him a smile. "Besides, you did just buy a new suit. It would be a shame for you not to get the chance to wear it."

"I was kind of looking forward to seeing you in your new dress too."

Amberlyn spotted Gavin's wife hurrying toward the entrance, another woman in her early thirties keeping pace with her.

Not wanting to risk being identified as a law enforcement officer, Amberlyn leaned into her current cover story. She put her hand on Luke's shoulder and kissed him.

The sensation of her lips against his was just like before. A ripple of pleasure skittered through her, the emptiness of a moment ago easing to tolerable.

Luke lifted his hand to her waist as though he didn't want the kiss to end. But it did end, and Amberlyn had to remind herself that this wasn't real. Or was it?

She eased back, her gaze meeting his. She didn't look over her shoulder, but out of the corner of her eye, she caught how Gavin's wife's friend slowed, her attention on Luke and Amberlyn.

She leaned close. "We have an audience."

A hint of disappointment flashed in Luke's eyes but was quickly banked. Apparently more than happy to keep up the ruse, he leaned in and kissed her again. Only this time, when his lips met hers, he lingered.

She barely noticed anything around her beyond the strength of the man currently holding her.

Luke's hand on her waist drew her closer, and a bevy of butterflies fluttered in her stomach. This time, when the kiss ended, he leaned forward until his forehead pressed against hers. "If you keep doing that, I might get used to it."

Amberlyn couldn't help but smile. "We should go."

"Yeah." He stepped back and put his hand on her car door. "We should."

Luke resisted the urge to take Amberlyn's hand when they walked into the pastor's house. Sometimes this relationship with her felt so real. He supposed parts of it were real. Over the past couple of weeks, they had surely become friends, but with every day, Luke couldn't help but want more.

Pastor Mosley was waiting for them in the kitchen. "I managed to find a bit of information that might help."

"What have you got?" Luke asked.

"I can tell you that he got a ride with Brad to Roanoke." The pastor's phrasing suggested he was aware of much more than he could share for privacy reasons.

"Which tells us how he left town without using his own car," Amberlyn said.

"Why would Brad take him?" Luke asked.

"He was driving Russ's car over there to get it serviced. I guess that was part of the deal with Russ and Brad swapping cars."

"Did his wife know that's who was driving him?" Amberlyn asked. "It doesn't make a lot of sense if she thought he was going out of town for work that a banker would pick him up for his trip instead of her taking him."

"I'm not sure if she knew, but I'd guess Gavin was trying to keep it from her because Brad picked him up from his office."

"That would make sense," Luke said. "He probably had his wife drop him off at work and then acted like he forgot to take his cell phone with him."

"How did you find out Brad picked Gavin up at his office?" Amberlyn asked.

"Marty, from Gavin's office, mentioned it at the diner. It was all the buzz that Russ's Corvette was in the garage and Russ wasn't with it."

"If no one else saw them, it's likely they took Park Street. Not many people are out and about over there during the day."

"I'll text Whitley and let him know what you found out," Amberlyn said.

"Did you get anything else from your sources?"

"According to Cynthia, there was a rumor a while back that Gavin might have been stepping out on his wife," the pastor said.

"You know more than that," Luke said.

Pastor Mosley gave him an apologetic look. "I can't say more than that."

"Sounds like we need to have another talk with Brad to find out where he dropped Gavin off."

Amberlyn lowered her phone. "I already texted that request."

Of course she did. Brilliant and beautiful.

"Did you know anything about Gavin having a side business?" Amberlyn asked. "Something having to do with cars?"

"I know he did a fancy paint job on his Dodge Charger a year or so ago, but I didn't hear anything about him going into business," Pastor Mosley said.

"That would explain why he had the equipment to repaint the Camry," Luke said.

"This is a small town. Maybe we can use traffic and ATM cameras to figure out where the car went," Amberlyn said. "Or narrow it down."

"Like you said, it's a small town." Luke shook his head. "I doubt there are traffic cameras in Pine Falls, and the only banks are all on Main Street."

"What about security doorbells?" Amberlyn asked. "Those are popular everywhere."

"A few people around here have them," Pastor Mosley said. "It's worth a try."

Amberlyn's phone rang.

"It's Whitley." She answered. "What do you have?"

She fell silent, the faint buzzing of her fellow agent's voice carrying to Luke, but it wasn't loud enough for him to distinguish the words.

"See if you can press him on that during the next interrogation." More silence. "It's going to be a long night for him, then." Amberlyn ended the call. "Apparently, Gavin's attorney is heading in from northern Virginia and won't be here until tomorrow morning."

"So, no more interrogation sessions today?" Luke asked.

"No. At least, not with Gavin," Amberlyn said. "Whitley did speak with Gavin's wife. She confirmed what we already suspected. She dropped her husband off at work along with his suitcase on the morning of October 1, assuming his office was providing him with transportation."

That would save Luke from needing to call her. "Did she say where she thought he was going?"

"Richmond." Amberlyn pocketed her phone. "She also confirmed that Hallie Norris had come by the house last weekend to get her car painted."

"Any chance she saw the license plate?" Luke asked.

"She doesn't remember the numbers, but she said it was a Kansas plate."

"That'll make it easier to spot if it's still around here," Pastor Mosley said.

"I hope it is," Luke said. "Because that would mean we could have everyone in custody who was involved." But the sense that this wasn't over had yet to dissipate.

"You'd better let the chief of staff know what we've found," Amberlyn said.

"Good idea. I'll do that now," Luke said.

"While you two tie up the loose ends on your workday, I'll start on dinner," Pastor Mosley said. "I think a celebration is in order."

Amberlyn sighed. "It's hard to want to celebrate, knowing what Gavin and his friends did."

"But finding him has very likely stopped another bombing. That is something to celebrate," Pastor Mosley said.

"You're right." Amberlyn nodded. But something didn't feel right, as though they'd put together an intricate puzzle but were missing the most important piece.

CHAPTER 32

DESPITE AMBERLYN'S BEST efforts to shake off her dark mood, Pastor Mosley's dinner didn't feel much like a celebration, not even with the ballgame playing on the television in the background and the Braves up by two runs.

Amberlyn and Luke had spent all afternoon searching through video feed without luck. She had hoped the video doorbells were more common than Luke and Pastor Mosley had expected, but they'd discovered quite the opposite. The few people who did have them lived in the newer developments. Only four people in Gavin's neighborhood owned the enhanced doorbells, and of those, one hadn't even hooked his up yet. In true Murphy's Law fashion, that was the only one between Gavin's house and the neighborhood entrance.

With the table clear and the leftovers stored in the refrigerator, Pastor Mosley grabbed his keys off the hook by the door. "I need to stop by the new youth center. Why don't the two of you come with me? It'll do you some good to get your minds off things."

Amberlyn wasn't sure anything could accomplish that, nor could she shake the sensation that they were still missing something . . . or someone.

"Are you up for a change of scenery?" Luke slid the dish towel he'd been using over the oven handle. "It might do us some good to get away from our research for a while."

Amberlyn couldn't argue with that. She nodded. "I could use a break."

"Let's go. I'll drive." Pastor Mosley directed them into the garage.

Luke opened both doors on the passenger side and motioned for Amberlyn to take the front.

"Thanks," she said.

"When did you buy a new car?" Luke asked after he settled into the back seat. "You were driving that old Subaru last time I saw you."

"I picked this up last month. It was time to splurge a little." Pastor Mosley pulled out of the driveway.

"My coworkers have been after me to do the same."

The pastor laughed. "Sometimes you are economical to a fault."

"So I've been told," Luke said.

The drive to the new youth center took only five minutes, but the structure in front of them was far grander than anything she'd expected. The main structure looked like a recreation center, and what appeared to be an oversized garage stretched from the back corner.

The pastor parked beside two other cars already in the lot next to what appeared to be a loading dock.

"What is this?" Amberlyn asked. "This part looks like a warehouse."

"It is." The pastor climbed out and waited for Luke and Amberlyn to join him before he continued. "We're part of an organization that helps feed the less fortunate. This warehouse will help with that as well as give us storage space for school supplies and other items for families in need."

"Where are your volunteers coming from?" Amberlyn asked.

"The kids," Luke answered before the pastor had a chance to. "Right?"

"You got it." Pastor Mosley and Luke exchanged a knowing look. "It helped you find your way well enough."

"That it did."

"What am I missing?" Amberlyn asked.

"Pastor Mosley believes that the best thing for people to do when they're struggling is to help others."

"Luke here was one of my best history tutors for the middle-school kids."

Amberlyn's heart warmed and ached at the same time. Luke's peers had clearly subjected him to intense cruelty, yet he'd spent his free time helping students younger than him. "I'm starting to understand how the two of you became so close."

"We may not have seen each other often over the years, but some bonds remain no matter how much time has passed," Pastor Mosley said.

"Weekly phone calls don't hurt either," Luke said dryly.

"Speaking of phone calls, I should check in with my office." Amberlyn pulled out her phone.

"You'll need to use the phone in my office," Pastor Mosley said. "The cell service doesn't work here. We think there may be a tower down in the area."

"I can wait until later, then," Amberlyn said.

"Come on. Let me show you around." Pastor Mosley guided them through the door that led into the storage area.

They walked inside the huge bay that was currently empty, except for a couple of folding tables, a tool chest, and three boxes labeled painting supplies. If Amberlyn had to guess, they would be able to park a couple of tractor trailers inside.

"This is huge," she said.

"We expect to need the space." Pastor Mosley headed for a door to his right. "Come take a look in here." He walked into a brightly lit room where a half dozen people stood along a long table, assembly-line style. Canned food was stacked on top, and the volunteers passed backpacks down the line, each person adding cans in turn.

"I brought some extra hands," Pastor Mosley said.

"We can use them." Reverend Bowman smiled when he looked up. "Good to see you both again."

"You too, Reverend," Luke said.

"What is all this?" Amberlyn asked.

Pastor Mosley gestured to the supplies. "When we're done, each of these backpacks will contain enough food to provide meals for a family of four through the weekend."

A woman in the middle of the line placed two cans of chicken into a pack. "We'll deliver these to the schools tomorrow to make sure the kids who are receiving food assistance will have something to eat through the weekend."

"That's amazing," Amberlyn said.

Luke took a spot at the end of the table. "I say we help first and take the tour afterward."

Reverend Bowman grinned. "Pastor Mosley, you trained him well."

Pastor Mosley nodded. "Yes, I did."

CHAPTER 33

SPENDING THE DAY delivering backpacks full of food to elementary schools hadn't been on Luke's agenda, but when one of the volunteer drivers had called out sick, Pastor Mosley had asked for a favor. The task had provided a welcome distraction, both from the upcoming game where he would return to his old high school for the first time since graduation and from the frustration that Gavin still wasn't talking.

Luke tugged on the simple gray hooded sweatshirt he'd bought at Walmart and grabbed his jacket, a sense of dread already spreading through him. Going back to his old high school would be bad enough, but going with Amberlyn when everyone would likely know she was law enforcement or, worse, believe the rumors that he'd hired her as his date, would be a new brand of torture.

Forcing himself to press forward, he plodded down the stairs.

Amberlyn waited by the door, a hat and a pair of gloves in hand. "Are you ready?" she asked. Before he could give an honest answer, she held up a finger. "And no, I'm not asking if you want to go. We *are* going."

"Then, I guess I'm ready." He headed for the garage. "Where's Pastor Mosley?"

"He already left for the game."

As soon as they were in the car, Luke asked, "How many people do you think know you're FBI?"

"It should only be Gavin, unless he told someone before he was taken into custody," Amberlyn said. "He wasn't allowed any visitors yesterday or today."

Luke fell silent. He drove to the hospital and parked beside Amberlyn's car so they could arrive in the vehicle everyone had seen them in.

Amberlyn settled into the passenger seat of her car. As soon as he started the engine, she put her hand on his. "I know going back to the high school is stressing you out. It can't be easy facing the demons from your past, especially knowing what people might be saying about us."

She hit that nail on the head. "Sometimes I forget how good you are at analyzing people."

"Talk to me. Tell me what you're thinking."

Like how he wished she really were his girlfriend? But he couldn't tell her that. "I spent high school trying to be invisible. Walking in with you is going to draw a lot of attention."

"You're worried about what people are saying?"

Luke shrugged.

"We've planted a few seeds to counteract the rumors," Amberlyn said. "Don't worry about what people might be thinking. Just remember that right now, we're a couple."

"Holding your hand in front of people isn't going to convince them that you're my girlfriend."

"Actually, it's better if you aren't holding my hand when we walk in. It'll look more natural."

"Then people will wonder who you are and why you're with me."

"Let them wonder."

Amberlyn shifted in her seat and laced her fingers through his. "You've held my hand before. You know what it's like to kiss me," she said. "You don't need to show people you can. You need to act like you already have."

He had kissed her, but only with an audience. He couldn't help but wonder what it would be like to kiss her for real, to hold her in his arms when it had nothing to do with work.

"It'll be fine." Amberlyn squeezed his hand before she released him. "I promise."

"I'm not sure that's a promise you'll be able to keep." Luke put the car in gear and drove the short distance to the high school. The building looked smaller now, less formidable somehow, but Luke couldn't keep the flood of memories from assaulting him. Every day dreading the moment he would walk through the front doors, the few teachers who had made life bearable, his graduation that had released him from his four-year prison.

Luke circled to the back parking lot by the stadium and chose a spot beside Pastor Mosley's car on the far side of the lot.

"I'm surprised Pastor Mosley parked this far from the gate," Amberlyn said.

"It's his first new car in fifteen years. He's probably making sure no one dings it."

They both climbed out and headed for the gate, the sound of a whistle blowing carrying to them.

"It sounds like we missed the opening kickoff," Amberlyn said.

"I always missed the opening kickoff." More specifically, he always missed the games.

"It's just a few hours." Amberlyn put her hand on his arm. "You can do this."

"That's what you keep telling me." Luke still wasn't so sure.

They reached the gate, and he handed the woman at the ticket table a twenty-dollar bill to pay for their tickets.

"Are you here for the reunion?" she asked

"Yes."

She took the twenty and handed Luke his change. "We reserved the third set of bleachers for your group. You'll see the signs."

"Thanks."

Luke waited until after they had passed through the ticket booth to ask, "We're going to have to sit there, aren't we?"

"Yes." Amberlyn entered the stadium and glanced over her shoulder. "Yes, we are."

Amberlyn wasn't watching the game. Based on the chatter around her, not many other people from Luke's graduating class were either.

The blonde woman in front of her leaned closer to her redheaded friend. "I don't know what Felicia is going to do. It was one thing when she just thought he was cheating on her, but a terrorist?" The woman shook her head. "Her poor kids."

Two men to their left carried on a similar conversation.

"I'm still not buying it," one of them said. "Gavin is an idiot, but he's not that stupid."

The other man's comment was lost in the crisp breeze, but Amberlyn suspected by his body language that he was in agreement with his friend's assessment.

Cheers from the surrounding fans indicated a touchdown, and Amberlyn glanced at the scoreboard as the number zero turned to a six for the home team. A moment later, they made the extra point, and the score changed to seven.

A shiver worked through her, and she rubbed her gloved hands together. Despite the blanket Luke had spread out for them to sit on, the chill from the metal bleachers seeped into her backside and the wind had most certainly turned her nose red.

Luke shrugged out of his jacket and laid it across her lap.

"Luke, you're going to freeze." She tried to hand it back to him.

"You're already freezing." He nudged her hand and helped her spread the jacket out again.

"Thank you." She scooted closer, hoping shared body heat would help both of them, and spread the jacket out so it covered both of their laps.

Luke put his arm around her. "If you're too cold, we can always take off early."

"We should stay through the halftime show." Amberlyn leaned into him. "Isn't that when the football team is being recognized?"

"Yeah."

The conversations around them continued.

"I just don't think Gavin cares enough about anything to get involved with something as crazy as blowing up a building," the redhead said.

The blonde nodded in agreement. "The only thing he cares about is his latest girlfriend and how to keep his wife from finding out."

"He won't be keeping any secrets after all this," the other woman said.

The first quarter drew to a close, and the players cleared the field. A few people filtered out of the stands around Amberlyn and Luke, several of whom were sporting championship rings on their fingers. Others climbed the metal steps with hot chocolate and nachos in their hands.

"Do you want some hot chocolate?" Luke asked.

"That sounds great." Amberlyn started to rise, but he waved for her to remain seated.

"I'll get it." He put his hand on her knee before standing. "I'll be back in a minute."

The two women sitting in front of them watched Luke go and then, as though waiting for him to be out of earshot, turned to face Amberlyn.

"Is that Luke Steele?" the redhead asked.

"Yes." Amberlyn pulled Luke's jacket more firmly over her legs. "Did you go to school with him?"

"We both did." The redhead lifted her hand to her chest. "I'm Savannah, and this is Chelsey."

"Nice to meet you. I'm Amberlyn, Luke's girlfriend."

The blonde leaned closer. "Are you really his girlfriend?"

Amberlyn's natural instinct to protect Luke flared. "What's that supposed to mean?"

"Well, you may not know this, but he wasn't the most popular kid in high school," the blonde said.

"More like the least popular," Savannah added.

The second-quarter whistle blew, but both Savannah and Chelsey kept their attention on Amberlyn.

Chelsey lowered her voice slightly. "We heard rumors that he hired someone to stand in as his girlfriend."

Choosing to use truth as a weapon, Amberlyn said, "It's starting to make sense why he didn't want to come this weekend."

Chelsey lifted both eyebrows. "He didn't want to come?"

"Not at all." Amberlyn rubbed her hands together in an attempt to warm them. "Coming here was my idea. I told him it would be good to face his past and see who his old classmates have become."

"Looks to us like he's trying to show everyone he's all important now," Chelsey said. "He's even telling people he works for the president."

"He does work for the president." Amberlyn could have pulled out her phone to show them the images Luke took of the two of them on Air Force One, but she didn't. "Do a Google search on Air Force One. If you watch the videos of the president getting on or off the plane, you'll most likely see Luke in the background. I know he was with him on the trip to Kansas City last weekend."

Disbelief filled Savannah's voice when she asked, "He really works for the president?"

"Yes." Amberlyn stretched the truth and added, "He showed me around the West Wing a couple weeks ago and even introduced me to the president."

Doubt clouded both women's expressions. "You've met the president?"

"I have. He's a very nice man."

Luke approached, two large Styrofoam cups in his hands. He handed one to Amberlyn and sat beside her.

"Luke, do you remember Chelsey and Savannah? They graduated with you."

"Nice to see you again," Luke said, not confirming whether he remembered them or not.

Hoping to dispel the rumors about Luke's profession, she said, "We were just talking about your boss."

"Deputy Director Hobbs?" Luke asked.

"No, the president."

"I work with the president, but technically, I'm under the White House Military Office."

His answer couldn't have been more perfect. That little detail must have sunk in because the doubt on both women's faces faded, replaced by a shocked awe.

Luke gestured toward the field. "Did I miss anything?"

"No," Amberlyn said. At least nothing he needed her to repeat. She took a sip of her hot chocolate, the warm liquid helping thaw her frozen core.

A few men in their section climbed down the bleachers and made their way over to the three-foot chain-link fence that surrounded the field.

As soon as the halftime whistle blew, the band marched onto the field. Two songs later, the performance ended in a huge half circle. The band played again, this time remaining in place while a crew moved a portable stage onto the field.

The homecoming king and queen were announced along with the rest of the homecoming court. As soon as they concluded that portion of the program, the men from the championship team strode onto the field.

The principal gestured to those now standing to the side of the stage. "And now, we would like to recognize Coach Zabrowski as he prepares to retire at the end of this season. And as part of that tribute, we have invited back one of our former football teams as we reach the fifteenth anniversary of their state championship win."

The crowd cheered, and the principal stepped back from the mic while he waited for them to settle before he continued. "Two of those team members are no longer with us. In their place, we have asked family members to stand with the team to honor their memories. Timothy Vincent is represented by his father, Montrell Vincent, and Kyle Moran is represented by his brother, Trevor Moran."

"Poor Trevor," Chelsey said. "That has to be so hard being down there."

"Maybe he's finally doing better," Savannah said. "It's been almost three years."

Amberlyn took a last sip of her hot chocolate and tried to be patient as the principal read the names of the former football team—all sixty-two of them—each of them crossing the stage as he did so.

Her heart cracked a little when Timothy's father reached the stairs and shook the principal's hand. Kyle's brother came next, his posture rigid, as though he wanted to be anywhere else right now. Amberlyn could relate.

The thawing effect of the hot chocolate dissipated, and she shivered again. Luke put his hand on her back. "We can leave any time you want."

Though Amberlyn would have liked to continue listening to the conversations around them, she suspected they were going to keep circling through the same topics. "I'm ready if you are."

He leaned close, and the warmth of his breath tickled her ear. "Oh, I'm ready."

―――――――――

Luke stepped into the warmth of Pastor Mosley's house, behind Amberlyn, his relief instant. "Thank you."

"For what?"

"For not making us stay until the bitter end."

"Tonight, you can thank the bitter cold." She rubbed her hands together. "I'm still freezing."

"Want some more hot chocolate?"

"Yes. Please."

Luke moved into the kitchen and filled the kettle with water. As soon as he turned on the burner, he opened the cabinet above the stove and retrieved two hot chocolate packets from the little basket where the pastor kept them.

Amberlyn sat at the table, her coat still on. "I'm surprised Pastor Mosley was willing to stay at the game. It was so cold."

"He's not sitting out in the cold," Luke said with a high degree of certainty. "I'm sure he's up in the announcer's booth. He's been helping with the stats for as long as I can remember."

"We should have joined him up there."

"That would have defeated the purpose of being around my old classmates."

"True, but it would have kept us from freezing."

Luke's phone rang, and he patted his pocket only to find it empty.

"I think it's in your jacket pocket." Amberlyn fished it out for him and handed it over.

"Thanks." Luke glanced at the screen long enough to read his co-worker's name before he answered.

"Luke, it's Tom," Tom said. "I just wanted to make sure you saw the updated schedule for next week."

"I've been so busy, I haven't had a chance to look, but I'm guessing Deputy Director Hobbs has me working Monday morning."

"Close. Monday afternoon. You need to report at four."

Luke retrieved two mugs and set them on the counter. "What about the rest of the week?"

"You have an overnight on Monday, and then you'll have the late shift for the rest of the week."

"Thanks for letting me know."

"Are you back in town yet, or are you still in Pine Falls?" Tom asked.

"I'm still in Pine Falls."

"I figured you'd hightail it out of there once they made an arrest."

Luke glanced at Amberlyn. "I thought so too."

"Enjoy your next couple days. The president has a busy schedule when you get back."

Undoubtedly, information Tom couldn't give him over the phone. "I'll do my best."

Luke hung up and poured hot chocolate mix into both mugs.

"Who was that?" Amberlyn asked.

"Tom, one of the other mil aides. He was giving me my report time for Monday."

"It seems like you should get a day or two to recover before having to go back to work."

"That's not how my job works." Luke added the hot water and stirred the mixture. "What time did you want to head back on Sunday?"

"I thought we could leave after the dedication of the new youth center."

"You're okay with staying for that?"

"Are you?" she asked pointedly.

He carried both mugs to the table. "It would mean a lot to Pastor Mosley if we were there."

"Then, we should stay." She accepted the mug he handed her. "Thanks."

"You're welcome." He sat beside her. "Do you want me to see if he has any whipped cream?"

"This is fine." She blew on the steaming liquid before she took a sip. Then she closed her eyes. "This is so good."

"It came from a powdered mix."

"That's how hot chocolate always comes."

"No, it doesn't. Real hot chocolate is milk and cocoa and sugar, and you heat it on the stove."

She lifted both eyebrows. "If you know how to make real hot chocolate, why are we drinking the instant stuff?"

"Because you were freezing, and this was faster." He took a sip of his own. It wasn't bad for instant. "Next time, I'll make you the real stuff."

"Any idea when the next time is going to happen?"

"No, but we should make it soon," Luke said. "I don't want you to go too much longer without knowing what real hot chocolate tastes like."

Amberlyn laughed. "I like the way you think."

CHAPTER 34

AMBERLYN REPLAYED THE conversations from the football game over in her mind and compared them to her own impressions after questioning Gavin. If she removed her emotions from the equation, she had to agree with one of the guys at the football game: Gavin didn't appear to be the zealot type. Selfish, dishonest, and unfaithful, yes, but a criminal? She wasn't sure.

She showered and dressed for the day, returning to her room as her cell phone rang. She snatched it up and answered.

"It's Justin Whitley. I wanted to let you know we're releasing Gavin."

"What?" Even though Amberlyn was having her doubts, she was convinced he knew far more than he was telling them.

"We don't have enough to hold him. All we can tie him to is the paint job on Hallie Norris's car. We haven't found anything that puts him in Missouri on the day of the photo or the day of the bombing."

"You know he's holding back."

"Oh, I know it. That's why we'll be tailing him for the foreseeable future, to see if he'll lead us to anyone else involved with Forever Freedom."

"Keep me informed."

"I will."

Amberlyn hung up and dropped onto her bed. If Gavin wasn't the man in the photo, where had he been when he'd been out of town, and why had those days coincided so perfectly with the bombing?

Luke knocked on her open door. "I was thinking about going to the shooting range. Are you interested?"

"Yeah. I need something to take my mind off this case." Or preferably, help focus it.

"What happened?"

Not, "Did something happen?" but *what*. Luke was far more perceptive than he first appeared.

"Gavin is being released."

"What?"

"That's what I said."

"We know he painted the missing car, he was out of town with no alibi for the dates we know our bomber would have been in Missouri, and we can connect him to Hallie Norris."

"Yes, but all of that is circumstantial. We can't find any evidence that he was in Missouri or that he knew about the bombing, much less that he was one of the key players."

"Maybe we shouldn't go to the reunion tonight," Luke said. "If he shows up, it's not going to be pleasant."

"I know we may have to admit that I wasn't telling people the truth about where I work, but I don't think Gavin will cause any trouble."

"You don't know him the way I do."

Amberlyn retrieved her weapon and her extra ammo and slid both into her purse. "There's something else that has me troubled."

"What?" Luke stepped back so she could enter the hall.

Amberlyn moved forward but didn't go beyond the threshold. "Savannah and Chelsey were talking last night about Gavin."

"Yeah?"

"So, everyone knows he's a liar and a cheat, but no one seemed convinced he would get involved with any kind of activist group. And the idea of him blowing anything up stretched everyone's imaginations. It's possible he painted the car but wasn't actually part of Forever Freedom."

Luke set down the case that held her spare gun. "Then why did he paint the car?"

"Maybe he didn't know what the car was for," Amberlyn said. Although the lack of bank records showing a payment from Hallie

Norris or even a large cash deposit after the fact worried her. "Is it possible he was being blackmailed? If he really was having an affair, he might have done the paint job to keep Hallie from telling his wife."

"Maybe, but I'm not sure he would go to that extreme," Luke said. "He used to get caught doing stuff all the time in school, and more often than not, he just talked his way out of it."

"That flows with what I saw in the interrogation room." Amberlyn leaned against the door frame. "He's clearly a compulsive liar."

"Oh, he's definitely that. It's more likely that he got paid in cash and already blew the money, or he traded a favor."

"What kind of favor would he want?" Amberlyn asked.

"A car he could borrow or a place to stay that his wife wouldn't know about."

"He wouldn't have had time to drive from Virginia to Missouri in time to be in that diner in St. Louis."

"Then maybe the story about the affair is true."

"Which means we're missing something," Amberlyn said. "Someone from that football team was in St. Louis."

"You're assuming whoever planted the bomb in Kansas City is coming to the reunion."

"They were all at the game last night, except the two who died."

Luke shook his head. "The principal announced all the names, but three of them were missing."

"Do you remember who?"

"Yeah. Keith Hickman, Lance Herrick, and Randy Cole."

"How did you remember that?"

"I don't know. I just did," Luke said. "But Lance didn't have a tattoo, and you said Randy was out of the country. That means Keith is the only one who was missing who's still on the suspect list."

"I'll send his name to the investigating officer. They can work on tracking him down. It's possible the reason we aren't finding a suspect here is because the bomber never came back home."

"Maybe." Luke held up the gun case. "We aren't going to the range, are we?"

"Sorry, but I should get this information out."

"I thought so." Luke turned back toward his room. "I'll grab my computer."

"Thanks, Luke."

He furrowed his brow. "For what?"

"For everything. You've been a huge help through this whole investigation."

"It's what I'm here for."

It was what he was here for, but something about his comment didn't sit right with her. He was here to help her, but he was far more than her ticket to the reunion. How much more, she wasn't sure.

Luke knotted his tie and took in his reflection in the oval mirror hanging on the bedroom wall. Too easily he could see the lean teenager of his past, his hair always a little too long because he didn't want to go to the barber shop and his pants an inch too short because his mom couldn't keep up with his growth spurts.

He lifted his chin. He wasn't that boy now. And it didn't matter what his former classmates thought of him at this point. He'd done what Pastor Mosley had always told him: "Don't prove yourself to others. Be your best no matter what anyone thinks."

In Luke's case, being his best was simply proving to himself that he had worth, that he hadn't deserved to be treated the way Russ, Brad, and Gavin had treated him. And tonight, he wouldn't face them alone.

He had no doubt that there would still be rumors, both a close representation to the truth, that Amberlyn was here as part of her job, and the fiction, that he had hired her as his date to impress them. Luke never wanted to impress anyone. He only wanted to be left alone.

Amberlyn's voice carried to him. "Are you about ready?"

Luke turned away from the mirror to face her. She was stunning. The dark-blue dress looked even better on her than it had on the model online, and Amberlyn had done something different with her makeup that put her in the irresistible category.

Okay, so maybe he didn't want *everyone* to leave him alone.

He managed to keep his jaw from dropping, but his thoughts slipped out in his words. "You're beautiful."

"Thank you." She offered him a slow smile. "You look rather handsome yourself."

Luke wouldn't go as far as calling himself handsome, but he was pretty sure he'd at least accomplished presentable. Moving away from the mirror, he grabbed his wallet, phone, and keys from the top of the dresser.

He escorted Amberlyn to the top of the stairs and waited for her to go down ahead of him.

Pastor Mosley was in the living room, his cell phone in hand. "Oh, don't you make quite the handsome couple." He motioned them forward. "Come over by the fireplace. I need to take your picture."

"This feels a bit too much like being back in high school," Amberlyn said, but she and Luke complied with the pastor's request.

They stepped in front of the fireplace, and Amberlyn slipped her arm around his waist. Luke took advantage of the moment and wrapped his arm around her shoulder. Then Pastor Mosley was taking one photo after another.

It really was like being back in high school, only Luke had never taken a date to a big dance. He'd never gone to any high school dance.

Finally, Pastor Mosley lowered his phone. "I'll send these to you."

"Thanks," Luke said. He rather liked the idea of having a photo of him and Amberlyn on his phone.

Amberlyn stepped away. "We should get going. We want to go for fashionably late, not so late that people are already leaving."

There were a few people he wouldn't mind missing tonight, but this wasn't really a date. It was work, and work dictated that they talk to everyone, even those who despised him.

"You two have fun tonight," Pastor Mosley said.

Luke wasn't counting on it, but he offered the expected response. "Thanks."

Amberlyn slipped her arms into her coat, and Luke held the back so she could put it on more easily.

"Thank you," she said.

"You're welcome." Luke opened the house door to the garage, and Amberlyn passed through, opening the garage door on her way to the car.

As soon as they were both settled in the car, Amberlyn said, "It's strange, but even though we've only been here a couple of days, I feel at home here."

"I know what you mean," Luke said. He'd always felt at home here. "I wish you could have met the pastor's wife. She was every bit as amazing as he is."

"He was married? What happened to his wife?"

"She passed away from cancer during my junior year of high school. She'd been fighting it for a few years."

Amberlyn put her hand on his before he could put the car in gear. "Wait. He helped you through high school, and the whole time his wife was either fighting cancer or he was grieving her loss?"

Luke had never really thought of it that way, but it was accurate enough. "Pretty much."

"He really is an amazing man."

"Yes, he is."

CHAPTER 35

SHEER WHITE CURTAINS hung from the basketball hoop in the high school gymnasium, flowing from the center to the sides of the open space to make a fanciful entryway, complete with twinkling lights and a muted spotlight aimed at the area on the floor just beyond the curtains. Katy Perry's "Roar" carried to them along with the underlying buzz of voices.

With her hand on Luke's arm, Amberlyn passed through the opening and into the spotlight. The music stopped in that moment, and it was as though everyone inside turned toward them.

More than two hundred people already occupied the space inside, some sitting at the round tables scattered around the edges of the gym, others crowded near the center of the basketball court, which was likely being used as a dance floor. Still others lingered by the bar at the far side of the room and the refreshment table that lay beyond it.

Amberlyn had always liked the movie *Cinderella*, particularly the moment when she stepped into the ball and all eyes were drawn to her. Now that she was living such a moment, she wasn't so sure she cared to be the center of attention.

Luke must not have appreciated the sensation either because he put his hand on her back and guided her forward. Her heartbeat quickened at his touch, but she tried to ignore it. She was supposed to be working—and not on the attraction she felt for Luke.

The next song started, Taylor Swift's voice now providing the background music.

Luke leaned closer. "Do you want something to drink?"

"Sure. A Sprite would be great."

"I'll be right back." He started toward the bar and made it halfway there when Gavin stepped out of a nearby crowd and pointed at Luke.

"There he is." Gavin strode across the room and cut Luke off. "You're the reason I spent the last two days inside a cell."

"It wasn't me."

"Then, your girlfriend over there." He pointed at Amberlyn as a crowd slowly formed around Luke and Gavin, Amberlyn getting pushed to the front of it as others moved in.

"She comes in here, throwing her badge around. Did you tell her to come harass me?"

Julia edged forward. "I thought you were a teacher."

There was no denying her true profession now.

"I was a teacher," Amberlyn said. "Luke and I thought people would be uneasy if they knew what I really do for a living."

"What do you do?" Russ asked pointedly.

"She's a fed." Gavin pointed again, only this time his finger came far too close to Amberlyn for comfort. She nearly brought her hand up to block his forward movement, but Luke stepped between them before she could react.

"She was doing her job," Luke said evenly. "If you'd answered her questions, you wouldn't have spent two nights in jail."

"My life is none of her business."

"It became her business when she found out you were talking on the phone with the woman who tried to kill us."

An audible gasp rippled through the crowd.

As though empowered by their surprise, Luke straightened his shoulders. "What else are you hiding, Gavin? Were you also helping her bomb the FEMA building in Kansas City? You were out of town that day."

Gavin's face reddened.

Amberlyn didn't know how Luke saw the punch coming, but when Gavin's fist flew at him, Luke ducked and let the punch catch nothing but air. The lack of contact threw Gavin off balance, and he stumbled forward.

Amberlyn took a quick step back to make sure she didn't end up in the danger zone. The crowd followed her lead, the circle widening as though everyone were preparing to watch a professional boxing match instead of an ill-tempered bully trying to flex his muscles.

Luke moved several steps to the side and held out both hands. "I don't want to fight you."

His calm voice was like a poker stirring embers into a flame. Gavin charged forward and swung again. Luke evaded again.

Gavin growled in frustration.

"Where were you?" Luke asked again. "Where did you go after Brad dropped you off in Roanoke?"

The obscenity that came from Gavin's mouth was both crude and predictable. He lifted both fists.

"I'm telling you, you don't want to do this," Luke said, his hands lifted in front of him as though he were surrendering.

Amberlyn knew better. No matter how much Luke might have been bullied during high school, he was a Marine now. The way he held his hands, the way he circled slightly to change Gavin's attack angle—everything in his demeanor was textbook defense.

Gavin charged forward again, but this time, Luke grabbed his fist. In a blur of movement, Luke twisted Gavin's arm behind his back, gripping it tightly while Luke hooked his free arm around Gavin's throat.

"Where were you the day of the Kansas City bombing?" Luke asked again.

Another expletive colored the air.

Luke tightened his hold. "Where . . . were . . . you?"

Savannah, the redhead from the game last night, stepped forward. "Luke, let him go."

Her friend Chelsey looked from Luke and Gavin to Savannah. "Oh my gosh. It was you. You're the one sneaking around with Gavin."

Anxious to uncover any information she could, Amberlyn stepped forward. "What makes you think that?"

"We were supposed to go to the spa that weekend, but then Savannah got the chance to spend the weekend at a cabin at Smith Mountain Lake, and suddenly, I wasn't invited." Chelsey shook her head. "You were there with Gavin, weren't you?" Not giving Savannah a chance to answer, she pushed on. "How could you? Felicia is one of our best friends."

"Is that true, Savannah?" Amberlyn asked. She sensed that Savannah was about to give her a practiced lie, and Amberlyn held up her hand. "And before you answer, I'll remind you that making a false statement to a federal officer is a crime."

Savannah paled, and she swallowed hard. "Fine. Gavin was with me at a cabin at Smith Mountain Lake." She cast a quick look of apology at Gavin's wife before she continued. "A friend of ours let us use it for free."

"What friend?" Felicia Pennington demanded. "Who was helping you sneak around with my husband?"

Savannah fell silent, but Felicia's question resonated with Amberlyn. The dates Gavin had been gone were the exact dates their bomber would have been in Missouri. Could the bomber have deliberately left Gavin without an alibi in case he needed a scapegoat?

She stepped forward. "Who gave you the cabin to use?" When Savannah didn't immediately answer, Amberlyn said, "You can either tell me here, or I can haul you down to the police station."

"It was Trevor Moran."

"Kyle's brother?" Luke asked.

"Yeah. He works for a property management company," Savannah said. "Sometimes he gets good deals on the vacation rentals."

"But you said he gave you this one for free."

"Yeah."

"Had he ever done that before?" Amberlyn pressed.

"No."

Amberlyn turned toward Luke, her suspicions reflected in his eyes.

"Does Trevor Moran have Kyle's championship ring?" Luke asked.

Savannah didn't answer, but Chelsey stepped forward. "He has it. He wears it all the time."

"Any chance he also has the tattoo on his wrist?" Luke asked.

Chelsey nodded. "He got one about a month after Kyle died."

Amberlyn focused on Luke again. "We've got to go."

Luke pushed Gavin toward Russ and Brad. "You'd best keep him away from me and Amberlyn, or he's going to end up back inside that jail cell."

The two men each grabbed Gavin by an arm and nodded.

Amberlyn turned toward the door, but Luke backed away as though ensuring no one was following. When they reached the gym exit, he turned and headed for the outside door.

"How long will it take to get a search warrant?"

"An hour. Maybe two."

"Someone in there is bound to call him," Luke said.

"Then, we'd better find out where he lives."

"Stakeout?"

"Oh, no. We're bringing him in for questioning."

"That works too."

———

Luke hadn't wanted to go to his reunion, but he could admit now that he was disappointed that he and Amberlyn had left before he'd even had the chance to dance with her.

She hung up with whomever she'd called to request the search warrant of Trevor Moran's house as they reached her car. "The sheriff is going to bring him in for questioning while we wait for the search warrant."

"Do you want to go to his house or straight to the police station?"

"His house." Amberlyn climbed into the car. "I don't want to take the chance of him getting away because they don't have enough backup."

He slid behind the wheel, his muscles still vibrating from the lingering adrenaline from his run-in with Gavin. He hadn't been looking for a fight, and he considered himself lucky that Gavin's friends hadn't decided to join in on trying to make Luke a punching bag.

As soon as Luke slid behind the wheel, he asked Amberlyn, "Do you care if we're seen in your car?"

"If someone calls him, it won't matter which car we're in. He'll notice us."

"True."

She turned her phone toward him to show him the address.

"That's on the other side of town." Luke put the car in gear and turned onto Main Street. "Sorry we had to leave so fast."

"We got what we went there for." Amberlyn glanced at him. "I hope."

"Me too." But he still would have liked a little more time to watch Amberlyn under the twinkling lights.

"I was impressed with how you handled Gavin," Amberlyn said. "That couldn't have been easy."

"He was too emotional to be a real threat."

"Maybe so, but you had the chance to get some good punches in, and you didn't take them. That takes a lot of discipline."

"It was common sense." Luke held up his right hand. "Gavin wasn't worth bruising my knuckles over."

"I'm glad you know that."

Luke pulled up to a red light and tapped his fingers on the wheel impatiently. Best case, it would take ten minutes to drive to Trevor Moran's house. Hitting the red lights along Main Street would easily add another minute or two.

"Do you think someone will call and warn him?" Amberlyn asked.

"Oh yeah," Luke said. "No one will believe he could do something like this."

"Most people are shocked when they find out their friend or neighbor or even a loved one was involved in a violent crime."

The light turned, and Luke accelerated so he could make the next light before it turned. He sped through as it blinked to yellow.

"Do you think he really set Gavin up to be the fall guy in case someone traced him back to Pine Falls?" Luke asked.

"That's exactly what I think," Amberlyn said. "He wasn't even on our radar."

"On a Saturday night, we won't be able to check his work records."

"Probably not, but we'll be able to hold him until Monday night. Hopefully, we'll find the evidence we need to tie him to the bombing."

"He certainly had motive," Luke said. "In a twisted sort of way."

"Terrorism—whether it's foreign or domestic—is always twisted."

"True."

When they finally arrived at Trevor Moran's house, two police cars were already parked out front. Luke parked across the street, and one of the deputies, a woman in her thirties, approached.

"I'm sorry," she said. "You can't park here."

Amberlyn held up her badge. "Special Agent Reiner, FBI."

"Is he in there?" Luke asked.

"If he is, he isn't answering," the deputy said.

"The search warrant should be here within an hour. I need someone to stake out this house to make sure no one leaves," Amberlyn said.

"I figured you'd say that." The deputy motioned at the car parked closest to the mailbox. "Branson there will stay. I'll circle back as soon as the warrant comes through."

Amberlyn's phone chimed, and she glanced at the screen. "Looks like we don't need to wait." She held up her cell. "The warrant came through."

The deputy leaned closer and read her screen. "In that case, let's see if he's in there."

Amberlyn climbed out of the car. She took one step forward before Luke was at her side. He put his hand on her arm.

"I know you'd love to be the one to put the cuffs on him, but you aren't exactly dressed for a confrontation."

She looked down at her dress, the fabric falling nearly to the ground. "I hate that you're right." She spoke to the deputy. "I'll cover you from out here."

Luke and Amberlyn both stepped behind her car so they were shielded in case Trevor came out shooting. They needn't have bothered. Less than two minutes after the two deputies entered the house, they came back outside empty-handed.

The woman they had spoken to before approached them. "He's not here."

"What about his car?" Amberlyn asked.

"Branson, check the garage."

The younger deputy disappeared back inside. He returned a moment later. "His car is still in there."

"Then what's he driving?" the first deputy asked.

Luke glanced at Amberlyn briefly before sharing his suspicions. "Best guess, a newly painted blue Camry with Kansas plates."

CHAPTER 36

AMBERLYN GRIPPED HER hands in her lap. They were so close. Again. Three times now, they had identified a promising suspect. She really hoped the third time was the charm and that the sheriff's department would locate Trevor Moran before he could strike again.

Luke pulled onto the road and headed back toward Main Street. "If he left right after the game last night, he could be halfway across the country."

She much preferred the possibility that he was still hiding somewhere nearby. "I'll put in the request to ping his cell phone."

"Probably ought to request his phone records too," Luke said. "If he is close by, that will tell us who told him we were coming."

Amberlyn added that to her request and sent it to Whitley. She suspected he was putting in nearly as much overtime as she was this week.

Luke continued past the turn into Pastor Mosley's neighborhood.

"Where are we going?"

"Since Trevor Moran wasn't home, I thought we would go to our next best source of information."

"Who?"

"Cynthia, at the diner." He reached the parking lot and gestured toward the white SUV parked by the entrance. "Looks like the pastor is here too."

"We can get insight from both of them." Amberlyn pushed open her door and headed for the entrance, Luke falling into step beside her.

When they walked into the diner, Pastor Mosley sat at the serving bar, Cynthia standing across from him.

Pastor Mosley glanced at the door. "What are the two of you doing here?"

Luke put his hand on the small of Amberlyn's back, waiting until they were beside the pastor before he spoke. "We're looking for information, and you're just the two who can give it to us."

The pastor motioned for them to sit.

Amberlyn took a stool beside the pastor. "What do you know about Trevor Moran?"

"Oh, that poor boy." Cynthia straightened the salt and pepper shakers on the counter. "Losing his brother the way he did. He just hasn't been the same since."

Amberlyn keyed in on Cynthia's comment. "How did he change?"

"There's just such an anger in him now." Cynthia shook her head. "It's like the light in him was snuffed out as soon as he heard the news."

"You don't think Trevor is the one you're looking for, do you?" Pastor Mosley asked.

"It's looking that way," Luke said.

"He wasn't home when we stopped by to talk to him," Amberlyn added. No need to announce to Cynthia that she was FBI. "Have you seen him since the game last night?"

Cynthia pondered for a moment. "I can't say that I have."

The bell above the door jingled, and Amberlyn glanced over her shoulder. To her surprise, Brad, Mikayla, Russ, and Julia walked in, along with Savannah.

"This place is all sorts of fancy tonight," Cynthia said.

Luke stood and squared off against the newcomers. "What are you all doing here?"

"Are you really with the FBI?" Russ asked Amberlyn.

Amberlyn stood. "Yes, I am."

"Savannah here needs to talk to you, then," Brad said.

"I'm listening," Amberlyn said. She cast her gaze at Pastor Mosley and Cynthia before motioning to an empty table in the far corner. "Maybe we can talk over there."

"Go ahead." Cynthia waved at the main section of the diner. "Just holler if you need anything."

"Thanks, Cynthia," Julia said.

They all moved to the table, Luke and Russ grabbing extra chairs so there would be enough for everyone.

Amberlyn sat across from Savannah. "What do you know?"

"The woman who you said tried to kill you?"

"Yeah."

"She was with Trevor when I picked up the keys for the cabin."

"Did you happen to see what car she was driving?" Amberlyn asked.

"It was a white Toyota Camry, but I don't think it stayed white for long." She fiddled with the saltshaker in front of her. "Gavin was supposed to paint it for her. It was like he was repaying the favor for Trevor Moran getting us the cabin."

"Any chance you remember the license plate number?"

"Part of it. The letters were OMW. I thought it was funny because those are the same letters Gavin would send me when he was coming to see me."

OMW. On my way.

"Any idea why Gavin was so uncooperative when we questioned him?" Amberlyn asked.

"He knew if his wife found out he was cheating on her again, she'd file for divorce." Her eyes teared up. "I didn't plan for this to happen."

"What else can you tell us about Trevor?" Amberlyn asked gently. "What happened to him after his brother died?"

Brad spoke now. "That boy was spouting off all kinds of crazy. Said it was the government's fault for not shutting the roads down when they saw the weather coming in."

"He was convinced that if Kyle hadn't left town, he'd still be alive today," Mikayla added.

"Did he ever say anything about FEMA?" Luke asked.

Mikayla wrinkled her nose. "Only that the people working there were a waste of skin."

The comment, though innocently shared, pierced straight to Amberlyn's heart. Chanelle had never been a waste of anything.

Luke stretched his arm around her and squeezed her shoulder.

"Anyone else he talked like that about?" Luke asked, saving her from forming the next question.

"Lots of people," Russ said.

"Yeah." Brad nodded. "Everyone from the football coach who helped him get the scholarship to Iowa State to the governor of Nebraska for not declaring a state of emergency."

"Do you know how he might have found out about me being FBI?" Amberlyn asked.

"I don't know," Russ said. "We didn't know that until Gavin told us."

"Was he here at the diner when Owen Lester told you Amberlyn's real last name?" Luke asked.

Julia narrowed her eyes. "Come to think of it, I think he was."

"How did you know about that?" Savannah asked Amberlyn.

"Like I said, I'm FBI."

CHAPTER 37

LUKE STOOD IN the guest room and debated whether he could negotiate another day in Pine Falls, but he already knew the answer. He had a job to do at the White House, and no matter how much he wanted to help Amberlyn, he wasn't a law enforcement officer. She was.

The conversation at the diner last night had lasted the better part of two hours, but by the end of it, he and Amberlyn still hadn't managed to narrow down a single bombing target.

Logically, the target would be in Nebraska. But if that were the case, why would Hallie Norris drive here? Surely she could have had someone in Missouri paint the car.

This morning, they had received the update from the sheriff to let them know that Trevor's phone had been left in his car. Whether the text from one of Trevor's former girlfriends had prompted him to hide or whether he had already left, they couldn't be sure. Regardless, the search for Trevor continued, so far without success.

Luke's new duffel bag lay on his bed, his clothing arranged haphazardly beside it. Amberlyn had packed her clothes before they'd left for church this morning, but Luke had put off that task, hoping he could change out of his suit before their drive home. He should have known he'd need to wear a tie to the youth center open house tonight.

He placed his jeans and a T-shirt on top in the hope that he would be able to change at the youth center before they headed north. He took one last look around before he carried his duffel bag downstairs.

Pastor Mosley sat in his favorite chair in the living room, the Bible open in front of him, a pad of paper at his elbow. He scribbled something down before he looked up.

"Didn't mean to interrupt your preparations," Luke said.

"I'm ready for tonight. This is for next week."

"Where's Amberlyn?"

"She went to put her suitcase in the car."

"I have a question for you." Luke sat on the couch. "Can you think of a reason why Trevor might want to frame Gavin?"

"One or two."

"Any you can tell me about?"

"I don't normally share stories that are mere speculation, but if this rumor is true, it may give you some much-needed insight."

Amberlyn walked in. "What rumor?"

Pastor Mosley steepled his fingers together and waited for Amberlyn to sit before he spoke. "A couple years back, Trevor's younger sister had a baby out of wedlock. She never said who the father was, but she'd been working for the same office as Gavin at the time she got pregnant."

"You think Gavin was the father?"

"I can't speak to that, but there were rumors to that end."

"In a town this size, you can be sure Trevor would have heard them," Amberlyn said.

"It's also possible Trevor's sister told him who the father is, but that's not much of a motive for framing someone for a terrorist attack," Luke said.

Amberlyn gripped her hands together. "Not for a normal person, but if he's really part of Forever Freedom, if he helped set off that bomb in Kansas City, he's a long way from normal—or balanced."

Pastor Mosley glanced at his watch and pushed to a stand. "We should get going. The program is going to start in an hour."

Luke turned to Amberlyn. "Do you want to stop by and pick up the rental car from the hospital now or after the program?"

"Let's get it now and turn it in beforehand," Amberlyn said. "That will save us from having to stop in Roanoke on our way home."

Pastor Mosley headed for the garage. "I'll see you both over there."

As soon as the pastor left, Luke said, "I can always use the rental to drive home if you need to stay here longer."

Amberlyn shook her head. "My job was to help identify who was in the photo from St. Louis. We did that." She stood. "And I'd rather not make that drive alone."

"That makes two of us."

———

Amberlyn added lemon slices to the decorative water dispenser that would be used on the refreshment table. She and Luke had barely arrived before they'd been enlisted to help set up. And for the past thirty minutes, she couldn't stop thinking about where the next target would be.

Luke entered the kitchen and motioned to the full water dispenser. "Is that ready to go?"

"Yes, but be careful. It's heavy."

He lifted it. "Can you grab the door?"

"No problem." She led the way into the large classroom that was being used to serve the refreshments.

Mrs. Bowman followed with a plate of cookies covered in plastic wrap. "I think that will do for now. We should get in there. The program will be starting any minute."

They headed into the multipurpose room, where all the seats were filled and several more people stood along the back wall.

"Wow. This is a way bigger turnout than I expected," Luke said.

Pastor Mosley offered an opening prayer and then turned the time over to Reverend Bowman.

"Reverend Bowman," Amberlyn whispered the name to Luke. "Wasn't he the one who helped Kyle get his scholarship?"

"Yes. He and the football coach. The Gomezes too."

Amberlyn spotted Mr. and Mrs. Gomez a few rows up. An unsettling thought surged through her. "Is the football coach here too?"

"It's possible." Luke stood up on his toes and scanned the room. "I don't see him, but there are so many people here, he could be up front."

Pastor Mosley made his way toward them. He motioned to the front of the room. "I have a couple seats saved for you two up front."

Her uneasiness still churning inside her, Amberlyn repeated her question to Pastor Mosley. "Is the football coach here today?"

"Yes. He's in the second row."

Amberlyn went over the basic floor plan in her mind. If her sense of direction was correct, the length of this room ran alongside the storage bay they had cut through the first time they'd visited the youth center.

Could this be Trevor Moran's target? Though improbable, Amberlyn grabbed Luke's arm and tugged. "We need to do a security check."

"What?"

"The reverend, the Gomezes, and the football coach are all people Trevor blamed for Kyle's death."

"The way this community came together to help Kyle succeed in school and find scholarships is the backbone of how we set up this youth program," Pastor Mosley said.

Luke's face paled, and he rushed back through the door they had just entered.

Pastor Mosley joined them in the hall. "I'm coming with you."

"Don't you need to be here for the program?" Luke asked.

"My work is done, and this is more important. It'll go faster if there are three of us." He moved toward the loading bay door. "I'll check out the interior."

"I'll take the front parking lot," Luke said.

"Then I'll take the side lot," Amberlyn said. "We're looking for a blue Camry, Kansas license plates starting with 'OMW.'"

Amberlyn and Luke both headed for the main entrance.

"I really hope you're wrong about this," Luke said as he headed outside.

"Me too."

———————

Luke moved toward the front lot and scanned for a blue Camry, focusing on the vehicles closest to the building. He located one a few spots over that fit the description and another a row over. Two more Camrys were also in the lot, but of different colors.

Luke approached the nearest blue Camry first. It had Virginia plates and a county inspection sticker on the windshield. He peered through the driver's side window. A car seat in the back, Cheerios spilled on the floor, a water bottle in the cup holder. If this car contained a bomb, it was camouflaged well.

Not wanting to take any chances, he tried the door handle. It opened.

"Gotta love small towns." Luke popped the trunk only to find a stroller and a few canvas shopping bags.

He closed the trunk and moved to the next blue Camry. This one appeared to belong to a teenager. Wrappers from various fast-food restaurants littered the floor, and both cup holders contained partially full drinks in paper cups with straws sticking out of the lids.

Music filled the air despite the soundproofing the pastor had told them about. If it was this loud, he could only imagine how bad it would be without the preventive measures.

Luke tried the door handle, but this time, he found it locked. He was debating whether to try to break in when he caught a glimpse of movement out of the corner of his eye.

He turned toward it, but before he could focus on the man's face, he spotted the weapon in his hand.

Luke dove for the ground in the same moment a gunshot rang out. The ping of the bullet impacting the truck behind him sounded a split second later. That muted sound brought with it a terrifying clarity. If someone was shooting at him here, Amberlyn was right. This was the target. He couldn't be sure if the armed man had planted another bomb or if he had another type of violence in mind, but the only reason to shoot at Luke was if he had gotten close enough to interfere with his plans.

Fear for those inside—innocent men, women, and children—rose inside him. He had to do something. He couldn't let those people die.

Unarmed and with the music masking both the gunshots and the man's movements, Luke had only one choice. He visualized where he had parked an hour earlier. Then, keeping his head down, he sprinted from the spot behind the Camry to the next car over. Another shot rang out when he darted behind an SUV.

Would Amberlyn and Pastor Mosley hear the shots? Luke wasn't sure whether he wanted the answer to be yes or no.

He needed to make it past three more cars to reach Amberlyn's SUV, three more times that he would be exposed to the gunman's bullets.

Amberlyn's voice rang out. "FBI. Freeze!"

Luke took advantage of the distraction and raced forward. Another shot fired, this one knocking off a side mirror as he passed.

"Luke, get down!" she shouted, two more shots ringing out from two different directions.

Amberlyn needn't have bothered shouting the warning. Luke dove for the ground as another gunfire exchange sounded.

Luke grabbed the car keys from his pocket and clicked the unlock button.

The music stopped, and Luke peeked around the edge of the SUV. He spotted the gunman crouched behind Russ's Corvette, two bullet holes in the front fender. Russ was not going to be happy.

Amberlyn wasn't visible, but judging from the direction of the earlier gunfire and the angle the gunman was facing, he suspected she'd taken cover behind either the silver Lexus sedan or the black Chevy truck.

Several cars behind where Amberlyn was hiding, a car door opened, and a man climbed out.

Luke started to shout a warning for the man to stay where he was, but when the man lifted his hand and Luke spotted the pistol he held, another warning burst from him. "Bryn! Behind you!"

CHAPTER 38

AMBERLYN SCRAMBLED AROUND the edge of the Chevy truck and ducked beneath it. A gunman behind her, another in front of her. She was trapped, and she was right—this new facility was Trevor Moran's target.

An image of Chanelle filled her mind, a reminder that no one should have to go through such a tragic loss.

With her heartbeat already racing, she debated her options. She needed a better angle, somewhere she could fire at the men trying to shoot her and Luke without being an easy target.

To the right or the left. Luke was already to her right, and though the thought of joining him brought a sense of security, she knew better. Just like Pastor Mosley had said, their cell phones weren't working, so there was no way to call for backup. They couldn't risk being together and possibly getting trapped, as she was now.

Dropping to her stomach, she engaged the safety on her weapon, drew a deep breath, and rolled to her left until she reached the spot beneath a silver sedan.

Another gunshot fired, and her breath whooshed out of her.

Fighting for calm, she remained on her stomach as she scooted farther under the vehicle, continuing until she reached the other side. Her shoe caught on the pavement, and she let the heel fall off. She toed off the second one and ignored the chill seeping into her.

Once again, she gathered her courage and rolled out from under that car and under the next.

The music inside the building had stopped, and she heard footsteps approaching. She scooted farther under the car, terror rising inside her. A new song started inside the youth center, once again masking the approach of the nearest gunman. When Amberlyn reached the far side of the car, she flipped off the safety on her weapon and rolled out from under the car, this time stopping when she was on her back. She lifted her gun, spotted the movement of the man shadowing her, and fired once.

A second gunshot joined hers.

Amberlyn didn't wait to find out if the man was hit. She rolled again, under the next car, and took cover.

The music had started again by the time Luke had squeezed off another shot and forced the man shadowing Amberlyn to take cover. The man ducked at the same time his partner popped into view.

Luke adjusted his position and fired again before dropping back behind Amberlyn's car.

Leaving the trunk open and the now-empty gun case beside their luggage, Luke rounded the back side of the vehicle and raced between the cars toward the man trying to shoot Amberlyn.

The line of cars protected him from the first shooter but would leave him vulnerable to the one by Amberlyn. It couldn't be helped.

Luke kept his weapon raised, ready to fire at the first sign of movement, as he continued forward.

The man remained crouched for several seconds. Luke was within a few car lengths of him when he emerged again. The gun appeared first, and the man fired blindly.

A window shattered, glass raining onto the pavement, but Luke kept going.

His focus entirely on the man trying to kill him, Luke ducked down as a bullet whizzed over his head and impacted the car right behind where he had been a second ago. He didn't see the high heel in his path until it was too late.

He tripped and fell to the ground, his left knee impacting the pavement a split second before his right. His left hand hit next as he used it to break his fall and protect the weapon still gripped in his right hand.

Pain shot through his knee, but he didn't have time to consider what damage the fall might have caused.

He righted himself and continued forward until he reached the car between him and the shooter.

The next song started, the electric guitar ringing out with far too much volume.

"Give it up!" Luke called out over the music.

No response.

Hoping to get a better handle on the man's position, Luke dropped down and peeked under the car in the hope of seeing the gunman's feet. Nothing.

Luke could circle the rear. He was closest to the back. If he tried to go around the front, he would be in the direct line of fire of the man's partner. He also wasn't sure what to think about the way the men were staying on the outer edges of the parking lot. Could that be because they were protecting themselves against an inevitable explosion?

Luke spotted Amberlyn peeking out from beneath the car. When she glanced his way, he pressed his hand to his chest and pointed toward the front of the vehicle. He then mouthed the words, "Cover me."

She nodded.

Luke lowered his head and crept forward until he reached the hood. Then he lifted his left hand, three fingers raised. He dropped his fingers one at a time until his hand became a fist.

Amberlyn fired a shot toward the other gunman. Luke popped up and sighted the gunman closest to him. The man stood beside the passenger door, his back to Luke.

"Drop it!" Luke demanded as Amberlyn fired off two more shots of cover fire.

The gunman in Luke's sights didn't comply, instead turning toward Luke, leading with his gun.

With no other choice, Luke fired his weapon, the bullet impacting the man's chest.

Luke ducked back down and took cover. The music stopped, and the wounded man dropped to the ground.

With the gunman closest to her neutralized, Amberlyn abandoned her spot under the car and joined Luke where he had taken cover between the red Mustang that no longer had its windshield and the silver Corolla. A piece of glass cut into her bare foot, and she winced.

"Are you okay?" Luke asked.

Her dress was torn, her knees were skinned, and her foot was bleeding, but she nodded.

"We need to make sure the guy on the other side of here is really down."

"I'll check him." Luke headed for the back of the vehicle, a slight limp noticeable every time he stepped on his left foot.

Amberlyn leaned down and pulled the small chunk of glass out of her foot, then carefully followed Luke to bypass the rest of the glass glittering on the ground in the opposite direction.

She reached the trunk at the same time Luke did. He now had a gun in each hand.

"He's still alive, but he's not going anywhere."

"Was it Trevor?" Amberlyn asked.

"No. I don't know who that guy is."

"With the way these guys are sticking to the far side of the lot, it makes me think there really might be a bomb in play here."

"I had the same thought, but we can't do much about that until we make sure we won't get shot." Luke surveyed their surroundings before bringing his gaze back to her. "Try to work your way over to that black Honda." He jutted his chin toward a car one row in front of them and three cars over from Russ's beloved Corvette, where the other shooter remained hidden. "I'll circle to the other side of the lot to see if we can flank him."

"You head for the Honda, and I'll circle to the other side of him," Amberlyn said, changing the plan.

"Why? I'm pretty sure I'm faster than you."

"Maybe under normal circumstances, but right now, you're limping. I'm not."

"You also have no shoes on."

"Which means it will be harder for him to hear me coming even when the music isn't playing."

Though Luke clearly struggled with the idea of her taking the more dangerous role in his plan, he nodded. "Be careful."

She put her free hand on his arm and squeezed. "You too."

CHAPTER 39

LUKE HAD TO give Amberlyn credit. She knew how to stay out of sight, and she was right. Without her shoes on, she was impossible to hear.

He fired a shot to cover her, first using the downed gunman's weapon to clear the bullet in the chamber before discarding it and reloading his own.

He scanned the parking lot for any sign of another gunman. He didn't recognize the man he'd shot. It wasn't Trevor Moran, and unless Kyle's brother's hair had darkened from blonde to dark brown after the game on Friday, the second shooter wasn't Trevor either.

The music finally stopped again, and Luke suspected Reverend Bowman would be starting on what would likely be a long-winded thank-you speech. Luke hoped it would be lengthy. The last thing they needed right now was a crowd of people coming out.

A door opened, but it wasn't the main entrance. Rather, the sound had originated from the warehouse, where Pastor Mosley was searching.

Fear for his longtime friend rushed through Luke, and he aimed at the remaining gunman in case he tried to shoot.

When the door slammed close, Luke glanced in the direction of the warehouse. Had the pastor heard the gunfire, or had the sound been lost beneath the beat of the drums? All of the exchanges had occurred while the music had been playing, as though the gunmen hadn't wanted anyone inside to know of the looming danger.

When the door opened again and slammed closed a second time without any movement, Luke suspected the pastor was aware of what was going on and was trying to create a distraction. Unfortunately, the gunman wasn't falling for it. He remained tucked safely behind the Corvette.

He wasn't moving. That fact registered as an oddity. The man was outnumbered and outgunned. He had to have figured that out by now. So why was he content to remain where he was, where he might very well end up trapped? Unless there really was a bomb and the man didn't want to enter the blast zone.

The bomb had to be close by. Amberlyn was sure of it.

A door opened and slammed a third time in as many minutes. At first, she thought it was the pastor trying to create a distraction, but now she suspected he was trying to signal them. But signal them for what, she wasn't sure.

She crept forward, her feet numb from the cold, the stickiness of the blood coming from the bottom of her foot leaving a trail behind her. Only another few yards.

She kept her body low as she moved into position and placed her left hand on the car in front of her. If she was right, the gunman should be in her gunsights only two rows in front of her. Or he would be once she gathered the courage to look over the top of the car.

The door in the distance opened and slammed again.

A sense of urgency rushed through her, and she uttered a silent prayer that she, Luke, and any potential innocent bystanders would be protected. Then with a quick count to three, she put both hands on her weapon, straightened, and took aim.

"Federal officer. Drop it!"

The gunman turned and aimed, once again ignoring her directive.

With only the briefest of hesitations, Amberlyn followed her training and squeezed the trigger.

The bullet impacted his shoulder, and his body jerked back, but the weapon remained in his hand. He lifted it again, and Amberlyn fired a second time. Another shot rang out in tandem with her own.

This time, the gunman stumbled forward, grabbing onto the side of the Corvette before sliding to the pavement.

Amberlyn rushed forward, her weapon still at the ready. She stepped on the gunman's wrist to ensure he couldn't get off another shot and kicked the gun free with her other foot.

Footsteps rushed toward her, and she glanced up as Luke approached at full speed despite his obvious limp.

The man on the ground was still breathing.

"We need an ambulance," Amberlyn said.

Luke pulled out his phone and held it up. "I'm not getting a signal."

Amberlyn nodded toward the nearby neighborhood. "We can use the landline inside."

"Not until we find the bomb and Trevor Moran."

Amberlyn looked up. "This isn't him?"

"No, it isn't."

Pastor Mosley called out from the warehouse door. "I need a little help over here."

"You help him," Luke said. "I'll finish the search of the parking lot."

"Be careful."

Luke nodded. "We need to spend time together when we don't need to tell each other that."

"I know."

"Amberlyn?"

"Yeah?"

"You be careful too."

"I will." She hurried across the parking lot as quickly as her numb feet would take her.

Pushing the door open, she stepped into the brightly lit storehouse area. Inside, a blue Camry was parked right beside the wall directly behind the multipurpose room, Pastor Mosley standing beside the open trunk, a pair of wire cutters in one hand and a flashlight in the other.

"How much bomb ordnance training have you had?" he asked.

"Just what they taught me at the Academy."

"Come here." He waved her forward. "Hold these wires for me. I need to get a better look at the detonator."

Amberlyn followed his instructions, though she focused on the door leading into the youth center. "We need to evacuate. There has to be over two hundred people in there."

"No. If Trevor is out there, he'll detonate before half of them clear the blast area."

"How would he be able to do that?" Amberlyn asked as the pastor shined a flashlight on the tangle of wires. "The cell service is down."

"I have a feeling it's a signal jammer causing that rather than a downed cell tower like we thought. Best guess is the only reason we're still alive is the signal jammer is within the blast radius. Trevor won't come too close until he knows if the primary detonator sets off the bomb." He motioned to the left side of the wires. "Lift that a little higher."

If the pastor was right, even if they did defuse the bomb, Trevor would be able to shut off the jammer and call the secondary detonator to set it off. Amberlyn pulled her cell phone from her pocket and checked the signal. Still none.

"How much time do we have?"

"Three minutes, forty-two seconds."

"Do you know how to defuse this?" Amberlyn asked.

"I hope so." He held the flashlight out to her. "Hold this for me."

Amberlyn set her phone down in the trunk beside the bomb and took the flashlight. "I'm praying that you'll cut the right wire."

"The Lord has been hearing that prayer since the minute I found the bomb."

CHAPTER 40

LUKE ROUNDED THE corner on the back side of the youth center and headed for the warehouse bay door. He made it only a step inside before he spotted the blue Camry with the Kansas plates, Amberlyn and Pastor Mosley on opposite sides of the open trunk, both leaning in.

Luke rushed forward and confirmed his fears. A bomb lay inside, only forty-nine seconds left on the timer.

"We need to get out of here." Luke put one hand on Amberlyn's shoulder and gestured to Pastor Mosley with the other. He'd haul both of them out of the building if needed.

"Another fifteen seconds," Pastor Mosley said.

"I've almost got it." Amberlyn continued to separate the wires. "You sure it's this one?"

Thirty seconds.

Twenty-nine.

"Trust me." Pastor Mosley slid a pair of wire cutters into place while Amberlyn pulled the others away. "This is the one."

Luke nodded. His analysis matched his old friend's.

Twenty.

Nineteen.

"If you're going to try, clip the wire now. You're out of time," Luke said.

Fifteen seconds.

Pastor Mosley drew a deep breath as the timer dropped to fourteen. He snipped the wire.

The detonator froze at thirteen.

"Help me disconnect the secondary detonator," Pastor Mosley said.

Luke stepped closer and gently lifted the housing of the two detonators so the pastor could remove the cell phone attached to it and eliminate any possibility of it being detonated remotely. "What can I do to help?" Amberlyn asked.

The pastor pulled his keys from his pocket. "Go inside and use my office phone to call the sheriff's office."

"I'll be right back." Amberlyn headed inside.

"That's one incredible woman you've got there." Pastor Mosley slid the wire clippers into place and disconnected the phone. "She's got nerves of steel."

Luke didn't disagree with Pastor Mosley's assessment, but he also didn't want to deceive his former preacher. "You know that this whole boyfriend/girlfriend thing is just for show, right?"

"It might have started that way, but I see the connection between you even if you don't."

Amberlyn returned a few minutes later, but she waited until the door closed behind her to speak. "The ambulances and the police are on their way. I also ran into Chaplain Miller inside. She's going to have Reverend Bowman drag out the program so the police have time to secure the crime scene before people start trying to leave. She'll guard the door to make sure no one tries to sneak out early."

"Smart thinking," Pastor Mosley said.

"Yeah," Luke added. "It really was."

She closed the distance between them and held up her hands. They both trembled. "I'm still shaking."

That made two of them, but Luke didn't mention it. "You were incredible out there."

"Thanks. You too." She looked at Pastor Mosley. "Both of you." She turned her attention back to Luke. "But just so you know, any time I hear you call me Bryn, I'm going to look for someone shooting."

"Good to know."

"Bryn?" Pastor Mosley asked.

Luke shrugged. He wasn't quite sure how he had shortened her name, but it had happened both times he'd needed her attention quickly.

When Luke didn't respond, Pastor Mosley asked, "Any sign of Trevor?"

"No," Luke said. "There were two men out there, but neither of them was Kyle's brother."

A cell phone rang. At first, Luke dismissed the sound since it wasn't his ringtone. Then logic caught up with him. Their phones hadn't been working a few minutes ago.

"Whose phone is that?" he asked.

"It isn't mine," Amberlyn said.

Pastor Mosley picked up the phone that still lay beside the explosive, the wire connecting it no longer intact. The phone went quiet, but the implication continued to ring loudly.

"He's got to be close by, or he wouldn't have been able to shut off the signal jammer and try to call the second detonator," Pastor Mosley said.

"I searched the parking lot and the area behind the building." Luke tried to visualize the exterior and places someone could hide.

"Maybe he was in one of the cars parked along the road," Amberlyn said.

"Or even behind one of the trees," Luke said.

Pastor Mosley nodded. "He'd want to keep some distance between him and the building to protect himself when the bomb detonated."

Sirens grew closer.

Gun in hand, Luke rushed to the door. Amberlyn and Pastor Mosley joined him.

The three of them emerged outside, all of them scanning.

"If he was by the front parking lot, he could have taken one of us out," Amberlyn said.

"So he has to be—" That was as far as Luke got before Pastor Mosley grabbed his arm and yanked him backward. At the same time, the pastor stepped in front of Amberlyn and yelled, "Gun!"

A gunshot rang out an instant later, and Pastor Mosley's body jerked as a bullet struck him, followed by a second.

"No!" Luke swung his pistol in the direction the pastor had been facing. Luke spotted movement behind a tree and fired.

———————

Amberlyn grabbed the pastor under both arms and dragged him back through the door. Luke fired several shots, but he was exposed with no cover.

She returned to the door as the gunman's weapon appeared from behind the tree, little more than the man's hand visible.

Luke kept shooting until his weapon clicked, his magazine now empty.

"Luke!" Amberlyn grabbed his arm and yanked him back through the door as more bullets flew through the air and impacted the door.

"Stay with the pastor," Amberlyn said. Some of those approaching sirens had to be police cars.

"But—"

"You're out of ammo, and I don't want you to go down too." Amberlyn glanced down at the pastor. She didn't have to be a medical professional to know that the shallow breathing and irregular heartbeat weren't good signs.

Luke holstered his gun and put his hand on the pastor's. "Just hold on, Pastor. Help is coming."

Determined to stop the gunman, Amberlyn sprinted for the door on the far side of the warehouse, which wasn't far from where she had spotted the shooter. Her bare feet throbbed from the cold concrete beneath her, but she didn't have time to worry about that now. The rescue personnel would be here any minute, and they had no idea what they were driving into.

Amberlyn flipped the lock open and slowly pushed the door wide enough to peer outside. No movement. The dumpster to her right became her first objective, and she sprinted the three yards to take position behind it.

A bullet pinged against metal, and she gripped her pistol. The man trying to kill her was the same person who had just shot Pastor Mosley. He was possibly the same person responsible for Chanelle's death.

A silent prayer for Pastor Mosley's survival circled through her mind and soared heavenward.

Amberlyn crept between the back of the dumpster and the building until she reached the far side. The rest of the space between her and the shooter across the street was open, except for a single delivery truck ten yards away.

The sirens continued to wail, and the first ambulance appeared down the road. Within seconds, it would come between Amberlyn and her target.

Amberlyn peeked out briefly, and instantly, another shot fired. She jumped back behind the dumpster, and her breath caught in her chest. She didn't need to look at the bullet hole in the wall to know it had struck a mere inch from where her head had been a moment ago. But she looked anyway. Her heart raced. That was far too close for comfort. Not that she would find any comfort while someone was shooting at her.

What was she doing? She was chasing an armed fanatic without backup. She should wait for the local law enforcement officers to get here before she abandoned her cover again.

But as soon as the ambulance drove between her and the shooter, creating a brief interruption in visibility, she darted out of her hiding place and rushed to the nearby delivery truck.

So much for logic.

She was now ten yards closer to the shooter, ten yards closer to danger. Crouching behind the hood of the large vehicle, she gripped her pistol with both hands. Then she popped up, using the truck for cover, and fired two shots.

Bark splintered beside the gunman as a police car raced toward them. A deputy jumped out, gun in hand, and aimed at Amberlyn rather than the man she was shooting at. "Drop your weapon!"

CHAPTER 41

THE SIRENS HAD stopped, and Luke rushed to the exit to find paramedics for the pastor, the pain in his knee shooting through him with every step.

An ambulance was parked on his left, and a deputy stood behind his car in the open space to Luke's right, his gun drawn. Luke followed the direction of where the weapon was pointed, hoping to see Trevor with his hands up or, better yet, already handcuffed. Instead, it was Amberlyn in the deputy's sights.

"She's FBI," Luke shouted. "The gunman's over there!"

He had barely spoken the words when Trevor burst from his hiding place and darted into the woods.

The deputy shifted his focus to the movement, but not before Trevor disappeared into the foliage.

Amberlyn lowered her weapon and took off in pursuit. Luke's stomach clutched at the thought of her running after a gunman through the woods, and in bare feet, no less.

Luke spotted a nearby ambulance attendant. "In here! Two bullets to the chest."

The ambulance attendant shouted at his partner before disappearing inside.

Satisfied that the pastor was now in more capable hands than his, Luke turned his attention to Amberlyn's retreating back.

With no viable weapon of his own, Luke waved at the deputy. "Circle around to the park entrance on Third Street. I'll go the other way." Luke didn't wait for the deputy to respond. Instead, he turned and sprinted toward Amberlyn's car. He dug the keys out of his pocket. A second ambulance pulled in as Luke reached Amberlyn's car, closed the trunk, and jumped into the driver's seat, starting it before he was completely settled.

He put the car in gear and hit the gas, the tires squealing when he reached the parking lot exit. He whipped the car to the left and sped down the road. If he was right, Trevor should emerge from the wooded area that divided the neighborhood right between his old English teacher's house and Mrs. Monahan's barn. Luke pulled to a stop twenty yards from where the path from the park ended, but he kept the motor running.

Amberlyn needed shoes, not that her high heels would have been much better when she was trying to run through the woods. Leaves softened the ground, but they also hid what was beneath them. She winced when she stepped on yet another pine cone, but she kept going.

The gunman's camouflage jacket blended a little too well with the trees, but he was still close enough for her to catch glimpses of him as he darted through the woods, always changing direction enough to keep Amberlyn from taking another shot.

He disappeared behind a thick pine, and his footsteps stopped.

Amberlyn took cover. A gunshot pierced the air and impacted the tree behind her.

Her breath caught, but her heart continued to race. This being-shot-at thing was not in her usual job description, and she was quite certain she could happily live the rest of her life without experiencing this sensation again.

Several seconds passed without any sound beyond the rustle of the wind through the branches above her and another approaching siren.

The footsteps started again, this time moving to their left, away from the direction of the siren.

Amberlyn counted to three before she peeked around the edge of the tree and spotted the gunman.

She took off after him, her thighs burning, her feet throbbing. She bypassed a protruding root and sidestepped another pine cone. The light filtering through the trees grew brighter as they approached a red barn on their right.

Amberlyn had to take only a few more steps to see the house on the other side of the path. The possibility of civilians getting caught in the crossfire suddenly became too real. She kept her weapon pointed down and prayed she could find a way to stop this man.

The road came into view right as the man reached the narrow sidewalk that preceded it. An engine revved, the man ran into the street, and then suddenly, a car struck him, braking immediately after contact.

Amberlyn spotted Luke scrambling out of the car at the same time she recognized the SUV as hers.

Luke scooped up the gunman's weapon and aimed.

The man on the ground moaned and rolled onto his back.

"Just try it," Luke said through gritted teeth.

Breathless, Amberlyn reached Luke's side and aimed at the downed man. "Is this Trevor Moran?"

"Yeah." Luke nodded. "That's Trevor."

A police car approached and screeched to a stop a few yards from them. In a replay of a few minutes ago, the deputy leaped from the car and pulled his weapon. He took aim, but this time, he must have recognized Amberlyn, because he pointed at the man on the ground.

She lowered her gun slightly. "Cuff him."

The deputy did so and pulled Trevor to his feet. Amberlyn stepped forward, looking Trevor in the eyes. "Trevor Moran, you are under arrest." She listed the charges, starting with attempted murder and escalating from there. When she stepped back, she nodded to the deputy. "Read him his rights."

———————

Luke paced the surgery waiting room, his emotions far too close to the surface. He and Amberlyn had driven to the hospital right after the deputy had taken Trevor into custody. They'd arrived only moments after the ambulance.

The pastor had made it to the hospital and immediately been rushed into surgery. Now Luke could only wait and worry.

An ache settled deep inside as fear overshadowed hope. The pastor had to be okay. He just had to. Had it not been for Pastor Mosley's quick actions, Luke would be the one on the operating table or, worse, in the morgue. And if not him, it would have been Amberlyn.

Amberlyn approached from the hall, where she had gone to make a phone call. She stepped in front of him, forcing him to stop moving.

He expected her to give him some speech about how everything would be okay, but instead, she opened her arms and embraced him.

Luke pulled her close, needing the physical contact. He held her as a minute stretched into two, taking the time to blink back the tears that threatened.

When he eased back, he looked down at her to see that her eyes weren't dry either.

Amberlyn swallowed hard before she spoke. "I talked to Ian. He'll get a message to the White House about the incident here and the arrest of Trevor Moran."

"Did either of the other gunmen make it?"

Amberlyn shook her head. "I talked to the sheriff too. Both men died at the scene."

Luke released Amberlyn, dropping his hands to his side. "I hope those people inside the youth center didn't walk outside and see the mess we left behind."

"They didn't. Chaplain Miller and Reverend Bowman kept everyone inside. The sheriff said they would wait until the crime scene was processed before letting anyone leave."

"Good thing we set up lots of refreshments for them," Luke said, trying to lighten his mood.

"Seriously." She looked down at her watch. "How long has the pastor been in surgery?"

Luke looked up at the clock on the wall. "Almost two hours."

The door on the side of the room opened, and a surgeon wearing scrubs and a downtrodden expression approached.

"Mr. Steele?" he asked.

A lump rose in Luke's throat, and all he could manage was a nod.

"I'm sorry. We did everything we could, but the damage was too severe," the doctor said gravely. "Pastor Mosley didn't make it."

The tears that sprang to Luke's eyes were instant. He looked up and blinked quickly, trying to stem them.

Though Amberlyn's voice was hoarse with emotion, she said, "Thank you, Doctor. We appreciate your efforts."

The doctor nodded. "I'm sorry for your loss."

The first tears spilled over, but before Luke could swipe them away, Amberlyn pulled him close.

"I'm so sorry," she whispered.

He buried his head in her shoulder as more tears fell. The pastor, Luke's oldest and dearest friend, was gone.

CHAPTER 42

AMBERLYN DROVE THROUGH the darkness, Luke at her side. Part of her couldn't believe he'd been willing to leave Pine Falls so soon after receiving the news about Pastor Mosley, but she understood the need to fulfill one's duty. And despite his loss, Luke was still due to report tomorrow afternoon.

She glanced at the clock on the dashboard. Make that later today. Midnight had come and gone twenty minutes ago.

Luke turned away from the window to face her. "Thanks for driving."

"You're welcome," Amberlyn said. "Are you going to be okay to drive home, or would you rather I drop you at your apartment? You only live a few blocks from me. You can pick up your car tomorrow if you want."

"I can drive home." Luke fell silent for another minute before he abruptly changed the subject. "I still can't believe he's gone."

"Are you going to go back for the funeral?" Amberlyn asked.

"I don't know. It's a long way, and I don't know if I'd be able to get the leave."

"Kansas City was a long way, too, but it was worth the trip," Amberlyn said. "Funerals aren't for those who passed away; they're for the living."

"In case you hadn't noticed, not a lot of people living in Pine Falls cared to see me."

"That's not true," Amberlyn countered. "Every person at the church dinner was thrilled to see you."

"I guess I always did do better with people who weren't my age."

"Sometimes it takes a while for people to see who we truly are." Amberlyn reached out and put her hand on his. "Whether people in Pine Falls realize it or not, you saved the lives of a lot of people today."

"*We* saved the lives of a lot of people today," he corrected.

"Okay, we." Amberlyn made the turn toward her apartment building.

"This is how you felt when Chanelle was killed, isn't it?" Luke asked.

Tears pricked at her eyes. "Yeah."

She pulled into the garage beneath her building and parked beside Luke's car.

Luke squeezed her hand. "I'm really sorry for your loss."

"And I'm really sorry for yours."

Luke limped into his boss's office, bracing against the possibility of being told no. Pastor Mosley had been a critical influence during his teenage years, a constant champion through college, and a huge support right up until the moment he'd died. And he'd died a hero. There had to be a way for Luke to get twenty-four hours of leave to attend his funeral.

Deputy Director Hobbs's secretary looked up when he approached. "He's on a call right now, but I'll let him know you're here."

"Thanks." Luke debated whether he should sit while he waited or remain standing. If he sat, he'd have to stand up again. His knee wasn't a fan of those transitions yet.

He stepped back beside one of the chairs lining the side wall but remained upright.

His wait was mercifully short, and within a few minutes, the secretary sent him into Deputy Director Hobbs's office.

Luke made it only two steps inside the door before his boss closed the distance between them, his hand outstretched. "I understand you did quite an amazing job yesterday."

His chest tightened. If he'd done an amazing job, Pastor Mosley would still be alive. Luke managed to nod, but he didn't trust himself to speak.

Deputy Director Hobbs motioned for Luke to sit in one of the chairs across from his desk. Though it pained him to do so, Luke bent his knee enough to lower himself into the chair.

Deputy Director Hobbs reclaimed his seat. "I was just updating the mil aide work schedule. I should have it finished by the end of the day."

"That's actually what I'm here to talk to you about." Luke tried to sit up straight without bending his knee fully. "I'm sorry to ask this, but would it be possible for me to take leave on Friday? Even just twenty-four hours?"

"For Graham Mosley's funeral?"

Luke had no idea how the deputy director had come to that conclusion so quickly, but he nodded. "Yes."

"He told me you two were close."

Luke lifted his eyebrows. "You knew Pastor Mosley?"

"We worked together quite a bit during his time with the agency." Deputy Director Hobbs leaned back in his chair. "He's one of the main reasons you're currently in this job."

"What?"

"I met Graham for lunch when he was up this way last December."

Luke's understanding heightened. "He took me to the tree lighting ceremony last year. He said he had a friend who was working here at the White House who got him tickets." Luke narrowed his eyes. "That was you?"

"It was." The deputy director tapped his fingers on the arm of his chair. "He mentioned you, gave me a bit of background, including how skilled you are at protecting confidences. Your interview proved he was right. You were the perfect fit."

"I had no idea."

Deputy Director Hobbs straightened, his chair creaking as he did so. "I have a family wedding this weekend, which will keep me from making the trip. I think it would be appropriate if you go and represent us both."

"I appreciate the opportunity."

"And, Luke?"

"Yes, sir?"

"Take the weekend. You've earned it."

Luke pushed to a stand, wincing slightly. "Thank you, sir."

CHAPTER 43

SHE MISSED HIM. Amberlyn stood at her apartment window and stared out at the Potomac River and the Washington Monument in the distance. She had chosen this apartment for the view and the easy access to DC. Now she knew Luke lived only four blocks away. Four blocks, and she hadn't seen him since they'd returned to northern Virginia three days ago.

The little ache that had settled in her chest expanded. She understood the psychology of how attachments formed, of how friendships developed. She also sensed the connection she had experienced with Luke was rare, one worth exploring.

Her phone rang, and hope rose inside her. She pulled the phone from her pocket and glanced at the screen. Disappointment surfaced. Ian, not Luke.

"Hey, Ian. What's up?"

"I wanted to give you an update," he said. "Right after you left the office, the Kansas City office sent an update. They've taken six people associated with Forever Freedom into custody, including the woman who funded the bombing. Her daughter was one of the people who died in the blizzard."

"You think we got them all?"

"I hope so. We've cut off their purse strings, and I suspect both Trevor Moran and the woman who paid for the attack will face the death penalty. That should make any remaining co-conspirators think twice."

Amberlyn couldn't keep the weariness out of her voice. "One would hope."

"You've been working this case nonstop for weeks. You should take a couple days off."

Amberlyn turned away from the river, looking in the direction of Luke's apartment. "I may take you up on that."

"Get some rest."

"I will." She ended the call. She would get some rest, but first she had some packing to do. It was time for another road trip.

The church parking lot was nearly full when Luke arrived twenty minutes before the funeral service began. He backed his ancient Civic into the empty spot three down from the hearse. He would have preferred to stay in the background, but as soon as Reverend Bowman learned Luke was coming to the funeral, Luke's name had been added to the list of pallbearers.

Two couples in their forties approached from where they had parked on the street. A family of four came from the other direction, heading for the door.

Luke stared at the entrance, his emotions in a spiral. He didn't want to cry in front of these people, but he could feel the tears right there at the surface, trying to escape.

This was how Amberlyn had felt after losing Chanelle. Like there was a deep, gaping hole that could never be filled. A chill deep in one's bones, like the first winter snowfall with no spring in sight.

He hadn't considered what it truly meant to have another person beside you when saying those last goodbyes to someone who meant so much, but he was glad now that he had made the effort to go to Chanelle's funeral. How he wished he had someone beside him today.

He sniffled back his tears once again and drew a deep breath. He could do this. He was a Marine, a soldier, a friend. He had to do this.

Straightening his shoulders, he climbed out of the car and headed inside. Reverend Bowman stood in the entrance, chatting with the newest arrivals. He shook hands with the man in front of him. "Will you excuse me a minute?"

The man nodded and moved toward the chapel with his family.

"Thank you for coming," Reverend Bowman said, his voice not quite steady. "I know you meant a great deal to Pastor Mosley."

Luke swallowed the lump that had formed in his throat. "He meant a great deal to me."

"I know." Reverend Bowman reached into his pocket and produced a bulky, letter-sized envelope that had been folded in half. "I don't know if you were aware that I'm the executor of the pastor's estate."

"No, I wasn't." Nor did Luke expect a conversation about the pastor's possessions before his funeral.

"Most of his belongings will be donated to our charity, but there was one item he wanted you to have." The reverend passed him the envelope.

Luke opened it. Inside were two sets of car keys. "His car?"

"Pastor Mosley knew you would never buy a new one for yourself."

"His car," Luke repeated. He'd driven nice cars before, from his parents' cars to Amberlyn's, but he hadn't considered indulging in something this nice for himself.

And even though he couldn't deny appreciating the gesture and even wanting to accept it, he couldn't help but ask, "Are you sure it wouldn't be wiser to give it to someone who needs it?"

"Take it," Reverend Bowman said. "Every time you drive it, you'll remember how much he loved you." The reverend's lips quirked up slightly. "From what I understand, that could be quite a few years."

Luke let out a short laugh. "That's true."

"I need to check in with the funeral director. Go ahead and wait here. This is where the pallbearers are meeting before the service."

Luke nodded, a new thought pushing to the forefront of his mind. "Reverend?"

"Yes?"

"Do you think there's anyone in the area who might need a car? I have one I don't have use of anymore. It's old, but it runs."

"I'm sure there is." Reverend Bowman shook Luke's hand again. "Pastor Mosley was right about you. You are one of the good ones."

The reverend disappeared into the chapel, and Luke held up the keys. A new car. He'd rather have his friend back.

The door opened behind him, and he turned. His jaw dropped when Amberlyn walked toward him.

"Hey there," she said.

Stunned, it took him a moment to find his words. "What are you doing here?"

Amberlyn took his hand and laced her fingers through his. "Someone once told me no one should ever have to go to a funeral alone."

His shock faded, and a glimmer of warmth crept through the chill inside him. He squeezed her hand as hope joined the warmth. "Thank you for coming."

"I wouldn't want to be anywhere else."

ACKNOWLEDGMENTS

MY DEEPEST APPRECIATION goes to Samantha Millburn, Amy Parker, and Chris Schoebinger for ushering me into this new chapter in my writing career, and thank you to Samantha and Chris for making my work shine.

Thank you to Lara and Scott Abramson for all your help during the early stages of this book, and thanks to my fabulous critique partners, whose insight is invaluable during the writing process, especially Ashley Gebert, Daniel Quilter, Eliza Sanders, and Emma Jackson.

I also want to thank Chris and Gretchen Ross for facilitating so many of my White House tours. My appreciation also goes to the CIA Publication Classification Review Board for your continued support and for helping me meet my deadlines. Your staff is always a delight to work with.

Finally, thank you to my family for loving me even when I disappear into my fictional worlds.

SNEAK PEEK

COMING APRIL 2025

SHADOW
MOUNTAIN
PUBLISHING